Pansy

UPROOTED

THE FLOWER LADIES TRILOGY 1

Pansy UPROOTED

D. A. SPRUZEN

Published By: 4 Horsemen Publications, Inc.

4 Horsemen Publications, Inc.
PO Box 419
Sylva, NC 28779
4horsemenpublications.com
info@4horsemenpublications.com

Cover Illustration by CD Corrigan
Typesetting by Autumn Skye
Edited by Kris Cotter

Library of Congress Control Number: 2025948197

Paperback ISBN-13: 979-8-8232-1018-8
Hardcover ISBN-13: 979-8-8232-1019-5
Ebook ISBN-13: 979-8-8232-1019-5

Murder is unique in that it abolishes the party it injures, so that society has to take the place of the victim and on his behalf demand atonement or grant forgiveness; it is the one crime in which society has a direct interest.

—W. H. Auden

Contents

1

Pansy

Pansy made her first kill at fourteen, albeit with the best of intentions. I'm not Pansy anymore. I became someone quite different, despite all the obstacles placed in my path by others, and circumstances that forced my hand and made a few more casualties inevitable.

I need to write everything down now—the things I had to do—and try to show the sense of it all. When people read it, they will understand that I had no choice and will not think so badly of me. After all, I never had anyone to stand up for me; I had to solve my own problems the best way I could. My solutions might be considered somewhat extreme, I know, but I couldn't lose everything I had always dreamed of and strived for.

I wanted a good life in a normal place, doing normal things. I wanted respect. That meant a good job, a good husband, and a nice home in a nice place. I used to look through fancy magazines in midtown drug stores until they chased me out. I gathered up a dream and held onto it: a white house with a solid fence and big old trees. Lots of green. The only trees where I lived were scraggy and half-dead from exhaust fumes, so my dream-trees were a vague impression of the kind I had seen in those magazines, hemming wonderful perfect gardens that encircled wonderful perfect houses. I imagined vases of pink and blue flowers posed on polished tabletops—generic flowers like children paint, because no one I knew ever had flowers in their home—unless you count dusty plastic ones, and even then I knew better. Drapes and blinds shrouded the windows; no one could spy on me, and only the invited could enter. I got all of it, but, as everyone knows by now, I didn't get to keep it. I had a good run, though. Not bad for someone like me. I can't complain because I did very well, considering my start—in a grungy family living on the roughest street in Hell's Kitchen. No juicy bite of the Big Apple for us.

A Washington suburb seemed like paradise to me—I could stay the same person for years. Too many people knew me in New York in spite of all the time and money I spent on hairdressers and cosmetics to change my look—red hair in a short pixie cut and Cleopatra eyeliner one year, and a nylon ash-blonde wig and false eyelashes (a strange 60s fashion fad) the next. Each time I changed jobs I changed my look, my apartment, and often my name, too. New everything. I had to keep my life smooth, you see. Bumpy rides are not to my liking.

There came a point when I wanted to—had to—get out of New York and I succeeded beyond my wildest dreams. But I'm getting ahead of myself.

I burned my old journal long ago—it was too risky to hold on to it once I married. Now I must begin again.

I'll be long gone by the time you read this, children—if they let you. Know that I did my best; suspend judgment until you are done. Don't bother looking for me.

2

Halos glowed through the mist and undulating masked figures hovered; the old ones come to guide her through to shimmering light. The light heightened and sharpened until the masks became faces. She closed her eyes again and listened for life, looked for a heartbeat. There it was, faint but steady.

"Rose, can you hear me? I'm Doctor Wallace. Try to keep still. You've had a nasty knock on the head. You're going to be all right. You're in the hospital. Can you tell me your full name?"

It was hard to make her mouth form the words; her tongue felt so thick and heavy and her head ached as if a little man were working a jackhammer inside it. The sharp, fear-tainted smell of the place seeped into her conscious-ness as she forced herself to respond.

It jumbled out slowly. "Rose Hale."

"Do you know what day it is?"

"Monday. Monday?"

She remembered Judy's dead eyes—rather like the live ones had looked as she gazed through the horizon when things didn't go her way—then a sudden burst of pain in her head and a dive into darkness. She didn't want to remember any more. If she closed her eyes and took a deep breath, she could force it all down and away until her mind closed off the fidgeting memories.

"What happened?"

A blurred suit and tie edged into view, a soothing view of beige against stark white.

"Mrs. Hale, I'm Detective Paglietti. Can you answer some questions, ma'am? This is a murder investigation or I wouldn't be bothering you just now."

Her eyes hurt as they strained open to incredulity. "Murder!"

"Yes, ma'am. Judy Roberts was murdered this morning, hit on the head with a statue. And you were found right outside her back door. A neighbor saw you and called us. What do you remember? Did you see who did it?"

"Can't remember much. Went for coffee. Came to the back door, like always." The words began to jell, fueled by adrenaline. "The door was ajar. I pushed it open and called her. She didn't answer, so I went through the kitchen into the family room. She was there. On the floor. Dead. I ran, wanted to get out, get away. Lights in my eyes. Nothing more."

"You got hit on the head, too. Didn't you see anyone?"

"No, no one. Least, not that I remember." She drooped her eyelids, a dramatic enough droop, she hoped, to get him to leave her alone. She was so tired and there was that little man in her head again, his pounding getting louder by the minute. She must focus, stretch her toes, flex her fingers, listen to her breathing and steady it, swallow her thoughts, suppress memories that must never see light again.

"You sure you can't remember anything, Mrs. Hale?"

She shook her head and winced, the shooting pains vicious.

"Let her rest now," the doctor said.

Dr. Wallace discharged Rose two days later with the provision that she take it easy until her family doctor pronounced her well enough for normal activity. Her son Andrew came to the hospital to take her home. A stocky young man, Andrew always tried to maintain a neutral affable demeanor, but today he looked pale and tense, his dark eyebrows almost meeting. Gone was his usual careful noncommittal smile that could never be interpreted as anything but appropriate. Even the ability to make bright-sounding observations on the weather seemed to have deserted him for the time being. She supposed he was tired out from the "what-ifs," tired of all the gnawing feelings. He had never liked to stir up unnecessary turmoil. The solemn young stalwart kissed her and gave her some flowers, standard florist stock—pink roses with long stems and no scent. Silly, really, since they just had to carry them home, but nice gestures had always been important to him.

He said little beyond "How are you, Mom?" before he vanished to fetch the car. She waited in the lobby on her wheeled throne. Everyone stared at her as if they all knew about the murder.

Andrew helped her in and out of the car, supporting her by the elbow to make sure she didn't stumble. Rose would have liked a good hug and that sudden neediness surprised her, but they'd never been a family of touchers. When they got home, he settled her on the sofa and brought the telephone and her current murder mystery, setting a glass of water within easy reach. He tucked a rug around her legs. He ordered Chinese food for dinner and made her tea. Then he sat with her and made a few desultory phone calls to his office, his voice rapping like a woodpecker at the secretary on the other end. He reserved his unctuous voice for clients and partners. She relaxed and even dozed a little, bored with the book, a book she'd been enjoying only a couple of days ago, but it seemed like trash now that crude reality had come to call.

After a respectable interval, the phone started to ring. Andrew answered and said the callers' names so she could make yes or no signals. There were so many of them, so very many friends. They all wanted to come.

"Tomorrow," she said. She wanted to look just right and to tell the truth, she felt dog-tired, too tired even to take a shower. Andrew called his brother Justin and his sister Lucy. Justin would take the weekend off and drive up from Charlottesville; Lucy would be over after work.

Rose lay in bed propped up on pillows, unable to sleep in such an awkward position, but lying flat made her headache worse. She thought about her children, usually a sleep-inducing exercise. She'd raised them to be responsible and independent. She wasn't a demonstrative mother, but loved them in her own way and had protected them from life's exigencies to the extent possible, especially Lucy—more than the girl knew. That boy would have dragged Lucy down with him. She liked being able to love them at a distance and respond to them as adults. Young children could be quite sweet, but a little of that went a long way. And you had to put up with their friends, of course. Other people's children.

What was in store for Lucy? She wasn't beautiful, but pleasing to look at and always on the go. A successful architect now, she could be unforgiving of those less intelligent than she. Her few friendships tended to be tumultuous. Everything looked black or white to her and she always knew what was best for people, her opinions usually at odds with those of her targets. She didn't look like either of her parents but, to Rose's annoyance, closely resembled someone whose name she didn't even acknowledge silently, someone she hadn't spoken to or seen in years. That's why she always felt sudden, sharp discomfort when she glimpsed her daughter after a long absence, like a sudden inhalation at the prick of a needle.

Andrew had been practicing law in Washington for a couple of years. You could tell just by looking at his impeccable dark suits, eternal white shirt, and quiet ties. One always found him "very well, mustn't complain." Partners were "my esteemed colleagues," and he could even make his "cautious optimism" sound genuine with his modulated voice and benign countenance. He worked hard, cultivated the partners and clients, and avoided undue risk with uncanny prescience. Not one of the brilliant ones, but, perhaps more importantly, not a serious threat to anyone else's career or self-esteem, either.

He was her favorite, visiting at least once a week and never arriving empty-handed, perhaps bringing a book he thought she would enjoy, sometimes flowers or chocolates, and he always helped with the dishes after dinner. At once undemanding and needy, she enjoyed doing little things for him. She insisted that he bring his laundry home and liked cooking him his favorite meals. His presence filled her with the glow of successful motherhood, happy he awoke such feelings in her. No one else could. And he looked the most like her of any of the children, except on a larger scale. Was he happy? Hard to tell. He seemed fairly content with his life, and maybe that was all one should expect.

She sighed as she thought of Justin, a fine cellist, although a waiter at present. Slim and tall, he was blessed with a handsome face—just like his father when Rose had first met him, although there was no resemblance in temperament. She feared he lacked the drive to succeed in the music world, as too many other passions distracted him from the necessary unwavering commitment. The most sensitive of her three children, Justin had an uncanny knack for tuning in to others' moods and emotions—except for those of his current girlfriend, whom he angered when he failed to echo her opinions. He frequently fell in love and, just as frequently, fell out of love after the crushing disappointment of finding that the young lady of the moment did not live up to his high ideals—or hers. He felt injustice keenly and was boyishly idealistic. She loved this sweet young man but, all in all, he was a pain in the rear end to be around for long. He never stayed for long as he found Rose's suburban life "stultifying." His mother felt the same way, although she never admitted it.

Rose considered herself fortunate on the whole. Her children were three good young people who loved their mother and missed their late father. They followed their own stars and allowed her glimpses into their lives as they saw fit, mostly by telephone. She would listen to Justin's anguish after yet another girl had failed to measure up, Andrew's triumph when a client had expressed her gratitude and admiration, and Lucy's current line of outrage. Best let them get on with their lives, she felt. But she needed them at home now—for a while, anyway.

Rose heard Lucy's car door bang and felt a little knot of anticipation tighten in her stomach. She hadn't seen her for a couple of months. Lucy didn't mean to stay away, but she always got so tied up with her work and there seemed to be a new young man, too.

Lucy swept through the door and pecked her mother's cheek, remarking how well she looked, considering. She stood in front of her brother, tapping her foot impatiently until he finished his call, her lip curling when she heard him say, "While Sam is a very, very competent lawyer, perhaps he isn't quite yet as well-versed in that particular area of tax law as I." Andrew reddened and scowled when he saw his sister's disdain.

"What are we doing about dinner?"

"I ordered it already from The Orchid Garden."

"Chinese. Oh, Andrew, don't you know they use lots of cornstarch and sugar, not to mention the mono..."

I can't take this tonight, Rose thought, and did the droopy eye look again. It worked again. "Mother mustn't be upset. She's not well yet, not herself," and so on, Andrew expostulated. He could always come through with the right platitudes. *Good for him, that's my boy.*

The next morning, Rose felt unsteady and still had a headache, so she was glad of Lucy's taking the time off. She needed someone to answer the door and make iced tea for the callers on this hot August day.

Rose settled herself on the sofa, feeling she looked soft and feminine in a powder blue silk robe that brought out her blue eyes and newly washed fair hair. Her makeup was just right, a little color on the lips and around the eyes, but nothing on her cheeks. Her lap rug was white and soft, her slim figure accentuated by its folds.

A group from the Women's Club got there first.

"Oh, you're looking simply marvelous!" Muffy Bigwell said. "So terribly brave, so dreadful for you!"

"No, I barely remember a thing," Rose said.

"Nothing at all?" Muffy asked. The woman's eyes looked almost fevered with anticipation.

"Nothing."

"Oh. Well, perhaps that's best for your own peace of mind." Rose smiled sweetly into the disappointed little frown and snapped her teeth.

"But look at you, so pale and delicate today," Jenny McLaughlin said. "Are you very shaken, dear?"

"Oh, no, I'm really quite all right, just a little headachy," Rose said.

"You do look a tad drawn. What can we do for you? Anything, just name it," Mary Treadwell asked.

"My children are taking care of me beautifully, thank you, Mary. So kind of everyone," Rose said. Them leaving soon would help. She thought she'd love the attention, but they were getting on her nerves. *Silly twitterers.* She allowed her head to sink back into the pillow.

"Well, we mustn't overstay our visit, dear. Simply marvelous to see you looking so well," Muffy said. "You have a lovely rest, now. Lunch soonest!"

There were several more visitors, and she smiled tremulously, murmuring sorrow for poor Judy and her family, and described making her shocking discovery and remembering nothing more. She allowed that it had all been a terrible experience, but that she would get back into things as soon as the doctor said her head wound had sufficiently healed. She repeated herself often and refined her phrasing with each telling. People kissed her cheek gently and patted her hand. They wore concerned expressions and brought flowers and chocolates. A couple of them even brought their husbands as a special gift of attention and concern. When she'd had enough and her tongue started to trip over her words, she laid back, allowing exhaustion—real enough—to show through. And having done their duty and discerned that no new information would be forthcoming, they left, voicing their hopes for her speedy recovery and she must come over for dinner very soon.

Her guests drank lots of iced tea and Lucy's sullen demeanor deepened. More little tea spills appeared on the tray as the day wore on and glasses were set down with increasing emphasis. Rose found it amusing to watch her daughter take the almost stoical approach, forcing herself to be stonily polite, and feeling she must suffer in silence after all her mother had been through. Her right cheek twitched as she clenched and unclenched her teeth and her frequent scowl looked downright unattractive. On the other hand, her daughter's silence was always a blessing. Lucy darted into the kitchen from time to time to take deep drafts of beer from a bottle in the refrigerator, which seemed to relax her as the day wore on. Rose could hear the bottle clink against the others and smelled the beer on her breath. Only one? Until they had children of their own, young people never seemed to catch on to the fine-tuning of a mother's ear for both catching and interpreting noises offstage. These women got on Lucy's nerves, especially when they wanted to know if she had met "Mr. Right" yet. Her response was a thin-lipped smile and another appointment in the kitchen.

In the late afternoon, Rose called Annie, one of her closest friends. "I'm absolutely exhausted, Annie. Too many people. Would you be offended if I told you I need a rest from visits tomorrow?" Annie, understanding, as always, said she'd deliberately stayed away the first day to give Rose the quiet time with her family she needed. "Would you mind telling the others, Annie?"

Andrew planned to come over after work, bringing dinner from a local delicatessen. The choices were made after a much-heated telephone consultation with Lucy, which, while probably entertaining for the other customers, had sent Andrew into a frenzy of irritation. Rose could hear his voice over the phone from the other side of the room. As Andrew's irritation mounted, Lucy's smirk widened. Rose was amused, if piqued, that her preferences had not figured into the discussion.

The next morning, Susan Lazare arrived armed with a lush bouquet of yellow roses. She didn't ring the doorbell but knocked twice, imperiously, and embarked on her fact-finding mission. Rose had put her off as more than she could deal with on the first day. She was received by a tight-lipped and silent Lucy, still at home helping, but showing her horns by this time. Susan sat herself on the Queen Anne armchair, clasped her claw-like hands on clenched knees, and locked eyes with Rose.

"Well now, we have been through some hard times!" she said.

Susan's eyes always looked beady behind the designer glasses she affected. Everything glistened—the gold rims, the lenses, her eyes, the anti-aging lotion she futilely slathered around her eyes—until a person would think she was looking at those marbles small boys used to play with instead of somebody's eyeballs. Rose couldn't imagine why she bothered with the lotion, as Susan showed no interest whatsoever in other aspects of her appearance.

People knew they shouldn't gaze into her eyes, but she possessed some sort of hypnotic quality, and they found themselves indulging in uncharacteristic bouts of frankness and honesty over the coffee cups. They told of friendships betrayed, husbands who strayed, children who sinned, and always heard about it later from another source. Someone they barely knew would express sorrow for a trouble they had borne courageously, and they realized that not only had they made a terrible mistake in talking to Susan, but they had known it was a mistake at the time. They didn't know what made them do it. The woman was a master of innuendo, butter-coated saber thrusts, and just plain malice. Gossip was Susan's hobby and her lifeline.

Rose remembered to pull away from those eyes, thinking that Susan had the uncanny observational powers of Agatha Christie's Jane Marple—although that was her only resemblance to that gentle spinster. Rose half expected her to extract some knitting from the antique sack she called a purse. The purse matched everything she wore, as her clothes were all a motley collection of drab earth tones, perhaps designed to emphasize her green eyes. Rose leaned her cheek on the cushion while Susan got started, gazing into the roses on the polished table next to her.

"I do hope you'll be well enough to come to Judy's funeral. It will be on Tuesday next and the press will be there and just about all of Salton, I should think."

"I hope so, Susan. I'd hate to miss paying Judy and her family my respects."

"No doubt. Do you know anything about Judy before she came to Salton?" Susan asked with an excited lilt in her voice.

"No. Now I come to think of it, she never spoke of her family."

"Well, I've done a little digging." *I bet you have.* "You know she was born in West Virginia? Dirt-poor, they were."

"How do you know?"

"Birth certificate. I know someone in Charleston. I had them check out the little town. Shantytown, just about, even now." *And how did she find the birth certificate? Oh, you'd find anything she wanted.* "Mother entered into a common-law marriage with a twenty-year-old when she was thirteen! Imagine! What kind of people let their daughter do that?"

"How on earth did your friend find that out?"

"Oh, talked to a lot of people?" *You paid for the information.*

"How much did that cost you?"

Susan colored a little and her eyes narrowed. "Whatever do you mean? I was just curious, and my friend's got a lot of time on his hands." *You don't have friends. Not real ones.*

"Sorry, go on."

"Well, Judy was the first of six children, all of them born within eight years. The woman had six children by the time she was twenty-one. Like farm animals!"

"Poor mother."

"Yes, well." Susan sniffed and snorted. "A neighbor told my friend that Judy had to take care of the last one, mother tired of it all by then. And they all had chores, plenty of them. They all dropped out of school, except Judy. Apparently, she had to borrow her brother's shoes that last winter and go to school wrapped in a blanket. No coat."

"She certainly had grit."

"I suppose you could call it that. Anyway, when she graduated, she moved to Charleston. No one's sure quite how she made it there, let alone set herself up. One can only guess. Something like Eliza Doolittle, I shouldn't wonder. Only way for a girl like that."

"Susan! We don't know that. We shouldn't put that about. It would hurt Davey's feelings if he heard such things."

"Hmm. She only went back to her old home one more Christmas. A woman who was her best friend in school said she was a different person. Talked differently, looked classy, total change. Said she was working in a flower shop and going to secretarial school at night. My friend was able to trace her through the local paper's archives. She worked as a secretary at a local college. Married the baseball coach. He died two years later, good life insurance. No children."

"Sounds like a Cinderella story. People do change. They learn and grow."

"They only change on the outside, in my opinion. We both know what a harpy she was." *Look who's talking!* "Would you believe she never saw her parents again? And they had a disabled son, paralyzed in a motorcycle accident, too. They couldn't afford the care he needed, so he didn't last long. They never knew where she was or even if she was still alive. They're both long dead now, of course."

"Why did she move up here?" Rose asked.

"I don't know. Maybe she wanted to be near Washington."

"She did mention working for the government once. That would have been in the sixties, I guess."

"Oh, she never told me that," Susan said, shifting in the chair, pulling herself straighter, clearly miffed. "She probably identified Salton as the sort of place she could meet the right kind of man. And she did. Volunteering for the Salton Symphony was a smart idea. Got her into the right circles. Kept her wits about her. That was just before my time here."

"Yes, poor Davey," Rose said with a sigh. Perhaps he'd had a happy release. She wondered how his two children would take it. Mixed feelings, most likely.

"Of course, I always knew she came from modest beginnings. There are always little telltale signs where people unknowingly show themselves up. Look at that tacky Beethoven bust she kept on that piano no one played—at least since her daughter's teacher said she couldn't take it anymore. The woman told me herself that she'd rather lose the income than put up with a child totally lacking talent, but whose mother thought her a prodigy."

Rose wondered what little clues about her own background she might have let drop. And what about Susan's? She never even talked about her late husband, let alone her family.

"I do remember her saying once that Beethoven was a kindred spirit. I thought it rather unbalanced," Rose said.

"And of course, it killed her. She was brained with that bust, did you know that?" Susan said. "So nasty, but if she had to go, strangely fitting."

"God, no! I didn't. And I think I know what you mean." Rose buried her smile in her cushion.

"She had some friends, you know, very, very close friends, who were happy to scratch her back if she returned the favor, but that is none of our business, of course, mustn't speak ill of the dead," Susan said.

"What sort of favors? You mean in Charleston, or here?"

"As I said, mustn't speak ill of the dead. Goodness, is that the time? I must be going. You must be exhausted."

Rose was indeed exhausted. Susan's visit had lasted over an hour.

"Just a little tired, Susan. So good of you to come. I don't know where Lucy is. Can you let yourself out?"

Susan was good at pretending to have information she did not, but on the other hand, she also excelled at concealing information that could be more profitably employed on another occasion. Inference was her major strength in the character assassination business. Promote uncertainty, cast doubt, and create smoke, without which there is no fire, as everyone knows. Rose saw her strategy, of course; Susan held the key to the murder—a ghost from Judy's past.

The long and expressive tip of Susan's nose had visibly quivered with suppressed excitement as she bustled away. Had Annie called Susan about not visiting today? Of course, she had.

Rose lay back and closed her eyes. It had taken her a couple of years to catch on to Susan's role in the community. When she had first started to socialize in Salton, she got the impression from all the gossip told and retold by her various new acquaintances that she had moved to a scandalously fast-paced community. She had expected safe, solid, affluent, provincial, and dull, dull, dull. It had taken her a couple of years to understand that dull facts and tawdry little events were often elaborately embroidered, and usually by Susan. There wasn't ever anything of significance going on in this upscale suburban paradise. Until now.

She recalled Simon Stottleman's supposed indiscretion with his secretary (he drove her home when she became ill with the flu), and Sarah Morgan's shoplifting (she picked up two scarves instead of one and discovered her mistake at the cash register), then the Barker girl, whose mother made her go to school in a short-sleeved blouse one cold December morning (she'd peeled off her outer clothing around the corner from her house to look more appealing to a sophomore she had a crush on), and last January they'd heard a story about Emily Channing who had made her poor old mother walk to the store in the snow (the old lady suffered from Alzheimer's and had wandered away from the house one afternoon while Emily was doing the laundry). People were always so eager to hear and spread the dirt, but didn't seem to share Rose's interest in ferreting out the truth and circulating that instead.

She had expected the usual political scandal. After all, this was the sort of Washington suburb where the people in her circle tended to be transplants into so-called power jobs who strove mightily for social position. They acquired massive tract houses, worthy charities, and rapidly established themselves as pillars of the community, forming careful groupings for dinners and hosting cocktail parties around artful patio furniture.

And how they latched onto their choice of civic volunteerism. Unemployed women were especially fond of this exercise in cutthroat one-upmanship. And they could never let the facade slip, not for a moment. Expressions of interest were made with slightly raised eyebrows; friendship was shown by keeping up the ping-pong of returned invitations and, if possible, the dispensing of occasional favors—nomination for appointment to a socially desirable board, for example. Disappointment was registered by muted reproach (so sorry, we're not on the same page quite yet), and anger by estrangement. Joy was measured in the phrases of nicely worded notes (so very pleased to hear your good news), tasteful flower arrangements (always seasonal, preferably themed), and "little celebrations" (we'd be delighted to have you join us, we're having a few friends over, oh, and Josh got into Harvard, you know). It was all very carefully choreographed. How could she be so keen on maintaining her status in a group she despised when it came right down to it? She treasured her membership with her friends on the symphony board—even Susan—but the rest of them could evaporate tomorrow, for all she cared.

Lucy used to have a gerbil with a toy that condemned it to live much the same way—scrabbling round and round and round. And it had a see-through tank with four walls, even a mesh ceiling. Did any of these people ever step back and look at Salton with the same detachment Rose often felt? Perhaps they couldn't bring themselves to that level of honesty. Perhaps, of course, they truly did feel part of a group. Rose watched the interactions at the social events she attended much as one peeking through a window, wondering if any of the others also felt like pretenders. That gerbil had come to a miserable end when its neck got wedged under the wheel.

Rose slept on the sofa for over three hours after Susan left, but woke tired. Her heart pounded, and she was short of breath, as if she had been fleeing some sort of danger. The memory of a dream began to surface. She'd been floating in the sea, so light and peaceful before her late husband's face loomed close to hers, distorted and agonized. His mouth contorted, and he gestured to her, to someone far off, to himself. He seemed frantic, as if he needed to tell her something she couldn't hear. She lay so rigid her body rolled face down and she tasted salt, although she could still breathe somehow, could see him, down on the seabed now. He glided up with arms outstretched as if to envelop her, but she woke up just as he touched her face. Rose spent the rest of the day alternating between agitation and depression. Poor man, he'd been fine until the last few years. *But he can't hurt me, at least while I'm awake.*

Lucy entered the room and slammed a vase of marigolds on a side table, their color an unwelcome jolt against the room's soft blue and cream hues. Rose saw she was fighting an ever-increasing urge to escape back to her job and boyfriend.

"Mother, I really have to go home soon, you know. I've got this project at work. It's the new government center. And my apartment's filthy, haven't had time to clean it, what with all the overtime I've had to do. I've got no food in the house, either. I guess you'll be all right for the weekend with Andrew here? Justin's useless, of course."

"Of course, dear. And don't be unkind about your brother. It was good of you to come. How's Steve?"

"Steve? Oh, him. No, there's someone else now. Steve wasn't a very stimulating person to be around. Good in the sack, but thick as a plank when it comes to current affairs."

Rose couldn't get up the energy to pretend to be shocked. Of course, Lucy had lovers at her age. So, poor old Steve hadn't passed Lucy's many tests. Probably dared to have an opposing opinion from time to time.

"And who is this one?"

"Martin. A lawyer in the EPA. Also good in the sack."

Rose wouldn't rise to the bait. "Glad to hear it, my dear," she said, keeping her face blank to Lucy's evident disappointment. They'd never discussed sex and Rose had no intention of starting now. There was really nothing she could, or wanted, to share.

Andrew had gone back to work after her first day home, but came back after work and slept at the house. He had admitted that he was afraid for her, although he hadn't wanted to say anything that might alarm her. Supposing the killer thought she could identify him, even though the news reports of the murder had said clearly that she could not? She must be careful, he said, and she must on no account open the door to strangers. It had been hard to keep a straight face. He'd make a good, if unappreciated, father.

She was still so tired that she refused visits for that evening and the next day. She suggested to Andrew that he return home, as she was feeling much stronger and fully able to cope. Justin would be with her for part of Saturday and Sunday, after all. Andrew's brow puckered.

"Justin's just not very practical, Mother, is he? I am concerned about you. I'll stay through tomorrow evening—if you want me to, that is. It'll be getting dark soon and you shouldn't be alone."

"Of course, my dear, I was just worried about you missing your weekend. You are so good to me."

Andrew's brow cleared as he basked in her approval and need. He would stay on for nearly a month.

It was a lovely funeral, and Rose knew she looked good in black—dignified, if frail. The press took lots of pictures and a good one of her had been in The Washington Post a couple of days earlier. Davey and the children looked grim, poor things. They held onto each other, jaws set and dry eyes fixed on the casket. The boy had recently married, and the girl was in her senior year in college. *They'll get over it*, Rose thought, *just like mine did*. Victor had died of a heart attack. Such a tragedy, everyone said, and she'd eaten donated casseroles and meatloaf for a month. The kids went back to college and got on with their lives. Rose stayed in Salton and got on with hers. She made the rounds and guarded her volunteer positions zealously although she wasn't sure why. Her life was stuck in this groove—but what would be better? She could marry another community pillar, but she thought not. She'd had enough of dinners and laundry. At least she was a somebody in this narrow place. She wouldn't want to be a nobody again.

The church was full and Rose and the other "Symphony Seven," as they called themselves, sat together in the front row, only six of them now. They were a close-knit group, and Judy had been one of them. They'd been founding members of the Salton Symphony about fifteen years before, and still volunteered at every concert, moving on and off the Board of Trustees as their terms expired and they were reelected after a decent interval.

Judy's family followed the casket to the graveside, and the Seven walked behind them. Sally started sobbing and Annie put her arm around her. Susan sniffed and walked a little faster, drawing ahead of the others. It looked as if she would overtake the family, but she seemed to realize what she was doing at the last minute and slowed down. Janet admired the flowers too loudly, saying they must have cost a fortune. Helen said nothing but linked her arm through Janet's. Janet's husband, Roger, dropped back. The wreaths covered the casket like a blanket and the lilies' heavy scent wafted over them in decadent waves. Rose started to feel slightly sick.

The minister's drone was all that broke the silence as the casket was lowered into its hole. Rose's heart thudded along with the handfuls of soil, and she tossed in a miniature Beethoven bust she'd concealed in her scoop of dirt while heads were bowed in prayer. She glanced around quickly to see if anyone had noticed before bowing her own head, which started to ache again, memories knocking for readmittance.

After the service, everyone went back to Susan's house for the obligatory cold cuts and cheap wine. Rose found herself the center of attention, even more than Davey

Roberts, Judy's husband, because she'd been at the scene, and a victim, too. Very satisfying, especially when she saw how hard Susan had to work to claim the spotlight, darting from guest to guest, offering snacks and reciting breathless clichés. She overheard Susan tell the portly and solemn Reverend Steinbeck, "Such a pity, such a waste... she'd done so well, after all, come such a long way from a difficult beginning..." He sniffed the air like the bloodhound he so closely resembled.

Rose chimed in, "Yes, she helped bring our orchestra a long way from its modest beginnings. And she was a key player in keeping it afloat during those hard financial times a few years ago when donations all but dried up. She worked for our community tirelessly, didn't she, Susan?" And thus deflected the arrow.

She met Susan's glassy, gleaming eyes for a moment and felt acutely uncomfortable under the shaft of what could only be described as speculative hostility. Susan had been upstaged and would hold that grudge.

"Nice touch with the baby Beethoven," Susan whispered as she passed. Rose wondered how long it would take for that piece of gossip to appear on the circuit.

3

Pansy

Saturday nights were special. He would tell my older sister Daisy to go out and have a good time. Daisy didn't even look back as she made her escape. She must have known it was my turn, now. He only used to read to me in bed before he decided Daisy was played out, too mature.

We moved to New York when I was eight. We'd lived in Pinner, a London suburb where Dad was a schoolteacher until he got fired—framed by jealous colleagues, he insisted. He never said what they framed him for, even when he was drunk and ranting about the injustice of it all. He'd go on about how they despised him for marrying beneath him. My mother was the daughter of the local fishmonger, and he seemed to despise her as much as he claimed his friends and family had. How his colleagues could have been jealous at the same time as looking down on him for marrying Mom,

I don't know. She probably wasn't so slovenly in those days, just "common" as he liked to point out. So why did he marry her? She showed me a wedding photo once and I could see how pretty she'd been. Gorgeous, actually. She told me she'd been twenty when she got married, but she looked much younger than that to me. Too young to know any better, she'd said. I could hardly believe it was the same person, and she could see what I was thinking. After that, she never talked to me unless she had to.

Dad taught in a New York middle school for a while, but lost that job, too. He worked one dead-end job after another from then on and got fired at least every couple of months. All bad luck, none of it his fault, but we'd never learn the truth of it. A drunkard who beat his wife and abused his daughters was our truth. But he had a beautiful speaking voice and was a stickler for good grammar and enunciation. At least he left me with something useful.

His shadow always looked monstrous in the faint night-light of the hall as it came slithering toward my room. The scraping sound of a metal spoon stirring something in a cup made my stomach knot. I curled away into the wall and kept as still as still could be. He'd whisper, "I know you're awake, honey. Sit up now and have your hot, sweet milk like a good girl. Your daddy loves you." He'd stroke my hair while I drank the milk, slow sip by slow sip, my breath shallow and raspy. When he got tired of waiting, he'd take the cup from my hand and set it down as if it were made of paper-thin crystal. He didn't treat me like crystal, but stroked and probed and rubbed and invaded and hurt until he flopped over onto his back, spent.

My mind would come back unwillingly, slower sometimes than others. Our class was taken to a ballet performance once. I must have been about six. The dancers were magical creatures, full of grace and beauty, gliding to the strains of heavenly music. It was another world, a world where wonderful things could happen, where nothing ugly penetrated. I would take myself away to that world and float there through the sordid pain.

Years later, I picked up a book about Hitler. I read several more, each account of his regime's atrocities more horrifying than the last. When I came to the description of Dr. Mengele's work, I suddenly wondered what those children used to think about while he performed his hideous experiments. Did they have some beautiful memory to hold on to, or was the agony too extreme for anything but screaming terror? What can a child do when she is betrayed so horribly? Nothing, of course. She is helpless. I realize there were boys, too, but somehow I only ever thought of the girls.

After it was over, Dad would say, "Goodnight darling. You know your daddy loves you, but remember, it's our little secret." Deathly afraid of his violent temper, if he told me to keep it a secret, I knew I'd better do just that.

After he left the room, I'd hear him washing the cup. I wanted to wash myself, but didn't move until sleep drew me under. In any case, I never felt clean, however much I scrubbed. And I scrubbed a lot. I bled a lot, too, sometimes from him and sometimes from the scrubbing.

When I got my period, all that bleeding was too much, I could hardly stand it. The first time I had it when he came to me, he was furious and slapped my face. "Filthy little slut," he hissed.

He never came to me again. But I had a little sister.

4

Annie Minhoff put down the phone with a sigh. Susan's tirades were tiring and annoying, but must be suffered if she didn't want to be her next target. This particular rant had to do with the appointment of committee chairs. Susan had wanted the Development Committee, but she'd been assigned to Finance. Susan had to be kept away from benefactors. She was too likely to tell them what was wrong with their company, or their house, or even their children.

Earlier, Annie had talked to Helen, who was depressed and confused. She just had to talk to someone, she said. Her life seemed to be out of control even more than usual. Money was tight. Her husband made a good salary but complained that she managed the housekeeping money badly and that she would have to go back to work.

"But I thought he said he didn't want you working. I remember you telling me that several years ago," Annie said.

"Yes, he did. He didn't want me to work because he said he's perfectly capable of supporting his family and wants to come home in the evening to a well-run house and a solid meat-and-potatoes meal on the table. But he says it's all my fault because I manage the housekeeping money badly."

"I was always under the impression that you were very careful, Helen."

"I certainly do my best. I don't know where the money's going. He cut down my housekeeping allowance months ago. He won't talk about it."

"What're you going to do?"

"I've found a clerical job in an office near the center of town, but I need to make my way to something better soon. I've got a master's degree in political science, but that's not much good. And I haven't worked in years. I think I'll have to go back to school if I'm to make a decent salary. What do you think, Annie?"

"I think you should sit down with Pat and have a calm conversation."

"That won't work. Pat will just clam up and leave the room. Well, thanks for listening, Annie. I guess I'll see you and the others on my lunch hour. I won't be able to stay out long."

"So sorry, Helen, I know it must be difficult. Let's talk later. But see if you can talk to Pat."

"Okay, bye."

Annie sighed again. Why couldn't people be kind? It was all beyond Annie's comprehension as she came from a family of reasonable and decent people and was married to a reasonable and decent man.

People tended to like Annie at once as her face radiated goodwill. Her only irritating quirk was a relentless pursuit of logic that kept her friends straight when discussions became emotional and unreasonable. "Let's just review the facts," she would say. Her only child, a daughter, was married and lived in Ohio, so Annie devoted most of her spare time to the Salton Symphony. She worked part-time in one of the town's fashionable clothing boutiques and kept her friends apprised of upcoming sales. She was a walking advertisement for the merchandise as the tailored outfits suited her trim figure. She always kept true to her values—decency and loyalty being chief among them—and was, indeed, the most likeable character in her circle and the only one who enjoyed a good marriage. Her husband, Tom, was an easygoing man who had a strong sense of integrity that he applied to all facets of his life. Many envied them. Susan said they were boring.

The friends usually gathered on Thursdays at the large round table against the back wall of the Salton Family Restaurant. They were not, for the most part, alike in character, or even particularly compatible, but they had adjusted to each other over the years and grown quite fond of one another, and it was a point of honor to "rally round" in times of crisis. They all continued to provide volunteer work to the Salton Symphony, without which no community arts group could survive. Of course, there were always many others involved, but this was the core. They had started calling themselves the "Symphony Seven" after the first year, and there had always been seven of them. Helen had filled her mother's place when her parents moved away, but there was no one waiting in the wings to take Judy's spot.

Annie arrived first with a glum Helen Gandy in tow. She noticed there were seven chairs and caught her breath in dismay; she put her purse under her own chair without comment. Helen was too wrapped up in her own problems to notice the anomaly.

Susan Lazare, the consummate busybody, arrived soon after. Annie should have been used to it by now, but the body language that asserted Susan's presence and made her seem taller and overwhelming as she approached still intimidated her. Susan always scanned the room when she entered so she could spot anyone she knew right away and waylay them for news snippets. Most of her acquaintances tried to hide behind the menu or seemed to be studying the opposite corner of the room, but it did no good. Susan was a heat-seeking missile on a permanent search-and-destroy course. Her long nose quivered, her marble-like eyes gleamed in anticipation, and her hands clutched her purse as a vulture might clutch a tree branch. Unusually, there were no intercepts on this mild September day. Susan strode over to the table and, with a stabbing index finger, counted seven chairs.

"That witless waitress has forgotten already. Oh well, we can hardly expect Judy to be mourned or remembered by most people; indeed, only the circumstances of her death ensure that she is remembered at all."

"Really, Susan, that's a terrible thing to say." Annie's outrage overcame her discretion.

"Well, let's not be hypocritical. I don't believe for a moment that you liked Judy any more than I did, Annie."

Helen said nothing. Annie pursed her lips and retreated behind the menu. When she needed to read, she would hook her wire-rimmed oval glasses over one ear so that the glasses hung under her chin; her swing-cut hair was always getting caught in the hinges and she always had to put the menu down and untangle it. Her friends no longer noticed this ritual. Susan moved a place setting to the coffee stand and set her purse on the chair next to her. Annie wondered if the other women would notice the extra chair. Even if they did, they would probably pretend they hadn't. Susan would find that very amusing, she thought with exasperation as she lifted the menu again. She glanced at Helen with concern, hoping the others would arrive before Susan had a chance to home in on her dispirited mood and conduct a cross-examination.

Susan sat in her usual spot at the back of the table, where she could survey the room. She adopted her mandarin position while she waited for the others, resting her fists on each side of her place setting and bracing her elbows firmly against her waist. Her posture was rigid and her face, with its long nose and darting eyes, kept watch. Her progressive glasses allowed her to see near and far with an infinitesimal inclination of her head. Susan was fifty-three and, as long as anyone could remember, had worn her gray hair in an old lady permanent wave—side part and tight curls. Today's drab and shapeless outfit, almost indistinguishable from all her others, disguised the tall, bony frame and any remnant of femininity. Susan was widowed, childless, and affluent. She didn't work for pay, but volunteered tirelessly. She seemed to know everyone in Salton, and everyone certainly knew her.

Annie silently applauded Helen for trying to put a good face on her low mood. A good-looking woman in her mid-thirties, she had a teenage daughter. She always looked tired these days, her face as washed-out as her clothes. She had recently had her chestnut-brown hair cut very short so that it would be some time before she would need to have it styled again. Annie thought it suited her wide-spaced hazel eyes and freckle-specked face—she had good bones. Helen had been brought up in Salton and had become involved with the symphony with her parents, who had moved to Sarasota some years before. Annie's concern for Helen's well-being derived mostly from her earlier friendship with her mother.

Janet Bakewell rushed in breathlessly.

"So sorry, everyone. Just as I was leaving, I got a call from our delegate's office. There's a fundraiser at—"

"Yes, let's get on with ordering, shall we, or we'll be here all day," Susan said.

While embarrassed for Janet, Annie was relieved. Janet liked nothing better than to name-drop, but a red spot centered on each cheek registered her pique. Annie wondered how long it would take before she reintroduced the subject.

Janet examined the menu with her customary care, extraordinary considering it hadn't changed in at least ten years. There were always two or three Greek specials, but the only woman who ever ventured to order one of them was Rose.

Janet was, as always, impeccable and over-dressed for a simple lunch in a simple restaurant. She wore high heels (she was already tall) and hard-edged clothes with a charm bracelet and various other bits of dangly, clanging jewelry. Her large rings set off her blood-red salon-enhanced talons. Annie could smell her heavy, sweet perfume from across the table, an aroma that always announced her arrival and lingered long after her departure. Annie rarely wore perfume, because Janet's turned her stomach sometimes. Janet's hair remained dark brown, suspiciously so, they all thought, so she looked like a well-preserved fifty-year-old, although Annie knew she was sixty-one. A vain and foolish woman, she would prattle on about her attractive, successful, and above-average adult children and her alleged little social successes until she was stopped—often not too tactfully—by Susan, who needed her own share of center stage. She was one of those women about whom people would employ those damning phrases "she means well" and "she has a good heart, really." She didn't have a job, but should have had, as her active mind needed a healthy outlet. Her husband was considered long-suffering, but he clearly adored her through all her tantrums and sulks. Everyone knew he forgave everything, and usually without comment. Janet was too wrapped up in herself to notice the empty chair. She hung her monogrammed leather purse over the back of her own chair.

Sally trotted in with Rose. A pretty woman in her forties, petite and blonde, she expended enormous amounts of energy trying to please everybody. She had small hands that fluttered often and a head of curly, fluffy hair that, she had once confided to Annie, her husband Jack had told her was not sufficiently sophisticated for their social circle. He didn't like the small mole on the corner of her mouth, either. There was nothing Sally could do about either the hair or the mole, though—she had discovered that sophistication could be very expensive, and Jack was very cheap. Sally was pretty good at pleasing the Seven—they were fond of her—but it seemed she could never get it quite right with Jack. She would cling to his arm and gaze up at him at parties while he told smug little stories about his triumphs and pointed out her perceived inadequacies. The Seven put up with him for Sally's sake, although they felt like kicking her sometimes for her downright stupidity in her willing sufferance of this unworthy tyrant. Sally married at twenty and Jack had pushed her into the group, quite without subtlety, as a way for him to penetrate Salton society. They always tried to protect Sally and make her feel good, although Susan and Janet sometimes had to be sidetracked from unfortunate trends in conversation whenever the subject of Jack came up—Janet would be condescending ("I suppose he can't help it, just doesn't know any better, poor thing.") and Susan would be cutting ("He doesn't seem to be aware of his own limitations, only everyone else's."). Annie did her best to reach out and bolster her self-confidence. Sally and Jack had two sons who were away at college and who rarely saw fit to return home. Sally was always saying how busy they were, but it was obvious to any observer that they despised their parents, one for dishing out the abuse, and the other for taking it.

Sally started when she noticed the empty chair and hurriedly placed her purse on it with the other two. Her eyes looked watery and Susan looked down her nose at her.

Rose Hale seemed to just materialize and took her seat after a serene "Hello everyone." She was a quiet and amenable woman who liked to order unusual dishes—compared to the others' tastes—especially if she had not tried them before. The others found it remarkable in one so determined to be conventional and ordinary in all other respects. Most of their circle had traveled abroad, but were not open-minded when it came to food. Rose was fifty-five and performed ballet barre exercises every morning at home to a tape. Since she abhorred all other forms of exercise, her friends thought this habit strange, but shrugged it off as a small eccentricity. She wore classic matching separates for the most part, but occasionally sported a surprising flash of bright color or glitter. Her facial expression in public was pleasant most of the time, but if her mind wandered, her brow might slowly crumple and settle her face into a sad frown—clearly her natural expression, as Susan had observed some time ago to Annie. And as Susan had told Annie that morning, there were definite signs that Rose had enjoyed her notoriety at the time of Judy's murder. "Still waters run deep," Susan was fond of saying.

Susan settled down to a close scanning of the menu's daily specials. She was as frugal with her money as she was extravagant with other people's business.

"Why don't we order now? It's getting busy in here," she said. "We're ready now, Maria," she commanded across six rows of tables.

As always, Susan ordered meatloaf and mashed potatoes; just water would be fine. Annie ordered a BLT on untoasted white bread, no mayonnaise, and iced tea; her order was so predictable that Susan smirked and even Helen managed a tight smile. Helen ordered a cheeseburger platter and iced tea. Helen and Annie drank iced tea at lunchtime as if they expected to spend the afternoon marooned in a desert. Maria, experienced with this group, placed a pitcher of iced tea and a saucer of lemon wedges in front of them. Janet ordered a chicken salad and, like Susan, water was just fine; Janet scrimped on anything that was not for show. Sally ordered a cheese sandwich; Jack kept her on a tight budget. Rose ordered moussaka and a glass of red wine. Then she sat back and watched the rest of them. Rose watched people a lot.

And so the friends ate and chatted. They talked about the next concert—the first of the season was a couple of weeks away—the constant gaze of the conductor upon one of the pretty young violinists, and the food for the next post-concert reception. They moved on to real estate. The house prices in Salton had risen steeply over the last couple of years, and interest rates remained low.

"Dear Jack is interested in buying a bigger house. It's quite exciting. He feels it would be a good investment," Sally said.

"Your boys are never home, so there are just the two of you. Not much of an investment, unless it's for show," Susan said with acid dripping from her voice.

Sally flushed.

Helen said, "I'm not sure if we can afford to keep ours. Pat keeps saying he can't afford the mortgage. If we sell it, though, we might not be able to buy anything near enough to Salton to keep Toni in her school."

Susan sniffed. "People should learn to live within their means."

This remark seemed to deepen Helen's depression and Annie, more in tune with people's feelings than the others, was concerned. She had been aware for a while that Helen was not herself, but that was natural considering the unease of her marriage. She had never been a particularly upbeat person, but, Annie realized, she must have been unhappy with Pat for a long time. No one whose wishes and needs were always discounted could be expected to be anything but despondent. Annie suspected that perhaps Helen had been mildly depressed for most of her marriage rather than coming by her quiet demeanor naturally. It was so hard to tell, she thought—she hadn't known her as a child. She decided that she would try to see a lot more of Helen and be a source of support whenever needed. Helen should get out more, too.

"You know," Janet said, "I've got that rental house, just opposite the Roberts's. A nice little house, and it might do for you, Helen, at a pinch, until things get taken care of."

"That's nice of you, Janet. And Toni would be able to stay in her school. I'll tell Pat. But don't you have a tenant?"

"I'm not sure she'll be there much longer. Gayle's behind in her rent. But, it's a little odd. She told me she lost her job last month, but had 'come into money' this month. Sounds fishy to me."

"Yes, it certainly does," Rose said. "Did she explain herself?"

"No. But I don't like the sound of it. I'm to meet her at the house in a couple of days—Saturday morning. She said she'd pay me in cash for the arrears and for next month, too. But I'm not happy about it and I might just ask the girl to go if I have another tenant."

"I don't blame you," Susan said. "After all, where would that kind of girl get that kind of money when she's unemployed? She's sure to be involved in something unsavory."

"Quite."

Annie was amused at the women's attitude. While it was true the girl was probably up to something, they liked to impose a strict morality whenever it suited them, and it suited them when the girl in question was young and sexy—undesirable characteristics in their minds. And, of course, Janet was a practical woman. If Helen wanted the house, it wouldn't stay vacant for long.

The chatter went on. Helen's daughter wanted a puppy. She worried that Toni wouldn't take care of it and didn't feel she had the time and energy to do it. Veterinary care could prove expensive, too. Annie was worried about her cherished old cat, who was becoming more stiff-jointed by the day. Janet, of course, didn't care for the odors and detritus of animals in the house. But, she announced, her daughter had just been promoted to director of the sales department in a pharmaceutical company, effectively closing the subject of pets.

Sally had found a marvelously economical recipe for a pseudo *coq au vin* in a magazine at the dentist's office. It combined vinegar and water mixed in with a little red wine, vegetable shortening in place of butter, and the cheapest kind of supermarket mushroom as opposed to a fancy mix.

"That sounds perfectly dreadful," Janet told her.

And Susan added, "Don't even think of serving it on any occasion when your friends might be expected to eat it. You should cook it for that husband of yours, though."

Sally blushed again and hung her head. Annie murmured that these economical recipes sometimes turned out remarkably well. Susan snorted and Sally sent Annie a tremulous smile.

Susan reported a rift in the thirty-year-old marriage of one of the symphony's major donors. The fifty-two-year-old woman had been having an affair with a younger colleague for over a year. Her husband was humiliated and furious—an attitude he had not thought reasonable on the part of his wife when he had had an affair with his secretary a couple of years before, she added. Annie and Sally were surprised; Helen was not. Janet and Susan bristled, and their lips drew into a thin line of disapproval. Rose's eyes twinkled, Annie noticed, even though the rest of her face stayed neutral and she said nothing.

And so another pleasant lunch of the Symphony Seven wound down and everyone went on her way feeling, for the most part, the warmth of old, comfortable friendship.

Gayle dragged her deck chair, book, suntan lotion, and sunglasses out onto the secluded tree-bordered lawn in the back of the house. The sun was out, and she wanted to boost her tan. The early September weather was lovely, not unbearably hot and humid, but just right. She settled herself down, took off her shirt to unleash her large breasts, and opened her novel. The birds chirped and sang and the sky was almost cloudless, but for a few wisps of white. She put down her novel and gazed at the sky, thinking about her little project. She would be able to afford to wait until just the right job came along now. *That stupid woman*, she thought. Did she really think she could get away with it without paying a steep price? She said she hadn't done any-thing wrong but didn't want to "get involved." Gayle thought differently—her binoculars were very powerful, and she had seen the shadows fighting behind the sheers. It was strange that the woman had not lost her temper or cried, as Gayle would have expected.

"I want ten thousand bucks," Gayle said.

"I don't have ten thousand dollars." She seemed too calm.

"Oh, come on. I know how you live."

She regarded Gayle with cold eyes for a few minutes while she thought it over. "No, it's too much," she said coolly. "Think again." She was unnerving, unnaturally still.

"All right, five thousand."

"Agreed. One time only," she said.

Oh, right! Gayle meant to make the most of it. The woman had been much more businesslike and cold than Gayle would have expected. A first-class rich bitch. She'd kick up a big fuss at the next demand for another five thou-sand. It never crossed Gayle's mind that someone who had killed once might not be averse to killing again. She didn't realize that those minutes of "thinking it over" had nothing to do with money.

Life around Gayle was busy. The birds were pushing their last fledglings out of their nests, the flowers opened toward their final glory, and the faint breeze through the trees fanned her sun-warmed nipples. The insects were also busy and their buzzing, humming, and whirring carried her into gentle sleep. A shadow blocked the sun's face from hers and caused her to stir toward wakefulness until the knife plunged her into the deepest sleep.

Janet arrived at the little house at the appointed hour. She rang the bell and knocked, but no one came to the door. She decided to use her key and go in. She had an appointment and Gayle was behind in her rent, so she felt entitled to make sure the girl had not run out on her. She wrinkled her nose at the state of the kitchen. Dirty dishes were on the table and meat set out on the counter was covered with flies. She went through the other rooms and found that all Gayle's possessions seemed to be in place and, in the bedroom, her clothes were either in the closet or on the floor. The rumpled bed was unmade and the bottom of the bathtub looked more gray than white. Gayle wasn't much of a housekeeper—the place hadn't been vacuumed in weeks and the bathroom looked as if it hadn't been cleaned since she moved in. The cottage should have been charming with its small irregular rooms, country kitchen, and enclosed garden. Janet looked out of the grimy kitchen window at the garden and a movement in the tall, weedy grass caught her eye. She rummaged in her bag for her driving glasses. There was a strange black cloud out there, and it seemed to be hovering over a canvas deck chair. The wind shifted, and the cloud undulated in perfect formation. She noticed a limp arm hanging and felt a sudden chill—something was very wrong. Then she noticed a dark stain on the canvas back of the chair. The best thing to do would be to call the police and stay inside; she did call, but a strange compulsion forced her to go and check on Gayle, an action she would regret for the rest of her life. She managed to stagger as far as the front garden before she passed out.

When Janet revived, the police and paramedics were there and there was a great deal of activity, some of it around her. But the only thing she could focus on was the horrific picture etched in her mind, as clear as if she were again standing in front of Gayle. Janet, like most people, had never had to confront the brute ugliness of violent death before. Nothing had prepared her for bloody bodies left out in the sun, the sharp smell of blood mixed with the foul-sweet smell of excrement, and the dreadful industry of flies over a carcass.

It was not like the television crime shows Janet watched; whoever found the body was comforted and medicated, had a good night's sleep, and seemed articulate and reasonably normal by the morning. Janet would be haunted by nightmares and flashbacks for many months to come. The sight of road-kill would be enough to nauseate her for the rest of the day. She would never eat her meat rare again and she could barely eat at all for a month. She became addicted to sleeping pills and drank a little too much in the evenings; her children became so alarmed by her distress that they showered her with loving attention, and, overwhelmed by their concern and tenderness, Janet finally began to speak of them with love rather than false pride.

Her family persuaded Janet to see a psychiatrist to help her overcome her phobias and fears. She called to make the first appointment with great reluctance, but she had warmed to the sound of the doctor's voice. He looked just like Janet had imagined from the sound of him—not tall and not short, neither fat nor thin, and he had gray hair and a stout build. He looked like anyone's grandfather when he smiled at her and folded his hands over his stomach. She talked a lot, and he listened a lot, and he guided her thoughts with gentle kindness. After they had exhausted the subject of the murder, he directed her attention to her behavior and addictions; she learned to listen to herself as others heard her. Over time, she learned to take a genuine interest in other people. She was never a bad woman, but had been a spoiled only child who had never been taught the value of people as anything other than a support system for her ego. It was a testament to her innate goodness that after a lifetime of enabled selfishness, she would be able to transform herself into a reasonable adult over the course of a year. She began to paint her nails in soft shades of pink—everything about her seemed softer.

5

Pansy

I woke to the sound of the baby crying. Mom worked nights and had just started back because we needed the money. I got out of bed to go comfort her, but froze when I realized Dad was already there. I crept to the door, which was ajar, and peeked through. The nightlight cast an orange glow over him as he stood by her crib wearing that devilish expression—clenched teeth and clenched eyes—I had seen so many times before. What I saw next spawned a lumpy sick feeling in the pit of my stomach that has never entirely gone away.

He sat in the rocking chair and laid the baby on her back on a cushion set on his lap. Then he began to play with her and himself, pushing against her so that she wailed in pain. His eyes were half closed as he lost himself in ecstasy, deaf and blind to the distress of his own baby. After he'd finished his desecration, he put her diaper back on and set her down in her crib. She cried like a newborn kitten, hardly able to catch her breath. I darted back to my bed and kept very still under the covers while he checked to make sure I was asleep. I didn't want him to know I'd been spying on him—the punishment would have been harsh.

Why wasn't I enough? Was this a new depravity or had he started on Daisy that young? He didn't bother her anymore. At least I didn't think so, so how old was too old, how young was too young? I had his monster blood in me, all three of us did—Daisy, the baby, and I.

When I heard his snores, grating like a rasp on my nerves, I crept back to the baby's room. The little one looked up at me with wide, pain-filled eyes—gorgeous, big blue eyes. She was quiet now, although her chest still heaved. "I'm your big sister. I have to save you from him," I whispered. I took the pillow Dad had used and pressed it over her face. The tiny perfect feet kicked a little but were soon still. I carefully placed the pillow back on the chair. I looked down at her once more. She was at peace now.

So pretty, she was. I wonder what she would have been like now. Could she have been happy? I doubt it. I wish she had died before she suffered so cruelly; I wish I could have spared her that awfulness. Well, I spared her years of pain and degradation. Of course, it released me from him, too, although I went on to other miseries. I can't remember her name now.

As soon as Dad left for work the next morning, I ran outside, flagged down a police car, and told them what I had seen that night, adding that I had seen Dad suffocate the baby. One of the cops cried as he looked down at the beautiful, motionless doll on the sheet.

Semen on the pillow and diaper clinched his fate. I didn't look at him while I testified, and I never saw him again. He died in prison, stabbed by another inmate; a worthless life brought to an ignoble end.

My mother's grief at the loss of her baby lasted about a week—I suspect she was relieved at some level. She blamed me for the loss of her husband's wages and the humiliation of it all coming out. It never occurred to her to blame herself for letting it happen. It never occurred to her to feel ashamed for letting him do that to his daughters, to feel sorry for us and our pain. Her own troubles were all that concerned her. She must have known. But she was scared of him and she needed what little money he gave her. Her betrayal angers me more than his. He was just a rotten pervert, but she was a mother, for God's sake.

She got drunk and gave me a good beating after the verdict came in. One day, she packed up and disappeared while Daisy and I were at school. The landlord wouldn't even let us back in the apartment. He'd changed the lock because he'd spotted her slipping out of the building with a suitcase and she hadn't paid the rent. He called the cops and left us standing crying on the street without so much as a kind word. I suppose he thought we were all trash. I suppose we were.

Daisy was sixteen, so she quit school and got a job. She never admitted it, but I'm sure she worked as a hooker, at least for a while. I saw her once on a street corner downtown, hanging out with a few girls who were definitely on the game. She didn't look quite as tarty as they did, but I saw her get into a car. Even at that age, I knew all about cruising and hooking. It isn't easy to support yourself in New York without skills, especially at that age, so I didn't blame her.

She was never very bright in school, so finding a white-collar job was probably not an option.

I wondered if having sex with those guys felt like Dad. Did they reek of booze, did they like it rough? Did they get crazy and beat her if they couldn't get it up? Did they whisper nasty words in her ear? Did it hurt, or had she learned to use baby oil like I had? I wondered about all those things that day before frantically pushing the wondering down and away. Thinking back on it, it makes me mad that I knew enough to wonder about things like that.

We didn't see much of each other after we went our separate ways, over forty years ago now. I can't believe she recognized me in that photo after all this time. She must have the instincts of a bloodhound. She would suddenly appear every now and then, even after I left school and started working, though I never looked for her and tried to cover my tracks each time I moved. I don't know why she would come, she never said, so I assumed it was just curiosity. She did say once that trouble seemed to follow me around, which I considered an odd remark at the time, because she couldn't have known anything about my life, or so I thought. Perhaps she was keeping better track of me than I knew.

I was only fourteen when Mom left, so I was abandoned to foster homes. Bad things happen in foster homes, too.

6

Helen Gandy sighed as she surveyed her daughter's room. The closet was nearly empty, and the floor was nearly full.

"Toni," she said, struggling for a calm tone. "What exactly do you need to take to the slumber party tonight? I don't see any clean clothes."

"Oh, it's all right, Mom. I saved the clothes I need from the last wash. See, I do plan ahead."

"You will not leave this house until your clothes are picked up. The things that need washing are to go in the hamper, and the others are to be folded and put tidily into drawers or hung in the closet. I mean it, Toni."

"That is so unfair. You'll make me late. It's not my fault you're in a bad mood."

How she hoped Toni would become a mother who would have such fruitless conversations with her child. She was apprehensive about this evening, so perhaps she had been more impatient than usual with her daughter. She was not yet used to working and running the house, either, although Pat seemed to expect everything to be done for him just as before. She was tired by evening and no longer wanted to cook anything but the simplest dinners, but Pat would not accept tiredness as an excuse—after all, it was her fault that she couldn't manage money and had to work.

When Pat heard that Toni was to be out all night, he had responded to Helen's suggestion that they go out somewhere by saying they should spend the evening at home. He had something to discuss with her. His expression was hard and neutral; not a good something, then, but she couldn't even begin to guess what it was all about. She hoped there was nothing wrong at work, especially since he would not answer her questions about why money was suddenly tight, except to blame her. His health seemed good, but he had been in a bad mood even more than usual these past few months and she couldn't do anything right in his eyes. Where was the money going? Oh, well, it would do no good to wonder, and it did no good to ask.

Toni's friend's house was a half-hour's drive outside town in a rural area and Helen felt uneasy as she wended her way through the narrow roads. There was a murderer at large, after all, and this was a lonely place. As she pulled into the driveway, she noticed a familiar car pulling up outside the small house on the opposite side of the street. There weren't too many Mercedes station wagons around, especially pale blue ones. Yes, that was Davey Roberts—Judy's husband—getting out of the car. He walked quickly up to the front door, looked around, and let himself in. What on earth could he be doing there?

After Toni had raced down to the basement to carve pumpkins with her friends—they planned a grotesque display for their school lobby—Helen asked the girl's mother who lived across the street, "I thought I saw a man I used to know going in there."

"Oh, is he back? We haven't seen him for over a month. That's Cynthia Pullman, the girl with the bleached, curly hair who works at All Green Thumbs—you know, that flower shop in the Salton Mall. You must have noticed her. He's been visiting for a couple of years now. We have no idea who he is. Do you know him then?"

"I think I used to know him, but I can't remember his name. Because of all the awful things that have happened in Salton lately, I'm a little worried. It's so quiet out here."

"Oh, don't worry, Helen. The girls won't be allowed to go anywhere, and I'll be sure to keep the doors locked. You knew the victims, didn't you? It must have been a terrible shock."

"I only knew one, but the girl was the tenant of a friend and she's in a terrible state after discovering her body. It might not even be the same person. There might be two murderers."

"How dreadful! Well, don't you worry, I'll take care of them."

So, she thought as she drove home, *Davey has had a mistress for at least two years, took a break from her after the murder, and was now visiting again.* How extraordinary! He had always seemed so quiet—almost mouse-like, especially around the ghastly Judy. Then she had a shocking thought. Maybe there was a motive for killing Judy in all of this. She ought to go to the police. But would she? She needed to think it over, maybe discuss it with Annie and Rose.

By midnight, everything was over—the discussion, Helen's marriage, and even the crying. Any thought of what she had seen at the little house that afternoon was quite forgotten. Pat wanted to leave her and had already done so.

"I'm just bored with my life, Helen, and I'm certainly bored with you. You've really become very dull. I have to be honest. I'm an honest sort of person, as you know. I don't love you anymore. Not at all."

Helen's stomach churned. Of course he didn't love her. She'd known that for years. Honest? He must be kidding.

"Is there someone else, Pat?"

"Oh, no, I'm not a cheat. There's no one. I just want to start a new life."

"What about Toni?"

"She'll get used to it, and I'll take her out some weekends. She's busy with school, anyway. You can tell her about it in the morning. I'm packing the rest of my stuff tonight and going. I took most of it while you were taking Toni to her friend's house."

"What's the next step?"

"Well, my attorney can handle matters for both of us. There's no need to waste money on two attorneys. Anyway, you don't have any money of your own, do you? My guy's already drawn up a settlement, and it's pretty fair. I'm sure you'll agree. We'll have to sell the house, of course. It's way too big for just you and Toni."

"And then where will we go?"

"Somewhere where you can live within your alimony. Which will end once Toni turns eighteen."

"What about college?

"Oh, she can get a scholarship. She's a bright girl. And I'll help out where I can, of course."

"That all seems to be pretty much in your favor." She was tearing up now.

"Well, you've had it easy all these years while I've been working my butt off. And you're still fairly attractive. You'll probably find someone suitable, eventually. Just take my attorney's advice and do things the easy way. Do what's best for all of us."

As she listened to him bluster on, her mind slipped from tearful recrimination into a strangely detached state. She heard and memorized his comments and would process them later. For now, she said nothing. Her long familiarity with Pat's mannerisms put him at a disadvantage—she knew he was lying.

She hadn't seen it coming. After he left, she gazed at her ashen face in the bathroom mirror for a long time. She stippled her clammy fingers over her skin, then ran them through her hair. She looked dry and colorless, as if the life were being leached out of her, though she used to be considered attractive. Perhaps she had grown plain because of age. Perhaps she was plain because she was not loved. Maybe she was not loved because she was plain. She could no longer tell how others might see her. She wasn't sure exactly what she was looking at—she looked like someone she used to know but had long ago lost touch with. Her shoulders sagged. She wanted to sleep and sleep and took a glassful of bourbon to bed with her. She fell asleep after gulping the last mouthful and dreamed dreams she had forgotten by morning.

The next morning's headache stoked her anger. Her first priority was to take care of Toni, and her mother-love spurred her into action. She called an old family friend who was an attorney. "This isn't a do-it-yourself job," he told her.

He recommended a divorce attorney who, in turn, put her in touch with a private investigator. She had an appointment with both the following day. She didn't believe for a moment that Pat didn't have someone else.

Helen then turned her attention to their bedroom—her bedroom. It was a gloomy room, even with the morning sun pouring through the window, because Pat had insisted on having it painted a dark, "masculine" shade of green. It would be painted white very soon, however many coats it took. Pat had removed his clothing but left a mess, as always. There were old receipts, underwear, odd socks, and other useless items he couldn't be bothered to throw out. She scrutinized each piece of paper in case it was evidence of his misdeeds; one receipt was for a motel in Maryland and she tucked it into her purse—she would give it to the investigator.

Helen cleaned his closet with disinfectant. She would paint it before she moved her out-of-season clothes into it. She wanted it sanitized. Indignant, she shouted out loud, "I will not move out of this house. This is my home, damn you!" She looked at her watch. Toni was getting a ride home, and she still had a few hours before she had to break the news. She didn't know how Toni would take it. Even through her anger, Helen realized she was scared—she hadn't been alone for a long time. Was being miserable with Pat better than being alone, perhaps forever?

Perhaps Toni would be afraid of what the future might bring, but Helen didn't think she would miss her father. It was not as if Pat had ever paid his daughter much attention. When he noticed her, the encounter often took the form of negative commentary—this grade wasn't good enough, that friend was not from the social circle he would have wished, and so on.

Helen sat on the bed. Later, she would wash the sheets and blankets and spray them with lavender water. His smell had to be erased. Thank God, no more sex with him. He'd never really made love to her, just fucked her with the finesse of an ape every couple of days. Never said a word. And the last time was three days ago. If he did have someone else, when did he fuck her? How many hours before he came home to fall on her? Had they mingled fluids? Helen ran to the bathroom and vomited. That kind of thinking was poison. It had to stop.

She looked in her own closet. She found a box of maternity clothes in the back and pulled out a silky maternity dress; she remembered the last time she had worn it. He'd made her striptease to music—she'd been eight months pregnant at the time and felt self-conscious and degraded. He had laughed all the while, and when she had finished remarked how fat and ridiculous she looked. She should have kicked him down the stairs. She took out all her clothes, examined them critically. The maternity clothes would be given to the thrift store. Some outfits were old, but of good quality and worth keeping. The recently purchased tops and skirts were not so good, but they'd do until she could replace them. Her new wardrobe would not be large, but would be classy. She still had some good shoes, bags, and plenty of scarves with which she could create different looks for the same outfits. She felt a twinge of excitement as she realized she had not taken an interest in her appearance for several years. A new look for a new life.

By mid-afternoon, Pat's former closet was painted with some leftover latex Helen had found in the utility room— dry in an hour. She found its slight residual odor pleasing. She would just have time to put her clothes away before Toni came home. First, she went downstairs to the kitchen to eat a late lunch. She couldn't see the glow in her cheeks or the new life in her eyes, which would diminish little by little as the time of Toni's arrival grew closer.

Toni shouted and cried in anger and fear. "The bastard, leaving us like that. Doesn't he care for me at all? You're not supposed to leave a kid, and did he really say we should move out of here? Bastard!"

Helen was shocked at the vehemence of her daughter's emotions and strong language, not that she could talk, even though she'd not uttered those things, just thought them. She should have expected it, she should have realized that children always hope they come first with their parents. When Toni calmed down, they sat next to each other on the sofa. They looked into each other's eyes that brimmed with tears. Toni clasped Helen's hands in her own in the manner of a mourner expressing condolences.

"Poor Mom, you must be so sad. I'm so sorry. I was only thinking of myself."

"Don't worry about me. I'm fine. It's you I'm worried about, how you feel about things. I haven't been happy for a long time, I think you know that. You have to learn to accept your father's limitations. He does love you, I'm sure, but I don't think he can love anyone a whole lot. He's just not capable of it. Tomorrow, I'm going to visit an attorney to make sure we are well provided for. I am determined to stay in this house. I don't want you to worry. I'll take care of things."

"We'll be fine, Mom. Dad was never around much, and when he was, he wasn't very nice. To tell the truth, I don't think I'll miss him much. I hope he doesn't expect me to spend a lot of time with him."

"I think that will be up to you, Toni. You need to have a relationship with your father. It would be a mistake to cut him out of your life."

"I love you, Mom. If you feel like crying or you're lonely, we'll just have a good hug."

Helen flung her arms around Toni and they held each other and rocked gently, each taking comfort in the touch and tears of the one who mattered most.

Toni went up to her room to change and start her homework. Helen wondered if she would be able to concentrate. She sprawled on the sofa, exhausted. What an outstanding child. No, an outstanding person. All those years hadn't been entirely wasted. If she hadn't married Pat, she wouldn't have had Toni. She had let Pat get away with too much early in the marriage. She had set the precedent for him to ride roughshod over her feelings and needs when she had gone along with the striptease. She had tried to keep his pouting, sulking, and tantrums at bay, and, before she knew it, it was too late to set another pattern. Pat had done a masterful job persuading her of her inadequacies as a wife and mother— it was easier to control her that way. She was sufficiently lacking in confidence and self-esteem that she always sus- pected he might be right, and by the time she was able to perceive his character defects clearly, she felt empty and powerless to change anything. She wasn't sure when the last vestige of her love had died—it had started to slip away years ago and had oozed steadily into an early grave.

She pulled herself together, stopped thinking about the past, at least for a time, and went into the kitchen to cook dinner. She had bought pasta and the ingredients for a classic pesto. She cleaned and ripped the basil with furious satisfaction. Pat hated pesto. Well, screw him.

Helen met with the attorney first and gave him the name of Pat's attorney.

"I want the house and enough money to enable Toni and me to live comfortably."

Next, she met with the investigator, outlined the situation, and passed over the motel receipt—very useful, as it turned out. The investigator started on her case immediately and got results in a week. When Pat was faced with undeniable proof of adultery, his ownership of another house in which he had installed his loved one, and proof of other assets acquired and concealed over the years, the original settlement offer had been substantially improved. Helen kept the house and he would pay. Helen briefly wondered how long the excitement of Pat's new romance would last in his straightened circumstances. Given his egocentric nature, Helen felt it would not be long before he started to blame his inamorata for their diminished situation.

News got out fast. Some of her friends stuck, and some did not. She had become "available." The Seven stuck by her, of course, and saw that she was invited to social functions and that Pat was not. Susan sniffed a lot—she had disliked Pat even more than she disliked most people—while the others commiserated. A few weeks after Pat moved out, Annie reminded Helen that it was time to help organize the Salton Foundation Christmas party. Helen had quite forgotten, although she had helped with that party for ten years, as had her mother before her. She called the committee chair, Phoebe Stevens, that evening to explain her preoccupation and offer to assist however she could.

"Yes, Helen, I'm sorry—I've heard about your troubles. I think we have most of our bases covered by now, so we won't be needing anything from you this year. But thank you for asking. See you very soon, I'm sure. Goodbye!"

This was the first of several snubs. Helen was tearful, then angry, before finding an even keel after she realized that she didn't care about such people; they and their petty insecurities weren't worth worrying about. Susan, to the Sevens' amazement, was furious with those who treated Helen so poorly—sooner or later, she vowed, they would suffer for it.

"I told that Phoebe Stevens that straying husbands are not unusual and hardly reflect on the character of their wives—as she might remember from her own experience a few years ago," she reported to Annie with gusto. "And when Marge tried to avoid inviting Helen to the Foundation Christmas party, I reassured her that her husband would definitely be safe, because if Helen had the poor judgment to want another relationship with a man she would be looking for someone younger, thinner, and better looking." Susan's arsenal of verbal weaponry was deadly.

It didn't take long for Helen to rediscover her naturally cheerful demeanor as the depression of many years gradually slid away, nurtured as she was by the love and concern of the Seven and her daughter. Annie was an especially good friend, giving the gift of frequent undemanding companionship. Helen's parents called and expressed dismay at her situation. Her father said she should have tried harder, and her mother sounded sympathetic, but couldn't say too much with her husband listening. Helen cried after she hung up. Why had she not recognized the pattern?

Helen was watching the news one evening when she was interrupted by a breathless phone call from Sally. The police were questioning someone in connection with Judy Robert's murder. A homeless man had been in the area on the day of the murder and had, in fact, knocked on a few doors in the Roberts's street looking for handouts. It was only then that Helen remembered what she had seen on the evening of her husband's thunderbolt. Should she tell Sally? She had to tell someone. No, Sally could be indiscreet. Best to call Annie.

The revelation shocked Annie into silence for a few minutes.

"Annie, are you still there?"

"Yes, let's have lunch tomorrow. Not at Salton Family Restaurant, there'll be too many people we know there. Let's go to Constantine's on Prospect. No one we know ever goes there."

"Okay, I feel I should tell the police, but I should have done it right away. I was just so distracted."

The friends met and went over it. The fact was that neither of them had liked Judy and didn't want to cause Davey trouble he might not deserve. They agreed, however, that the matter was so serious that Helen must come forward.

"I'll come with you, Helen. I'll tell them what's been going on in your life and that it was only when you heard news of this arrest that you remembered."

"No, I'll tell them everything. You can just back me up if they ask you questions."

So off they went. Helen met with Detective Paglietti and did her civic duty. She explained to him the sequence of events in her life that caused her to forget to come forward with what she had learned the evening of the Halloween party and how the phone call from Sally had jogged her memory.

Things took a very ugly turn for poor Davey and his mistress.

Davey sat at his kitchen table, crumbling toast between his fingers and looking out over the garden without seeing it. He was still shocked by the feeling of helplessness and claustrophobia he had suffered over the two days he was interrogated by the police. The interrogation room was small, sludge brown, and had two small windows set very high. After a couple of hours, it stank of men's sweat—the product of a cop's kinetic questioning and Davey's growing panic. The smell would linger in his nostrils for hours and in his mind for months.

He told them the same thing over and over again. The morning of Judy's death, he had left home at about seven-thirty to meet with a client who had to catch a flight to Rome later in the day. The meeting was scheduled at eight and the client had left at about nine-thirty. The police said that Judy had been killed between about nine and ten in the morning. Until nine, there had been no one in the office except the two of them. This client was in Rome again when the interrogation started and Davey didn't know where he was staying. He could only leave urgent messages at the man's office. Finally, after two days of questioning and accusations, the client returned and established Davey's alibi. Other staff members could vouch for him after nine o'clock.

Cynthia was not so lucky. She had been at home until it was time to go to work at ten. She had slept late that day and hadn't arrived at work until ten-thirty. She had no alibi but had, as the police brought up many times, a strong motive to get rid of Judy. There was no evidence against her, however, so they had to let her go. The flower shop didn't want to keep an employee suspected of murder, although, as Cynthia pointed out, they must consider their legal position—she was innocent until proven guilty, wasn't she?

"Cynthia, this is Davey. How are you? Are you all right?"

"I suppose. It isn't very pleasant being dragged into a police station and accused of murder. The shop wanted to fire me, too, but I put a stop to that. Threatened to sue them."

"I'm so sorry. I didn't love her, but I wouldn't have wished such a terrible end for her."

"Well, she was a horrible woman by all accounts, and you're well rid of her."

"You shouldn't talk like that."

Cynthia remained silent.

"Do you think we should see each other as things stand?" Davey asked, not sure what he wanted to hear.

"Better wait until they catch the one who did it. I might have to go away, too."

"Go away? Where?"

"The shop people won't be very nice to me now. I'll make sure they give me a good reference and then look for a place somewhere a long way away from here. I've got no ties, after all."

"What about me? Don't I count as a tie?"

"That's not exactly a tie, is it? It's not as if we're engaged or anything. It would look funny after all this."

"I suppose you're right. Can I call you next week?"

"Let's leave it a while. I'll call you when I'm ready."

They hung up after a final awkward silence.

Davey sat for a while, feeding on his thoughts. Suddenly, he lumbered to his feet and began the odious job of sorting out his dead wife's clothing. He hadn't asked his daughter if she wanted any of it. He would give it all to charity, get it out of the house.

Who could have found out about him and Cynthia? He had been very discreet, but perhaps she had not been able to resist telling a friend. He didn't believe she could have had anything to do with the murder. She was so gentle. He had met her at the flower shop. He used to stop every Friday on his way home to buy flowers for Judy in an effort to thaw the chill before the weekend. He loved to watch her caress the flowers. Her touch on their petals was so delicate and her look so tender, like a lover's. When he pictured it now—now his feelings were cooler—her flower fondling seemed odd, even creepy. But back then he had found it enchanting, per-haps because he hungered for that touch, that look. Every Friday he stopped longer to chat and, one day, she had asked him to come for dinner at her little home outside town. Meeting in a local restaurant was out of the question; she understood. Suddenly he felt bold and accepted. They had become lovers that first evening two years before.

Cynthia caressed his face as she did the flowers, and it soothed his soul. Her body was white and plump, but not particularly responsive. Her caresses never strayed from his face and back, however much he tried to guide her hands where he wanted to feel them. He was aware that she did not have the capacity for deep love, but she was capable of giving him affection, and that's mostly what he wanted. They talked a lot, but about what he could not now recol-lect, except that she had been at him to leave Judy and didn't understand why he couldn't bring himself to do it.

She didn't know what his wife was like. Judy would have hounded him until she had destroyed him, and Davey was not courageous. Judy had had a way of making his protests on any subject sound unconvincing and childish, and she could make him feel an inch tall. Her voice would become high and sharp as she made chopping motions with the edge of her right hand to add emphasis to each cutting remark. She stood over him while he wilted in his chair until she took on the aspect of a giant bird of prey. She had made a wreck of him and emotionally stunted the children.

They hadn't had sex for six years. That last time, she'd been in a towering rage and she'd grabbed at him and ground her hips into his—it had been predatory and violent, and he couldn't perform. Her disdain had been withering, and he'd gone off to the guest bedroom, where he'd slept ever since. He didn't even move back after she died. It didn't feel right. He'd wondered if he'd ever be able to do it with a woman, if it would always be a solitary event from then on. At least Cynthia had dispelled that worry.

And he'd let it all go on and on. In all likelihood, it was boredom with him and disappointment with his career that had turned her so shrewish. He had done well and made a good income, but he knew she had wanted real wealth and realized she was not going to get it. She tried to push him into a number of entrepreneurial schemes. He knew that he did not have the personality to make a success of that type of business. At least he had stood up to her on that count, although mostly by ignoring the issue until she shut up.

Davey stared at the snowy landscape hanging above the fireplace and, as the morning wore on, he became more and more focused on it, finding the beauty of the snow-covered mountains soothing and almost hypnotic. His mind wandered back over other snow scenes. He thought of his first girlfriend, Amy, so pretty and sweet he had fallen in love with her at once. He remembered walking through the park with her on their first date as the snow was falling. She had delighted in the silent massing of a million flakes. The sun hung in a slate sky, the trees sparkled under their frosting, the world was peaceful, and they were happy, so happy. Davey had always been quiet, although a smile had never been far from his lips in those days. Amy had died in a terrible car accident not long after. The memory that had started happy became sharp and painful. A bad death, and the death of real passion, too. The affairs that followed were sometimes born of affection, but more often than not, just scratching an itch.

After graduation, Davey had moved to Salton to start work in an accounting firm in the town center. He rented an apartment only a ten-minute walk from the office. He remembered winter mornings when he trudged through messy, slushy, slippery snow under a dead sky; sitting at his desk and watching through the third-story window as cars skidded, people struggled and sometimes fell, dogs peed little yellow pits and left their droppings on top of the snow as gifts to the unwary. Taxes were too low in Virginia to provide such amenities as efficient snow removal, and so the snow blanket remained, white turning to dirty gray.

He remembered a ski weekend in the mountains with friends, his first time to try the sport. His first experience of the exhilarating, cold, frightening flight down a slope had made Davey feel gloriously, differently alive. The second and last time down, he fractured a kneecap. He still had a slight limp, especially in cold weather. Exhilarating experiences seemed to take their toll. Cynthia, for example. Amy, too—her love had been beyond exhilarating.

He remembered another snowy weekend spent hibernating with Sylvia, another accountant in the firm. She had rented a cottage with a fireplace. They made love on a quilt in front of the fire, ate scalding soup, drank mulled wine, and slept the sleep of the satiated. She later got a better job that took her to Chicago. They wrote for a while, but it petered out after a few months. There'd been nothing between them other than sex.

When the children were small, a snowfall brought excitement, snowsuits, snowballs, snowmen, sleds, snow angels, and rosy cheeks—some of the makings of a sweet childhood. Judy always spoiled it, though. These happy ordinary events—the ice tracked into the house, the wet clothing that had to be put in the drier, the clamor for hot chocolate—provoked the woman to seething anger. Not even his efforts shoveling the snow pleased her, as the results never satisfied her exacting requirements. "Can't you even get that right?" It didn't take long for any remaining affection to erode and all their feelings to flatten. Davey became morose, and the children kept their emotions strictly in check. Davey cursed the impulse that had taken him to the concert where he had met Judy. It was snowing that night, too, and he had walked her home, holding her by the arm so she wouldn't slip. It was hard to believe now how charming she was then, and attractive, too; she had made him feel like a prince. Her transformation into a harridan had started almost immediately as she tried to change him to fit some formula she had clearly had in mind all along. Davey wondered about his son's marriage. He had been an affectionate little boy, at least with Davey, when his mother wasn't around. Was he able to give and receive love, or had Judy trampled all that? His wife seemed happy enough and was a sweet girl, nothing like Judy, who had inevitably disliked her.

When Davey shaved that morning, he'd seen a gray face staring back at him, gray sparse hair, and no laugh lines at all, although his forehead was scored. The man he used to be had died long ago, suffocated. He had been grateful that Cynthia seemed to enjoy his company. She told him she had been abused by boyfriends in the past and felt safe and comfortable with him. Yes, he supposed he was a comfortable person to be with, most people would say boring. He again pictured Cynthia caressing her flowers and knew he was finished with her, didn't want to feel that touch ever again. The thought of her repelled him, suddenly. What he wanted was to be left alone to live in peace. No women. He would make an effort to see more of his children, though. They might welcome his visits now because he could come alone.

Davey looked away from the painting and out of the window at his garden, no snow here, nothing beautiful and unsullied. Just falling leaves, moldering and slippery.

7

Pansy

Sukie had been quite beautiful, but not anymore. She got in my way, gloated, and stole my boyfriend. The morning before she died, Sukie taunted me for the last time. Yet again she asked me if I was having my period because I looked so terribly bloated, especially my face. And then she laughed her nasty little shrieky laugh that stretched my nerves to the breaking point. People should never, ever, laugh at me. I didn't have the drive or interest to do whatever it took to win him back, but Sukie couldn't be allowed to get away with it.

Bloated! That word and that laugh kept running through my brain until I couldn't concentrate on my work or any-thing else. One night I even dreamed of her chasing me through the streets of New York shouting "You're so bloated, bloated, bloated!" and my face swelled up to monstrous pro-portions as I tried to escape her. It had to stop.

This wasn't so tidy—there'd have to be a closed casket. They couldn't do anything to patch her up, I didn't think. It was her face that looked bloated now—disgustingly so. It didn't take much strength, just rage and a good weapon—his fingerprints on the poker and the little leftovers of recent love-making. I had watched it all, had seen him use the poker to stoke up the fire, and then use her in front of it, that double-crossing son-of-a-bitch. After he left, Sukie was startled, then scared, to see me emerge from the closet. A blow to the head, a little bruising around the thighs, some stage management, and then the final killing blows. It felt so good, like getting out a splinter after it has festered. I replaced the poker, threw apron and gloves in the fire, on went the blonde wig and dark raincoat (soon to be burned elsewhere), and off I slipped into the foggy Brooklyn night.

I had no more use for him. I despised him. When I'd confronted him about Sukie, he told me he hated my possessiveness, that it was over, that I was crazy. But it would never be over, not for him. He'd pay for it with the rest of his life. I wonder if he ever guessed what really happened? Of course, I didn't visit him in prison, so I have no idea what he thought. And I wasn't crazy, just angry.

I resigned from my job in Brooklyn because I was "so unnerved by the tragedy." They were very nice and understanding and gave me an extra two weeks' pay. I guess that's what people call a win-win situation.

I have often thought back on the Sukie business. It was over the top. Not necessary, and dangerous, too. The baby I saved—you could call that a mercy killing. Certainly a mercy killing. But why did I start to hurt other people?

Because it was an obvious solution to the problem at hand. Those other times—the other deaths—were to save my life, my *way* of life. Self-defense. I am courageous, not afraid to do what needs to be done. And most people are soon forgotten, you know.

Before Sukie, when I was angry, I would get hot behind the eyes, my stomach would knot, my fists clenched, and I couldn't see properly. I'd turn away and take some deep breaths to force myself back to self-control. Self-control is essential if you want to lead the good life and project the right image; but Sukie taunted me, got under my skin, and I shouldn't have let her. And it's not as though I had any intention of sleeping with him—I couldn't bear the thought of it—so I would have lost him, anyway. But on my terms.

The day after Sukie first told me I looked bloated, I lay in bed and planned it all. Then I felt much better and finally had a good night's sleep. The rage spilled over only at the right time, when I needed it, when I was killing her. I didn't feel it again for a long time. I felt much better about myself, calmer, and I had a sort of serene self-confidence. I didn't have to worry about self-control after that. It came easily. Just a little stomach cramp, a little shortness of breath, and a promise to myself to plan a grand solution (not always killing, by the way). It's all a matter of mastering self-control, you see. And good planning—but I faltered on that front and it has cost me.

8

R ose leafed through her program. The Salton Symphony's second concert of the season presented a music program remarkable only in its predictability. That spring, the board had had the usual annual discussions with the music director. The musicians wanted a challenge, and the audience did not. Rose, tired of the meandering discussion, had finally offered up the blunt opinion that if the symphony were to survive in these financially troubled times, the seats must be filled and the preferences of their supporters must be accommodated. This audience didn't like surprises and certainly did not appreciate any music that could be considered contemporary. They liked tunes. Shostakovich drove them away, and Tchaikovsky beckoned them. No doubt about it.

Rose thought the patrons seemed edgy tonight—the recent unpleasantness had skewered their complacency.

She nodded pleasantly to her numerous acquaintances and found her seat as soon as she arrived. She was not in the mood for breathless speculation.

The conductor entered with his usual aplomb to polite applause. The audience pasted on a collective expression of classical inspiration and sat through the first half with relatively little fidgeting, considering the determined output of the guest soprano. She sang a selection of syrupy arias from the mighty depths of her breast with appropriate gesture and fervency, shrilly proving herself unfit for the world of grand opera.

The second half opened with a popular work, the "Charge of the Light Brigade." As the orchestra approached the first crescendo, a little furry form—later identified as a rat—darted onto the stage, followed closely by a dog of uncertain heritage but a one-track mind. Dog and rat wove a path underneath the players' legs and raced to the brass section. They collided with a large tuba and its larger owner, both of which arced backward off the edge of the risers in a synchronized somersault, knocking the acoustical panel behind them sideways into the next one. Down the panels went, one by one, in a slow-motion ballet, exposing a paunchy plaid-shirted stagehand frozen in the lights. The audience sportingly applauded him as he pulled himself together and scurried into the wings.

The conductor made the fatal mistake of hesitating, then resuming. The strings gallantly forged ahead, the brass fell behind, and the winds caught up with cacophonous determination. The charge became a rout. Tim McDonald, a *Salton Times* reporter—*the Salton Times* reporter, actually—clicked away wildly, determined not to miss anything. The audience murmured, torn between horror and pleasure. The narrator stood in stunned stillness at her podium, depicting a near-death guppy. One of Salton's most distinguished citizens, president of the symphony board Caroline Smythe, was captured on film half standing and half sitting, backside suspended in global disbelief—a burlesque version of Lot's wife. Rose's neck ached from its sharp pivoting as she committed each catastrophic delight to memory.

The chase progressed toward the conductor's podium. A pot of chrysanthemums was tossed into the air like a soccer ball and landed on the conductor's left foot, upon which he let out a screech that rivaled the best and worst of the soprano. Prey and predator brushed against a cellist who, startled, pulled his instrument back and up and lodged its very pointy end in the backside of the hapless musician in front of him.

By now, people in the audience, finally undone by mirth, were holding their stomachs and weeping helplessly. The conductor acknowledged defeat, gathered himself to his full sixty-three inches, and limped off the stage with the musicians straggling off after him like a drunken parade of hobos. The concertmaster was left to her own devices. She had unwisely climbed onto her chair during the melee, and it had succumbed to her mass; she neatly passed through the seat and, thighs trapped but mouth wide open, brandished her violin aloft whilst caroling her fear and outrage. The rat and the dog had disappeared, presumably to continue their dispute offstage. Rose sat motionless for a full ten minutes. She had not so much laughed as exulted—the feeling had been almost orgasmic. Slapstick at its finest.

The concert did not resume. The post-concert reception hostess was surprised by the early arrival and ebullient mood of her guests. They were a happy cohesive group who had very recently undergone the ultimate bonding experience—a glorious five minutes witnessing the demolition of the Salton Symphony. They were blood brothers, sharing mirth, horror, and exultation on the most fundamental level of banana-peel comedy—and they had forgotten all about murder. As Rose muttered quietly to Annie, the diversion couldn't have come at a better time if it had been planned.

The fallout was gossiped about for weeks. The concertmaster needed therapy for her heels, thighs, and psyche. The recipient of the cello's pointy end slept on his stomach for a week. The tubist resigned—back, dignity, and instrument badly bruised—and the tuba evidenced the ultimate and fitting resting place of the rat, whose limp, furry little body was later found in the depths of that mighty instrument. The conductor walked with a pronounced limp for at least six weeks. He never, to anyone's knowledge, referred to that concert and preserved an icy silence when anyone else tried to. No one asked for his money back—that would have been ungrateful after such generous entertainment.

An emergency board meeting was called for the following evening. Rose reported that she had visited the theater to drop off the programs at approximately six o'clock and that everything had seemed quiet and in good shape at that time. The theater manager, full of righteous indignation and Scotch, spluttered that he had never before seen a rat anywhere near the theater, which was, as always, spotlessly clean. He swore that nobody had seen that dog before or since, either. The acoustical panels that surrounded the back of the stage to project sound forward were supposed to have concrete weights placed in the base of each to keep them steady. The theater manager accused the stage manager of failing to place these weights, but the latter protested tearfully that he just knew he had done it in the morning and had the backache to show for it.

The sacrificial stage manager was a short, thin young man, slight in every way. He said he had arrived at seven and everything had been in order. His hands shook as he left the room so that the board could discuss his future—none, as it turned out. Rose felt sorry for this pathetic little man-boy, but voted for his dismissal along with the rest of them, for Caroline would not have taken any dissension lightly. Her voice was still shaking from the humiliation of having her first season as president of the board marred by this spectacle. The conductor did not appear at this meeting but nursed his grievances and toes in the privacy of home and hearth.

Peggy Trimball, the symphony manager, was told to call "lucky" Tim at the Times to ask him to drop the story and come back for the next concert. She called Rose later to report his response—"Fat chance!" The Times actually held up the press so they could run the story, not to mention a whole page of pictures. The paper was sold out by noon and the Associated Press picked up the story. Rumor had it that Tim was up for a Pulitzer; unfortunately, even the unique travails of the Salton Symphony were not Pulitzer material, but merely grist for Salton's rumor mill. Tim had taken some marvelous pictures, for sure. He had caught Caroline from the back in perfect composition: a fat bejeweled hand in the lower right corner clutched a mangled program, the flower pattern outlined in metallic thread tightly stretched across her rear end occupied front and center, and the other hand stretched out to the top left corner as if trying to ward off the evil eye. Her metallic threaded bottom danced and sparkled in the camera's flash. Thus it was that the greatest chapter of the Salton Symphony was not only written but fully illustrated.

That night, as Rose brushed her hair before bed, she smiled into the mirror. "Well, Susan," she said aloud. "What an interesting month this has been, and I wasn't bored for once. The best of it was that you weren't there, but will have to listen to the ever-changing stories of everyone else. And the story gets better with each telling. What fun we had, what laughter penetrated our silly little social skins."

Rose turned her head this way and that. She looked pretty; her face glowed, and a glint in her eyes made her look almost happy.

I have a sharp mind, much sharper than Daisy's. I got a job as a file clerk in a small import-export firm in Manhattan and worked my way up to bookkeeper. I was ambitious, so I watched and listened, worked long hours, and took accounting classes at night. When the senior bookkeeper left, there was no doubt in my mind that I deserved that promotion. Dorrie had been screwing the boss for six months, so Dorrie got what she wanted. When I heard the news, I was full of rage—murderous rage; I took some deep breaths and promised myself a long evening of planning. I spent that evening stretched out on my bed, eyes closed, my mind working furiously; I didn't stop for dinner. By morning, I was calm again and prepared to wait until the time was right. I worked and watched and listened some more. I wrote a detailed plan, which I worked on at night at home. When

I decided I had it right, had thought it all through again, ironed out all the wrinkles, I memorized it, then burned it.

I made secret little changes to the books. "Reluctantly, forced by company loyalty," I brought gross irregularities to the attention of the division manager. There was an investigation and two positions came open. I was promoted to senior bookkeeper. I'd done my work well, as usual. I should have been promoted the first time around, so it was their fault. I did what I had to—I had to get on and make my own way in the world. And there was no one left who was smart enough to spot any further slight irregularities that might occur from time to time. I needed to build a safety net for myself and make sure I hid my precious nest egg well. Who else was going to take care of me, after all?

The firm merged with another and there was an outside audit. I got a year and did nine months—nine months I try never to think about. There was this awful little rat of a woman. Her name was Judy, believe it or not. She had an entourage of sorts and was strong for her size, stronger than I was. Besides, her cronies helped hold me down when I fought back. She was nice at first, seemed to take me under her wing. I was grateful. You can imagine what being in prison was like for a well-spoken person like me. She stared at me a lot. They all did. Creepy. But I still didn't get it. Until the night I awoke to find her straddling me.

It was never entirely dark in that place, there were always some neon lights in the hallways outside the cells and they flickered obscenely over her emaciated body, naked from the waist down but for some sort of belt with a penis-like attachment. I tried to scream when I realized what she intended to do, but one of them gagged me. It was a filthy, painful experience. Her breath was foul, and she grunted with each push before shuddering to the finish line. She was as bad as Dad. Worse, because of the leering onlookers. I endured that every night for three weeks before some other poor new kid claimed her attention. There seemed to be an unspoken agreement with the guards—mostly male—that they wouldn't interfere. At least they left me alone. They preferred the more voluptuous types. I could hear the noises coming from other cells as I lay trying to sleep.

Yes, those months were humiliating and my anger seethed more than it ever has, before or since. But I kept my nose clean as I wanted out at the earliest opportunity. God, I should never have written about that. It's given me a headache. I'll go to bed early and resume tomorrow. Some things are best left buried. I try to take the philosophical approach when things go wrong; mice and men and plans and all that.

My nest egg enabled me to make a new start—they never found it. I had enough for a name change with all the necessary supporting documents. I had plenty left over, but I would still need a good job because I had to save for my future. I made some useful connections in the forgery business in prison, so was able to provide myself with good references. They are not friends, you understand—such people can never be friends—it's just business. They don't know my real name and I doubt I know their real names either as they are very discrete—have to be in that line of work. I kept up with them, too. You never know when the course might have to change once more.

Off came my beautiful dark hair. I now had red, very short hair, and I took better care with my diction, too, which I'd let slip after Dad was out of my life. I used to listen to television newscasters and repeat what they said right after they'd said it until it sounded about right. I've had a lot of compliments about my speaking voice since. Someone even told me once that I sound a bit English sometimes. I thanked the gentleman and told him that my father, the youngest son of a vicar, had been a teacher in London as a young man. That is true, by the way. What kind of vicar brings up a son like that?

I bought some dark suits and crisp blouses to make sure I looked the part. I got a good job with a real estate developer, and did just fine, as I was an excellent bookkeeper and always maintained a professional demeanor. I was determined to better myself, whatever it took. It took a lot. If I'd had the money to study full-time, I would have been an accountant. I like working with numbers. You know where you are with numbers.

I rented a tiny apartment in a lovely brownstone in Queens, not far from where I worked. Daisy showed up on my doorstep just as I was getting home from work one day. God knows how she found me. She looked me up and down in my navy suit, hose, and high heels, and laughed as if her sides would split. She looked more like a tart than she had the last time I'd seen her and stood out like a clown in a convent in my middle-class neighborhood. Now I look back, I realize she looked remarkably like my mother, minus the sags and bruises, wheezes, and body odors. She even had a cigarette dangling from her lower lip. I opened the front door and shoved her in—I didn't want anyone in my new life spotting me with someone like her. I was no longer someone of her ilk, would never be again. I have brains and that made all the difference. Brains meant I could get on in the world, while she got left behind in the gutter.

I made her a grilled cheese sandwich and got rid of her as quickly as I could. That was the last I saw of her until she stirred up the whirlpool that sucked me under.

10

Susan had been visiting an old aunt in Baltimore, an aunt who had been dying for at least two decades. This time she'd meant it, though, and had given up the struggle the previous night, the eve of her eighty-fourth birthday. The old woman had been cantankerous and demanding, but Susan, recognizing a kindred spirit, had been patient with her throughout the years of regular visits to the emergency room and the nursing of a difficult patient that followed. She thought of that little bell that Aunt Mildred seemed to ring every five minutes for a different book, a cup of tea, a shawl, help to the bathroom, and so on. Susan had understood that what she really wanted was reassurance that her niece cared enough to answer the summons.

She assumed she would be Aunt Mildred's only heir—she was the only family left, as far as she knew, and there were no friends. Looking down at her aunt in the narrow hospital bed, Susan surprised herself by shedding a tear or two. Aunt Mildred had experienced the loss of her husband and five-year-old son in a train wreck while still in her early thirties and had allowed the agony of her loss to twist her. Susan understood twisting bitterness only too well. She closed her eyes fiercely and clenched her fists, determined not to remember the loss of her own child. She felt orphaned, somehow—stranded and abandoned. She looked again at the depleted shell of her aunt. She had become emaciated in her final years and her sharp bones showed through the sheet, pushing up like a moonscape.

Susan went back to Aunt Mildred's house for the night. It was cluttered and musty, full of upholstered furniture and side tables protected by crocheted doilies. She found that her aunt had kept up photo albums of the family and even had some of Susan's elementary school report cards. A few more tears rolled down her cheeks and Susan clenched up again. How was it possible that she still had some tenderness left in her?

In an effort to stop her tears, she decided to search the house as briskly and efficiently as possible. She found the will in the roll-top desk, and, yes, she was the only heir. There were ornaments and books she remembered from her parent's house. She even found the mother-of-pearl box her father had bought in Cairo in his adventurous youth. He had told her lots of wonderful stories about his travels, and although she was never sure if they were true, she hoped they were. There were silverware and dishes, lace tablecloths and embroidered ones. There was a silver tray with her parents' initials engraved in the center, a wedding present from his company, she remembered. All of this should have come to her, though, not her aunt. But then she remembered that at the time her father died, she couldn't handle anything and hadn't cared about anything except her dying child. Instead of disposing of them, Aunt Mildred must have saved them for her. Susan felt a rush of affection for the old woman and her thoughtfulness, even in the face of her own miseries.

She went upstairs and opened the dark hall closet that seemed to go a long way back into some sort of black hole. Her heart skipped a beat as her mind rocketed back through the years to a closet just like this one. Her father had been away and was due back that evening, and she missed him so much that she was determined to stay up and wait for him. He had been away for her eighth birthday the week before and had promised to bring her a present. Her mother was a cruel woman who couldn't stand the fact that the child loved her father better than she loved her mother. She'd locked her in her room and ignored her cries to be let out to go to the bathroom. Later, when she came in and found that Susan had wet her pants, she spanked her and locked her in the closet, still with wet pants. Susan was terrified; it was so dark and stale, and everyday objects began to assume the aspects of ogres. She tried to be quiet in the hope that her mother would calm down, but soon panic took over and she screamed without stopping until her father came home. His wife, who cowed him somewhat, informed him that Susan was being punished for disobedience and that she was to be left in the closet. He rushed upstairs, his wife in hot pursuit, unlocked the door, and got Susan out, clasping her to his chest. By this time, she had defecated as well, and she was weak with fear, her little chest heaving.

Her mild-mannered father turned around and struck his wife on the face, causing her to stagger and fall. He turned his back on the woman and carried Susan to the bathroom, where he cleaned her off. He ran a bath and washed and soothed her, then put her to bed and gave her the promised gift, a beautiful doll—the most beautiful one Susan had ever seen. She still had it, wrapped in white linen, in the bottom drawer of her dresser. He sang to her until she slept.

She didn't know what had passed between her parents that evening, but her father changed his job to one for which he never had to travel, and her mother spoke to her only when necessary for the rest of her life. At least she didn't punish her anymore.

Susan's mother had died from a fall down the stairs while Susan was home from college for Thanksgiving the year she turned eighteen. Her father had been out when they'd had a fight about unmade beds. Susan, used to a curt reprimand every now and then, had been taken aback by the sudden verbal assault and slap to her cheek. Years of resentment and fury boiled over, and she gave her mother a hard shove. She watched, unmoved, as her mother's face, screwed tight with hatred, opened into surprise, then fear as she somersaulted down the stairs. "She must have lost her footing," she said as her horrified father came through the front door. "I didn't see it happen, just heard her scream." She hadn't screamed, surprisingly. All Susan heard was a series of thuds and exhalations as her mother slammed into one stair after another.

The following Christmas had been the first Susan could ever remember enjoying. It had been just her and her father as she'd asked him to turn down invitations. They'd giggled over their first try at cooking a turkey (horribly chewy and dry) and watched television in peace all evening. He gave her a dainty necklace of pearls, which she never wore now, as she couldn't bear the thought of it coming to harm. The pearls rested with the doll. Although she had loved him, her father had died of lung cancer quite alone. At the time,

Susan's little girl had been very ill, and she had been unable to cope with caring for, then losing, both of them.

Susan took a deep breath, releasing herself from the bad memories. She looked inside the closet, and, to her relief, found a light switch. There were towels and hand-embroidered sheets and dozens of containers of over-the-counter remedies for everything from colds to wasp stings. She liked the idea of sleeping on the exquisite sheets, but wasn't sure if she wanted to have to iron them. She didn't want the nice things to go to strangers, though. They were hers.

Intriguingly, there were hundred-dollar bills secreted in and under just about everything. She counted just over fifteen thousand dollars by the time she was through, and there would perhaps be more to be found when she searched again in the morning—her sadness was no barrier to the gleeful thought that this was all tax-free.

She would call the attorney whose name was on the will's letterhead and visit him first thing in the morning. He would, no doubt, be able to recommend a funeral home and a real estate agent. In the afternoon, she would pull the house apart in search of more banknotes. Susan felt better.

The attorney's office was only a five-minute drive from the house and Susan found it without much trouble. It was in an old white house on a wide street lined with oak trees. A stolid middle-aged secretary with a gray permanent wave just like Susan's greeted her with unwelcome touchy-feely warmth.

"Why, you must be Mrs. Lazare, so sorry about your aunt. We didn't see much of her, but she'll be sorely missed, I'm sure." She patted a horrified Susan on her arms and shoulders.

"Yes, quite. Is Mr. Cartwright ready to see me?"

"If you'll just take a seat, I'll check," and the woman gave a strange little trilling laugh as she disappeared down the hallway in a swirl of new-age, flowing cotton layers.

Susan sighed, her irritation rising. She couldn't stomach annoying little laughs—they got on her nerves more than just about anything.

"Mr. Cartwright will see you now, down the hall, second on your right."

"Thank you."

A very tall, fat man with small, black eyes greeted her. "Good morning, Mrs. Lazare. Please accept my condolences." The smell of cigarette smoke emanated from his clothing in nauseating waves as he moved. He sat behind his over-sized desk and indicated the easy chair in front of it. Susan perched on the edge of it, grasping the top of her purse as she usually did.

"Thank you. I brought my aunt's will. I found it in her desk. I assume you have a copy of the same document." Susan passed it across to him.

He scanned her copy before handing it back. His tone changed from solicitous to brisk. "Yes, indeed so, Mrs. Lazare. In fact, we have the original. You are your aunt's only heir and, as she put all her assets into a living trust, there will be no need to go through probate. You may dispose of her property as you see fit. I have prepared several notarized copies of the death certificate for you."

Susan took the envelope without comment and stuffed it in her bag.

"I have taken the liberty of contacting an excellent real estate agent, a woman who is conversant with your late aunt's neighborhood. She should be here to meet you at any moment. And here is the card of a very reliable funeral home. I have already contacted them and they are expecting your visit after we have concluded our business here."

"Well, Mr. Cartwright, you seem to think of everything." *Pompous twit. Probably gets a kickback. Too oily by far.*

Susan heard the front door open and the secretary greeting and trilling.

"That secretary of yours laughs a lot, doesn't she? She sounds like a bilious pigeon. Not very professional."

"I'm sorry it upsets you, Mrs. Lazare. My wife is an amiable soul, always has been. Your aunt didn't take to her either."

"Ah."

The door opened and a vivacious little woman with short, red hair strode in. *Oh God, revoltingly perky.*

After introductions were made, the three of them sat at the conference table.

"When do you want the house to go on the market, Mrs. Lazare?" the agent, Maria Fentle, asked.

"I have some decisions to make about what to keep and what to sell. Then I have to get rid of the stuff I don't want. Do you know anything about estate sales, Ms. Fentle?"

"Oh, yes. Please call me Maria. I can recommend two firms that handle that sort of thing." Maria went on to describe how she would handle the sale. In spite of herself, Susan found herself warming to this woman. She was neither abrasive nor cloying and explained everything in a coherent manner. Susan signed the agreement and Maria left with a bounce in her step.

Mr. Cartwright and Susan shook hands, less cordially this time, before parting. He came to the door of his office and Susan could feel his little eyes on her back as she walked to the front door. She thanked Mrs. Cartwright in passing as she hurried out, pursued by a cascade of trills.

The funeral home was the usual sort of combination of a cozy family home with a nefarious outbuilding connected to the main by a closed corridor. The pale, young, male receptionist looked as if he were newly risen from the dead. He rose ethereally and extended his hand and his sympathy to Susan in slow motion. He beckoned her to follow him, and she complied with a feeling that she might be floating off the edge of the world right along with him. They came to a room full of caskets where a more solid gentleman awaited her.

"Ah, Mrs. Lazare, I presume? I'm Sidney Burbank. Mr. Cartwright called to say you were on your way. I am so sorry for your loss. We will do all we can to ease the way."

Susan closed her eyes briefly. When people die, it's all over, and memories soon fade. Of course, in her aunt's case, there was no one to remember but Susan. Her aunt had despised sentiment, she reminded herself, and had thoroughly approved of thrift.

"Thank you. I am my aunt's only living relative and she had no friends that I know of. I want a very simple and quick cremation. She wasn't religious, so no church service. And no flowers—she hated them. You can take care of it all here, I assume?"

"Yes, of course," said the clearly disgruntled Sidney. "Let's choose a casket now."

"Show me something simple."

They stopped in front of a shining mahogany monster with brass handles.

"A dignified resting place for your aunt."

Susan's irritation almost boiled over. He doubtless earned a commission on what he persuaded the recently bereaved to buy. Most of them were probably pushovers, easily nudged by "dignified" and "fitting" and "we know you'll want the best for her." Everyone these days seemed to be selling something to someone else, whatever the circumstances.

"I said, show me something simple." Sidney's face dropped until his condolence mask held an undertow of surliness.

They stopped beside a very plain design, no more than a box, really.

"This will do. Let's go and sign whatever we have to sign."

"As you wish, Mrs. Lazare."

Susan breathed out, then took a deep breath as she stepped out into the sunshine. The part of the funeral home that she had visited was not connected with the grisly mortuary part of the business and was scrupulously clean and filled with fresh flowers, but she had imagined the stench of death all the time she had been in there.

She stopped on the way home and bought a bottle of white wine and some sandwiches. She didn't drink every day, but drank a couple of glasses most evenings. She would occasionally consume a whole bottle in one evening when she couldn't settle down. The next morning's headache could be cured by a couple of painkillers in the space of an hour, but she would still be listless for the rest of the day. This was going to be one of those evenings, she could tell. She wandered around the house with a full glass in her hand, hunting for cash and deciding what she wanted to keep. She tried to avoid thinking about death until the wine took over her mind. Tomorrow would come soon enough, and she could stay in bed until her headache went away. Then she'd get on with the sorting and packing.

Mid-morning, her headache banished, Susan felt the need to hear a friendly voice and called Annie. She got the answering machine and hung up without leaving a message. It was Thursday, so the Seven were probably on their way to the Salton Family Restaurant for lunch. She pictured them sitting around the table, only five this time—Janet talking about her children, Sally fluttering her hands and talking about "dear Jack," Helen not saying much, although her troubled face might clear a little, Annie bright and chatting about community affairs, and Rose interjecting quiet comments from time to time and watching the others. Susan considered her need to make that connection with her friends this morning. She astonished herself by conceding that she needed them and missed them. Until now, she had always thought of them in terms of props rather than friends.

Aunt Mildred had lived in this house quite alone except for Susan's infrequent visits and she'd had no friends. The bereft house was starting to close in on her, so Susan drew back all the drapes and blinds, flung open the windows, and got down to work.

The cremation was a sorry affair. No flowers, as requested, and Susan was the only mourner—and she did mourn as she watched the coffin roll toward the curtain and the fire beyond. Burning seemed too brutal, suddenly. But the body was finished, wasn't needed anymore. The dead don't care, so why should she? Funerals weren't for the dead, though, they were for the living, so that survivors could feel they'd done their duty by their loved one. Aunt Mildred would have approved of this, Susan felt sure. Approved with her own particular brand of grim satisfaction, no doubt.

Susan wiped her tears and, infuriated by the piped-in organ music, ran outside and drove off, screeching out of the gateway at breakneck speed. The fire could do its work without her.

The following week, Susan was back in Salton and soon heard about the revelations concerning the affair between Davey and Cynthia. Before she even went to the supermarket, she drove to the flower shop, where she lingered over the selection of arrangements and plants for some time before deciding she had seen enough of Cynthia. "Common little thing!" was her verdict.

Her friends noticed that Susan was less acerbic than usual and even, at times, cordial. People outside the circle were one thing, but she had lost the desire to mistreat the Seven. She called Helen to see if she needed anything and Sally to ask if she was all right. All the Seven visited to welcome her back and pay their condolences. She couldn't bring herself to tell them she'd missed them, but she had.

The memory of the funeral parlor with its white flower arrangement and hovering hopeful Sidney would often flash into her consciousness over the months that followed. Her dreams would sometimes reveal the male receptionist floating over the desiccated remains of Aunt Mildred, beckoning her to join him. Sometimes she would be tempted to.

11

Pansy

A handsome young accountant called Sven joined the firm and was assigned the cubicle next to mine. He was what I would now label an Adonis, although I wouldn't have known that name then. The other girls used to gossip about him, and I overheard one of them say he looked like a Greek statue. I wasn't sure what a Greek statue looked like and didn't know how to find out. If I'd asked someone, they would have thought I was an idiot.

There hadn't been any room for culture in my life until then. I'd learned to present myself well, and learned about bookkeeping; quite a heavy load for a girl like me. I was only twenty. I'd never been to any of the museums, but thought they probably had statues. I didn't do anything for a couple of weeks, but was still so intrigued by the idea that I went to the Metropolitan Museum of Art one Saturday morning to check it out. The place was huge. It took my breath away. I determined that I'd see the whole collection one day, but I never got around to it. There was always something going on.

He did look like one of those splendid, smooth, white young men, although their genitals looked a bit small from my admittedly limited perspective. So much the better. As I stood looking up at those marble beauties, I wondered how Sven would look naked, lounging on black satin sheets. I couldn't believe I entertained such thoughts about him. I'd always thought I'd rather die than be touched intimately by a man again. It didn't make sense to me then and still doesn't now.

It was a jolt to realize I had a crush on him. I'd never had one before. He crowded my mind. I imagined he was watching me, loving me, approving of me, no matter what I was doing. It was a bit exhausting, actually. I'd even wake up in the middle of the night, unable to go back to sleep because my mind immediately jumped into fantasies of the most ridiculous kind. I was imagining a Sven that didn't exist. I liked it, and I didn't—I was off-kilter, and knew it. You might say I was off-kilter when I killed people, but that was a different thing altogether; I was able to compartmentalize my thoughts and feelings when I had that kind of business to conduct.

I took the initiative one day and asked him if he would like to join me for lunch. We had a good time. He was intelligent and had a sense of fun that was almost infectious. He loved the movies, and we started to go together a couple of times a week. I cooked for him sometimes, and he for me. He had all kinds of tasty pasta recipes, and I developed quite a taste for it. My cooking expertise was limited, but he had cookbooks and helped me along when it was my turn.

He took me shopping, too. He had a good eye for fashion and seemed to enjoy picking outfits for me. I really looked good and felt good, too. He liked me to wear black, said it showed off my figure and made me look sophisticated. I still like black. It always looks chic and comes in handy for cocktail parties and funerals, too.

He persuaded me to have my hair done. He stood over me while I called the salon he'd suggested and booked the appointment. He came with me and just about dominated the proceedings until the stylist, in high dudgeon, asked him to leave him to do his job. "I'm considered an artiste, not just a hairdresser, you know," the little peacock declared as he bounced around my chair. My eyes met Sven's in the mirror, and we both had to suppress our giggles, which bubbled over as soon as we walked out. The artiste had done a good job, and I felt on top of the world. On cloud nine, too. I had to stand my ground about makeup. Sven thought I wore too much. He couldn't know why.

Everyone at work knew we were an item, and I was deliriously happy. For the only time ever. And he himself often said I had a wonderful glow about me. But he never touched me, except to kiss my cheek hello and goodbye. I thought perhaps this was the way decent people went about a love affair. After all, I'd only known how it was to be forced into sex by hateful people. So, I longed for him in silence, even got into the habit of pleasuring myself while I fantasized about what our first time would be like. I bought some satin sheets, too, only dark blue, because I thought they'd bring out the arctic intensity of his blue eyes.

One day I told him I'd almost dropped by the evening before because I'd bought some strawberries, the first of the season. His face tensed as he turned to face me. "Never drop in without calling," he said. He must have seen the confusion on my face. "I'm a very private person. I only like to have guests when I invite them. I'm sorry, that's just how I am."

The butterflies in my stomach were uncontrollable. I was devastated. There was someone else. That's why he didn't touch me, make love to me. I looked at him as calmly as I could and walked away. He'd given me a key once when I was to drop off some groceries for one of our dinners. I never returned it and he never asked for it back—forgot, I suppose.

A couple of nights later, at around ten, I stood watching his West Side apartment from the little park across the road. Although it was May, the drizzly rain chilled my feet and hands, and my teeth chattered as I tried to stay focused on the building. I had to remain alert to my surroundings, too, a New York City park with concealing shrubbery and a blanketing gray night—irresistible to the drug addicts who had infested just about every neighborhood by then.

I knew he was in there, and I knew he had a visitor, but I couldn't see what the woman looked like as it was too dark and she'd bundled herself up in a bulky overcoat. His apartment was in the front of the building, so I could see when he turned on the light in his bedroom and drew the drapes. I watched two hazy shapes disrobing, and I thought my heart would break. I crossed the road and let myself in. Silent as a cat, I crept up the hallway to the bedroom. The door was ajar, so I had the equivalent of a front-row seat.

His lover was a young man, almost as beautiful as he. I watched, enthralled, as they entwined and moved over each other. They caressed with a gentleness I had thought to experience, kissing and stroking each other in every crevice and across every curve, seeming to move in a trance. They reminded me of those slow-motion films of flowers opening. As they finished their lovemaking, it was with sighs and low moans, before they rested in each other's arms. I was in a state of languorous arousal myself by that time.

I have never, to this day, witnessed anything more exquisite or erotic. Of course, I was too naïve to realize that this was only one of many ways they might interact, but for the moment I found them incredibly romantic and sensual. I hadn't known until then that enjoying sex without aggression, without pain, was possible. I saw two people making love, and the difference was a healing revelation.

I walked in. Sven paled when he saw me, even forgetting to cover himself, although his boyfriend scrambled under the sheets like a cockroach does when you turn the lights on. "What in the hell do you think you're doing? Didn't I tell you never..."

"It's all right, Sven. I had to know. You're both gorgeous fellows, and I enjoyed watching you."

"You were watching us? Are you sick or something?"

"No, Sven. I thought I was in love with you. It puzzled me that you never touched me. And then you behaved so strangely when I mentioned I almost dropped by that time. I knew there had to be someone else."

"Are you going to tell everyone? It'll ruin me. I'll get fired and I'll never find another job." He sounded whiny then, and I got impatient.

"No, don't be silly. It's none of their business. We could still go to the movies and do all the other things we enjoy together. We can still be friends. But why didn't you tell me? Or were you using me as a cover?" That thought had just popped into my head and the old hot-behind-the-eyes feeling started to flood over me.

"No, I love spending time with you. I didn't tell you because I've never told anyone. Anyone straight, that is. Most people hate people like me."

"I've got things I can't tell people, either. Most people hate people like me, if you did but know. I'm going now."

I walked out of there, leaving the key on the hallstand by the door. I didn't know how to feel. I was devastated by the loss of my fantasy, but still awed by the vision I'd seen. I'd heard about homosexuality, but it had always been spoken of in a derogatory manner as something unnatural and filthy. I'd never thought much about it until then. I didn't see how anyone could believe that what I'd just witnessed was wicked or bad in any way.

I wept several times over the next few days. The last paroxysm felt as if I were hemorrhaging my lungs, but when I was done, I felt purged. It was time to heal myself and put the yearning to rest. The wound stayed raw for a while, but it soon closed over, although it festered a little for a long time, maybe does still.

I regretted saying that about my secrets. Asking for trouble. But I wasn't angry, I had no thoughts of revenge, just harrowing regret that my dream had washed away. All so out of character. I'd become a new person over the past couple of months. A person who'd experienced the sort of happiness that normal people take as their right. When I came to my senses, the old me didn't take long to reemerge, though.

Sven and I maintained our friendship until I moved on. We never spoke of that evening, although I thought of it often, still think of it. When my husband used to make love to me, he was also gentle and loving, although somewhat clumsy; I would close my eyes and think of those two Greek gods, and I would enter their erotic domain, much as a phantom might, and climb Mount Olympus along with them.

12

The Salton Foundation had yet again launched its annual Christmas fundraising party. The foundation had been started twenty-five years before by a wealthy philanthropist to assist local charitable groups carry out their work. Most of the new income was raised by this event, and just about anyone active in Salton community life was there. It was always held in one of the huge mansions and competition to host the party was fierce, if furtive. As soon as the new foundation president was installed in May, the lobbying began. This year's president, Marge Lanley, had appointed a fundraising committee to handle the matter, claiming that her time was better spent working with the grants committee. She earned the undying resentment of half her board, most of whom would have rather mucked out a stable yard than tiptoe through this social minefield. They would exact their revenge, however, making sure that none of the groups that Marge favored supporting would receive a grant this year except, of course, the symphony, the group in which Salton's socialites would always want to be visible.

Susan had not been asked to participate in the planning, so she expected to find the event wanting in most respects. This year's party was at the home of Samantha and Toby Elantro, one of the newest and wealthiest couples in Salton. The house was crowded and noisy and decorated for the season with a heavy hand. When she entered, her vision was blurred by a profusion of red and gold mirrored baubles that slowly spun in the air currents, sending little flashing rays of light dancing and reflecting off every surface. The Elantros and Marge had formed a reception line at the door to welcome the guests shortly after Marge's husband escaped to the bar. Susan greeted them coolly and, on full alert, went to look around. Rose followed soon after and strolled through the rooms behind Susan, clearly amused both by the extravagant display and Susan's reaction to it. Susan greeted Janet and Annie and left Rose to chat with them for a while before they fanned out to mingle.

Susan had been watching Rose even as she was aware that Rose was watching her. She knew Rose had enough malice in her to be entertained by her acid behavior. She noted how at ease Rose was with this crowd; displaying a masterful mix of bonhomie and distance was one of her most valuable social skills. She had been a widow long enough and had made her lack of interest in finding a new mate so apparent over the years that she was accepted as a non-threat to the local institution of marriage. Rose had a good memory for names and little personal tidbits that flattered people she barely knew. Her mind was a fine-tuned filing system, which gleaned, stored, and quickly retrieved information when needed. Susan wondered if Rose cared for any of these people, but thought she probably disliked most of these over-hearty, over-confident, and over-loud men and their status-seeking, small-minded wives. What would be important to her was that she had a slot in their social system where she was accepted as a well-bred, well-educated, civic-minded, and well-to-do woman. Susan assumed this because she felt the same way herself. Rose and Susan had their place in Salton, Virginia; they needed a place. Most people liked Rose in a low-key sort of way—she was a quiet but ubiquitous presence. Susan knew that almost nobody liked her, and she didn't care.

The immaculate Janet's jangling jewelry caught Susan's attention as it reflected in the dance of the ornaments. Her brunette tones had been renovated to a hard, wavy sheen for the occasion, and she stood chatting with her daughter and a couple of local politicians she had ensnared on their way to the buffet table. Susan drifted over and stood behind them.

"Hello there, how nice to see you again! Have you met my daughter, Katie?"

Sarah Hance and Mike Myles both greeted Katie with the caution born of suffering Janet's previous monologues regarding her exceptional offspring.

"Sarah," Janet went on, "I heard that your son was accepted to West Point. How splendid! He must have done very well—how proud you must be!"

Neither Sarah nor Mike responded immediately to this expression of seemingly genuine and yet uncharacteristic interest in someone else's good news. There was a momentary awkward silence before they regained their composure and conversation flowed. They began to respond warmly to Janet, and she reciprocated. Susan realized Janet was unused to the idea of not having to impress people to be liked. She had been prattling about her therapist at lunch the other day, telling them that he had said most people are egocentric to some extent and like to hear their own successes and virtues echoed back to them from time to time. Mike and Sarah excused themselves to make their rounds, and Katie wandered off, saying she needed a drink.

"Well, Janet, you have softened up, haven't you?"

Janet jumped and turned around, coloring when she saw by her little smirk that Susan had been listening.

"Why don't we wander around together?" Susan suggested.

Janet, enthralled, pointed out the plush furnishings to Susan as she imprinted the details of the house on her mind. Susan understood that in spite of her partial rebirth, Janet was still fascinated by wealth and in some way felt that when a large sum of money was spent on expensive decor, it must be in good taste. For once, Susan did not comment. She was watching Sally now and led Janet in her direction.

Little Sally Hartington painfully made her way around the party with Jack. Susan saw how Jack made sure she stayed on his arm and gave her no opportunity to strike out on her own. Susan knew what he was thinking. He did not trust her friendships—he was afraid she might tell people things he would rather they not know. He was too shallow to recognize loyalty in others, and Sally was loyal to a fault. She never criticized Jack to her friends. Neither of them realized that Jack's behavior told her friends all they needed to know. They saw bruises sometimes. Sally "fell down the stairs" and "walked into a door" too often to be believed and her tone as she related these little accidents seemed too lackluster, her eyes too busy avoiding theirs. She sometimes seemed sore as she moved and her friends assumed that Jack probably avoided her face most of the time and hit her where her clothing, with its usual long sleeves and high necklines, would conceal his assaults. Susan stalked them as they made the rounds.

She hung back and watched as Jack accosted one of Salton's most prominent citizens, a tall and austere woman by the name of Betty Tomlin. She was a woman who, with generations of family wealth and position behind her, as well as at least seventy-five years, was in the habit of speaking her mind without concern for the consequences because there were none—for her, that is.

"Good evening, Mrs. Tomlin. How wonderful you look tonight! Such elegance and taste! You must give Sally some pointers. She's always looking for improvement."

Betty Tomlin, to her credit, looked down her nose at him and said, "Good evening, Sally, your husband's customary tact betrays him. You look very nice tonight, as always. Jack, speaking of looking for improvement, look to your manners!" She turned her back and sailed off to the dining room. Poor pink-faced Sally simpered and Jack's smile stretched wide and rigid as he ground his teeth in the face of the widely observed insult. Sally winced as his fingers dug into her forearm.

Susan greeted Sally warmly and Jack less so. "Betty can be most direct, can't she? Yes, Sally, you do look very nice this evening, unlike many here tonight. Your wife has good taste, Jack."

"Yes, quite. Well, we must be going. We have another engagement. Goodbye, Susan. Nice to see you again."

They left the party in haste and Susan reckoned that Sally would garner a fresh bruise or two that night.

Susan joined Annie and Tom Minhoff, who were chatting in a quiet corner with some of the musicians. Tom was an insurance company executive, but had played the cello since he was eight and was considered accomplished enough to play at the semi-professional level of a community orchestra. He would occasionally play in a concert to fill in for a missing cellist, although he said he didn't want to make a habit of it given the onerous rehearsal schedule. He and Annie were very committed to the symphony and gave generously of their time and money. They were equally committed to each other and their daughter and led the rich lives of the contented and fulfilled—a nonconformist lifestyle in social Salton. They were both quiet and unassuming people, so no one stopped to think how unusual it was that everybody liked them without reservation. No one had ever been heard to say a bad word about them. Even Susan had never criticized Annie in public, although her evenness and benevolence got on her nerves sometimes. She wondered how they did it. She supposed marrying the right person helped, and never knowing tragedy helped, too. The luck of the draw.

Bored, Susan looked around and spotted Helen Gandy wandering around aimlessly until she found Annie and Tom's group. After she had greeted everyone and chatted awhile, she and Annie drew a little to one side. Susan could just hear what she was saying. She was telling Annie how she was still unused to socializing alone and was afraid of seeming too friendly with anyone's husband. God knows she was not interested in finding another man, but women could be very insecure, especially the younger ones. Susan reflected that if older women seemed not to mind much, perhaps it was because they had ceased to love much. She was glad she had made sure that Helen had received an invitation and that Pat and his girlfriend had not. She guessed that Helen could hardly afford to be there at a hundred dollars a ticket, but this Salton social scene was all she had right now, and she could not become estranged from it and isolated. She also confided to Annie that Toni had helped her with her makeup, and Annie remarked how it gave her face more form and color and that black suited her, too. Helen said she had found this old black dress when she was cleaning out her closet. After dry-cleaning and the addition of tiny black beads around the neckline and cuffs, Toni had insisted that it looked slinky and sexy. She whispered, giggling, that she did think that several men had looked her way with more than passing interest, but she could have been mistaken. Annie told her that she indeed looked gorgeous and the young woman's back straightened and her chin lifted. She was on her way back. Susan walked away, leaving Helen with Annie and Tom where, now more relaxed, she would be able to enjoy herself.

Susan would have made a good journalist. She noted the buffet table, laden with dishes from the local delicatessen, the menu choices made by one with limited tastes and lots of money. She noted the Christmas decorations with their department store look of a professional interior decorator—no tree ornaments handmade by the children here. She made a mental list of the guests present and those absent (declined or not invited?). She surveyed the clothes worn by the women (old, new, costly?), together with their jewels (costume or real?). Then she cornered the hostess.

"Good evening, Samantha. Big crowd, although I'm surprised to see some of the usual people missing."

"Hello, Susan. Nice to see you. Apparently, everyone on the symphony's database was invited."

"Yes, well, some people are slower to accept newcomers than others. They like to wait and see, judge for themselves, you understand."

"Oh, I see."

"All these shiny hanging things quite assault the senses, don't they? Do you usually put up so many? Or did a decorator do it?

"Our decorator did it. She thought it would make a wonderful splash of color. We think it's very festive."

"You may possibly be right, Samantha. Who's your decorator?"

"Leslie Truman."

"Never heard of her. Who catered the food? Nice and basic, I see, should please the menfolk."

"Saving the Day. They're new in town, like us. I wanted to give them a chance."

"I see. Well, you do travel the world, don't you? You seem to acquire a collection of trinkets from everywhere you go—the natives must love you. One can't turn around without seeing some object from one of those tourist traps the guides always steer one to," asserted Susan, who had never traveled abroad herself.

"We love looking at these things and thinking of the happy times we shared. It's one of our favorite things to do in the evenings."

"What sorts of things do you remember?" Susan asked.

"Well, there was a lovely, romantic restaurant on the beach in Greece last spring," Samantha said. "And a camel tried to bite Toby in Cairo one time. Thank God he missed! Then he made sounds like a stopped-up drainpipe. But those pyramids were something!"

"Sounds like a lot of fuss and bother to me." Samantha's sentimentality disgusted Susan.

Thus, with her invincible choice of words and inflection, Susan let her hostess know that she had noticed everything and appreciated nothing. Samantha's eyes filled with tears, leaving Susan free to search out her next victim.

Susan closed in on the wearer of a rather unfortunate homemade dress that was meant to say "Christmas" loud and clear; it was bright red and spattered with a pattern of green holly sprigs. It could not have been more unsuited to the lady's physique, which, in profile, could only be described as ovoid, the crown of her head forming the apex. The back profile was formed by a round head, round shoulders, and a flat backside that curved under; the front, by a high sloping forehead and significant nose, followed by sagging breasts and a soft round belly. The dress made her look like a surreal Easter egg.

"Good grief, what does that silly woman think she looks like?" demanded Susan of the room at large.

"I don't believe we've met. I'm Susan Lazare. I saw your dress from across the room. It rather stands out, doesn't it? Unique. Quite extraordinary, in fact." Susan looked her up and down.

"I'll take that as a compliment," replied the woman aggressively. "I've heard your name—people talk about you a lot. You have quite a reputation for compliments." The woman turned her back on Susan and joined a group of friends.

The riposte felt like a slap in the face. For many years, Susan had wielded an unfettered aggression that was never challenged. It comforted her to torment people, especially at times like Christmas, for she loathed family festivity. She pushed her way through the rooms to the reception line to find out who the woman was. She would find out all she could about her and decide how to handle it. Who did the woman think she was? Susan had never seen her before, so she must be a nobody. An ugly, tasteless nobody.

The day after the party, Susan received many phone calls from people who knew she would appreciate their comments. A few of the superficially polite but vicious guests were laughing with each other at the excess, the decorations, Samantha's dreadful red dress that someone said made her look like a London bus—a double-decker at that—and especially her house. Samantha and Toby loved to travel. They had been nearly everywhere and seemed to have bought just about any ethnic artifact they came across and installed them indiscriminately around their home, as Susan had correctly, if unkindly, pointed out. Salton despised the Elantros for what they had been and what people assumed they were trying to become, even though few of the critics' backgrounds could bear close scrutiny, despite the legends they had created for themselves. Salton did, however, respect Elantro money. Given that level of wealth, most of Salton was willing to tolerate and accept the Elantros, even as they belittled them behind their backs.

The fundraiser made more money than it ever had before. Previous wealthy, yet less generous hosts, had not underwritten the entire event as the Elantros had done. Some people, including Susan, felt that Samantha and Toby had tried to buy their way into social acceptance—a view particularly espoused by earlier and thriftier hosts—and sneered. Others said that the couple could easily afford it, they would use it as a tax write-off (true), and that they owed it to their community; they sneered, too. Susan sneered along with everyone else.

And so Susan confronted Christmas, the season of goodwill, the worst part of the year as far as she was concerned. She would spend the day in front of the fire with a wine bottle, fuming at the hypocrisy of it all. These people, these worthy citizens, shopped, wrapped, decorated, and cooked with insane intensity and then ate and drank and loved and fought beyond reason. Some wallowed in domestic discord and some just sank into somnolence. The children were alternately excited, happy, irritable, and discontented. At least, she thought, murder had been put on hold.

No one had invited her for the day. Annie had in the past, but Susan had always rejected the invitation. She'd stopped trying. Susan could not abide being with people who were open to the Christmas spirit, content with the year past, and looking forward to the year to come. Annie and Tom were among those fortunate few souls. They were always delighted that their daughter and her family could spend the holidays with them. Susan had overheard Annie inviting Helen and Toni for Christmas Day, which must have added to the festive spirit.

13

In the empty period just after New Year's Day, Annie invited Samantha and Helen to lunch. Annie chose a little Victorian restaurant she said she liked because it was cozy and quiet and served old-fashioned comfort food. Samantha arrived before the others and sat down to hold the table. She ordered a glass of white wine and looked around with some satisfaction. This was a classy place. Annie and Helen arrived together, and they busied themselves with their orders.

"I like their Christmas decorations—sparse and in quiet, good taste," Helen said. "Every year, I'm surprised how Christmas decorations that looked so cheerful and pretty before Christmas look gaudy and seedy almost immediately after."

Samantha was surprised to notice Annie frowning at Helen. She didn't really agree with Helen, she liked plenty of color at Christmastime, and she continued to enjoy her decorated house long after the New Year was welcomed in. But each to their own.

"Samantha, the party was wonderful. Everything was so festive and well organized. Everyone had a good time. It was so very generous of you and Toby to underwrite it," Annie said.

"Yes, indeed," Helen said. "Everybody's talking about it."

"I don't think Susan thought much of it," Samantha said sadly.

"Oh, don't take any notice of Susan. She's always unpleasant at things like that. She doesn't like anyone or anything much. She's a very unhappy woman, you know. We don't know why, and she never talks about the past."

"We think the party was lovely—quite the best ever," Helen said.

Annie said, "The reason we arranged to get together for lunch is that we wanted a chance to get to know you better. There's never time to really talk at these big functions, is there? Especially when the hostess has to busy herself with her guests."

Samantha was ecstatic. The three of them had a wonderful two-hour lunch and talked about everything under the sun. Samantha's self-confidence rose and her sadness dropped away. She was amused to hear the women describe themselves as the "Symphony Seven" and secretly resolved to become one of them. It would help her feel she belonged in this town and she had noticed how they supported each other, especially Sally. Even Susan was kind to Sally. Annie and Helen asked Samantha if she would volunteer with them at the next concert and she was over the moon. She would be in charge of ticket sales, and Helen would help.

Samantha tried so hard to fit in. She and Toby both came from poor, uneducated families who lived in a small Arkansas town. Entertaining on this scale did not come easily to her. Toby was expansive and comfortable; he had his fabulously successful software business and did not care what anyone thought beyond that realm. He had started his company in Little Rock and had done well, almost from the beginning. As time went on, more and more of his clients were based in Washington, so it made sense to move, especially after their children were grown and on their own. Samantha was the only one to feel completely uprooted, and this social circle was all she had. Toby was wonderful, but he had to be out a lot. She wished she had never moved to Salton. She considered her dirt-poor relatives more mannerly and much kinder than most of these pretentious social climbers. She knew she could never hold her own with these people. Many guests had said kind things to her about the party, but Susan's biting comments had been more convincing.

Annie and Helen wanted to do some window shopping, but Samantha had a doctor's appointment so couldn't join them. They waved to her as she drove off.

"Samantha is a very nice woman. There aren't too many around like her," Annie said.

"I agree," Helen said. "She'll make a nice addition to the group, in spite of Susan."

The friends smiled mischievously at each other.

"I'm already so late getting back to work, it won't make any difference if I walk a little with you, Annie. It's pretty slow at this time of year, so I don't expect anyone will mind."

"Good. Now that the holidays are over, let's see if the china shop has a sale on. Did you hear from your parents?"

"I haven't been with my parents at Christmas for years, and now Aunt Barbara rules the roost, it's never going to happen. Pat always managed to spoil the day, too. Toni and I had the best Christmas I can ever remember with you and Tom. I have to say I'm glad my marriage is over. Are you shocked to hear me say that?"

"No, Helen, I'm not shocked. I'm happy for you. I have to confess that I never liked Pat and didn't think he was good enough for you. What are your plans? You have to work, of course."

"Yes, but I don't mind. I know I'll have to go back to school. A master's in political science isn't terribly useful. Believe it or not, I'm thinking of applying to law school. But I don't know if I could handle all the required reading as well as hold down a job, even a part-time one."

"Other women have done it, and so can you," Annie said. "You are still young, you are very intelligent, and you have plenty of energy. Now is the time to make a new life. By the time you finish law school, Toni will be off to college."

"Will anyone hire me, though? Law firms expect new associates to work nearly around the clock and I've been told they are always suspicious that older graduates can't handle the workload. And lawyers are getting laid off right now—did you know that?"

"Well, you don't know what the situation will be when you graduate. You could apply to federal or state government agencies, for example. That would mean saner hours, at least. Don't waste your time thinking of reasons why you can't do it. Instead, think of all the reasons you can and should do it. If you don't make yourself a career and a fulfilling life, who else will? Your life will seem empty and you will have wasted yourself. Make it happen!"

Annie watched Helen gazing at a window full of porcelain rabbits and birds, clearly seeing only the long road ahead. Annie was exhilarated and, at the same time, riddled with anxiety on her friend's behalf. The idea of Helen's transformation was exciting and Annie liked the idea of helping ease it along and watching it firsthand. She was glad she didn't have to go through it—she was content with her life—but she wanted her friend to be happy.

Susan sat at her kitchen table looking through a large stack of mail. There were a few bills, but the bulk of it was catalogs promoting the New Year's sales. She leafed through them as a matter of habit. The last one was a toy catalog. On the cover was a picture of a beautiful little girl clasping a teddy bear to her chest and beaming into the camera. She looked just like Molly on a good day. The shock incapacitated Susan, and she put her head on her arms and wept for hours. Spent at last, she took a bottle of chilled white wine from the refrigerator, went to her bedroom, and changed into her pajamas, although it was only seven o'clock. She kneeled at the bottom drawer of her dresser, lifted out a package wound in linen, and unwrapped it with infinite care. She got into bed and propped herself up on pillows, holding the precious doll under one arm and the bottle under the other.

Susan spent the bulk of the next day in bed. "A touch of stomach flu," she told Annie, when she called her to cancel lunch. "Nothing serious."

There were three rental apartments in my brownstone in Queens. The owner, Mrs. Layding, occupied the basement and first floor, my apartment was on the second floor, and there were two small efficiency units on the third. I knew my landlady had been in my apartment the day I decided to have a gin and tonic in the bathtub. I had just been promoted from administrative assistant to human resources officer, which is really funny when you come to think of it—considering how many human resources I've demolished over the years. The gin had been watered down so much that I could hardly taste it. I rushed to my bedside drawer and looked at my journal. The little lock was intact. Everything else appeared to be in order.

Mrs. Layding was a peculiar woman who always referred to her late husband as "my poor dear late departed husband" without pausing for breath. She had an amazing array of locks and bolts on her door and, nevertheless, insisted that people got inside somehow and looked through her things. Apparently she herself liked to get into other people's apartments and look through their things, and was not above doing a little pilfering.

I went downstairs, positioned myself in front of the peephole, and knocked on Mrs. Layding's door. The woman stuck her craggy head through the narrowest opening possible—she almost never let anyone into her apartment. I had been allowed in only once, the day I signed the lease and paid the deposit. It had been sparsely furnished, colorless, and dusty. I'd expected a cluttered old lady room, full of knick-knacks and photos. There wasn't a single photo, and nothing on the walls, either. I'd found it a frugal, sad sort of place. Actually, it was rather like my apartment, except mine wasn't dusty.

"Mrs. Layding, someone has been inside my apartment and watered down my gin. Nothing else seems to be missing. I would feel more comfortable with a new lock."

"What nonsense! No one comes in this house without my knowing about it." Mrs. Layding realized that had perhaps been the wrong thing to say. "Well, if you really think so, I'll think about it. Locksmiths cost money, you know."

I felt that perhaps that exchange would warn the gorgon off. But the next month, I came home to find my journal open on the coffee table, its lock broken. My heart started to race and almost stopped when Mrs. Layding knocked on my door.

"Well! A nice thing for me to find in my own house! I think I should call the police."

"Why, Mrs. Layding? Why did you violate my privacy like that? What gives you the right?"

"I'm entitled to know what kind of person I've got living in my house. And I've got a madwoman living in my house, apparently!"

"Mrs. Layding, I am trying to write a murder mystery. You didn't seriously think that was a real story, did you?"

The hatchet face dropped. "Well, I've got to think about this. I don't like it. Young girls shouldn't even know about such things. It's just not suitable!"

After slamming the door behind the wretched woman, I sat and thought things through, taking a few deep breaths now and then to calm myself. I packed a little bag with my few special keepsakes and, of course, the journal, and locked it in the trunk of my car. I traveled to Brooklyn and bought some kerosene at a hardware store. After dark, I poured it onto the porch at the front door and against the old woman's bedroom wall in the back, and tossed latex gloves on top of it. I wasn't sure there was enough, so added the contents of a large bottle of vegetable oil for good measure.

The woman never went out after dark. I drove to a neighborhood bar where, as expected, I found some of my friends from work—acquaintances really, because I can't say I ever remember having any friends, except for Sven, and he wasn't there that night. I didn't drink as much as they thought, and certainly not nearly as much as they did. I bought them a lot of drinks. I excused myself to go to the ladies' room, went out the back way, and drove to a dark street very close to the house. After I cut the phone line, a couple of matches were all it took and I made my way back to the bar in less than ten minutes. Incredibly, the same parking space I had before I left was still free. *The gods were on my side tonight*, I exulted. Combing my hair and touching up my lipstick, I reflected, well, probably not, just dumb luck.

"A little too much to drink," I said to explain my absence. "I'd better just sip some water for a while before I drive home."

I sat with my friends for another hour or so. I waited to hear the sirens. It took twenty minutes. I didn't say much to anyone that evening, as I'd never been on the same wavelength and I didn't share their interests and concerns. I considered them rather flighty. Of course, they didn't have my worries. And they always acted so happy; I guess they started life happy. I don't think my sort of tribulations could have ever entered their heads as anything but fiction.

I was never a suspect, although they knew it was arson, of course. The hateful woman was dead as well as the middle-aged math teacher who lived in one of the third-floor efficiencies—as far as I knew the other was vacant. I'd forgotten about the teacher, but she had seemed to be a fairly sour and miserable sort of person, so no great loss. Anyway, she would sometimes have coffee with Mrs. Layding, and who knows whom that woman might have said about my journal if left to her own devices. My secrets were safe.

I acted suitably dejected and enjoyed plenty of sympathy from those who thought I had lost everything. I even stayed with Sven for a few days. His friend stayed away while I was there; I guess I made him nervous. Maybe he thought I might want to watch again. He had a point. Sven helped me find another apartment, and there was no nosy landlady living in the building this time. He helped me pick out a couple of pictures for my walls. A bit of color makes all the difference.

I bought a stout box with a sturdy padlock for my journal.

15

It was freezing outside on this January morning, and a glint of ice crowned the grass and trees. Annie's kitchen had a fireplace with a loveseat and two chairs set in front of it. The countertop was tiled in terracotta, the floor was pine, the walls painted a soft cream, and sliding glass doors led out to a screened-in porch that looked over a wooded hillside, a favorite summer spot. The aromas of warm gingerbread and coffee and the throat-catching scent of burning wood filled the room.

Susan and Rose were having coffee with Annie and discussing refreshments for the February concert reception.

"Do you think we offer the same dishes too often? A couple of people complained last time," Rose said.

"Well, one has to look at who complained—Janet and that little violinist our maestro seems so fond of," retorted Susan.

"You know the caterer has a limited number of options for what we can afford to pay her, so we can't be too choosy," Annie said, ever practical.

"We certainly don't want to start doing the food ourselves again," remarked Rose. "It was a real pain to have to do that along with everything else."

Annie sighed. They had this conversation every year, and every year, nothing changed. The truth was that most people just wanted the opportunity to get together and see one of the big houses and didn't pay as much attention to the food as they did to the size of the rooms and the furniture. Annie said she would call the caterer to ask her if she could do one different dish.

"Who's in charge of the wine?" Annie asked.

"We don't have anyone so far. How about asking Caroline's husband to coordinate it this time? He hasn't done much over the past couple of years," Rose suggested.

"Oh, Allan really resents the symphony now that Caroline is president," Susan said. "He can't stand the time involved and the airs she puts on. We won't get anything out of him."

"What about Roger? He's always nice about helping," Annie said.

"Good idea," Susan said. "And I'll ask that nice Detective Paglietti to help. He seems to take an interest in the symphony nowadays, although I can't imagine why. Perhaps he thinks there's a murderer in our midst!"

"Susan, really, that's in the worst possible taste!" Annie said, her cheeks flaring red.

"Well, we can ask. All he can say is no," Rose said, sounding uncertain.

"I don't think he'll say no," Susan said, smirking.

Annie felt anxious. What was Susan up to? Planning some troublemaking for sure.

"I'll be responsible for the paper goods," Rose said. "We'll have to tell everyone to adhere to a strict budget. We're very short of corporate donations this year."

"Of course," remarked Susan snidely, "we could always ask Samantha Elantro to pay for the reception."

"That would not be appropriate," exclaimed Annie, even more irritated. "And well you know it, Susan."

"You know, I was thinking about her the other day. All these awful things that have never happened here before are probably connected with a newcomer to Salton. What do we really know about the Elantros after all?"

Annie and Rose looked at her incredulously.

"Do you seriously think that nice, simple woman could be involved with such things? Or Toby? Are you out of your mind?" demanded Annie, uncharacteristically furious by now.

"Well, think about it. What did she do before she married? What did he do before he started that business? I've always thought he was a shady character. Why don't we ask her if we can go over to her house tomorrow to discuss our volunteer needs for the reception? She would be so happy to be included, and we could get onto the subject of what we all did before we came to Salton and before we got married."

"I don't know," Rose demurred. "It all seems so underhanded."

"Well," Annie said, "I would rather be there than leave her to your tender mercies, Susan, because I know you're going to do it with or without us. All right, let's call her now."

Tom and Annie were sitting in front of their kitchen fireplace that evening as Annie told him about her morning with Rose and Susan.

"I don't know how to deal with those two these days. There always seem to be these undercurrents I can't quite catch. I never know where they're coming from. In fact, everyone seems different these days. I don't think I've changed at all, do you?"

"No, Annie, you don't change, thank God," Tom said fondly. "Some of those women are very unhappy, you know. In fact, most of them are. And a lot of things have happened recently. Judy's death was the first shock. And then look at poor Janet finding her tenant murdered. And Susan losing her aunt, her last relative. I'll bet she's a lot more upset about that than she's letting on."

"That's true, and Helen's had to deal with her separation from Pat. Sally hasn't changed. Unfortunately, she still buckles under to her dreadful husband. I feel uneasy, somehow. I'm used to everything happening in the usual way at the usual times. I guess I don't handle change very well. I like predictability. It's as if Salton is wobbling off its axis."

"Well," Tom said. "Life will throw in some surprises from time to time, and we have to go along with it. I don't think it's a good idea to be too complacent."

"Maybe you're right. I even found myself getting upset with that new Japanese landscaping next door when I saw it finished this afternoon. It's so out of keeping with the gardens in the rest of the street, although I have to admit it is beautiful. It jarred me, because it's different, very different. I suppose I shouldn't be such a stick-in-the-mud."

"No, you shouldn't. We must all keep ourselves open to new ideas and different ways of doing things. I've got a funny feeling there's a lot of stuff going on that we don't know about, and I think these murders might be connected in some way the police haven't figured out yet. I mean, how many murders have happened here in the last thirty years? None. And now, two so close together? Stands to reason. Anyway, let's go on up to bed and get stuck in the mud together." Annie thought that was quite a good idea.

Rose arrived at Samantha's a little early the next morning, apologizing for coming straight from the grocery store and explaining that her shopping had not taken as long as she thought it would. Samantha was visibly flustered by the early arrival.

"Can I help you in the kitchen, Samantha?" Rose asked.

"No, no, please just make yourself comfortable. I won't be a minute."

"Please take your time. I know I'm much too early."

"There are plenty of magazines on the coffee table. Help yourself."

"Thanks, I can see some really nice ones."

Rose made herself comfortable and looked through the magazine collection with amusement. These were the textbooks used by those who desperately wanted to have the right house, the right furniture, and the right clothes. *Poor thing*, Rose thought, *she doesn't realize that you need to have some innate sense of style before these so-called fashion gurus can even begin to guide you on the path to sophistication.* She looked around her—at gaudy Egyptian papyri, crude wooden African statues, shiny Asian silk pictures, brightly colored Greek "local" paintings, and there was even a Spanish painting of a bullfight on black velvet.

They could have bought so many beautiful artworks in all of those places. But they chose those objects they thought best represented that particular culture and would remind them of their visit.

Well, if it makes her happy, why not? Who am I to judge? Taste isn't something instinctive, it's imposed by others and you follow according to your icons: the assertion of old money or the show of new money, celebrity, ethnicity, or whoever you wish to be at that time in your life. Rose's own taste ran to the lusterless reassurance of middle-class affluence—she recognized that, half-mocking her pretensions.

Susan arrived just as Samantha was bringing in a heavy silver tray set with an elegant porcelain coffee set. They exchanged muted greetings. It was obvious that Samantha still smarted from Susan's cruelty at the Christmas party and that Susan despised Samantha.

"Samantha, could you please show me the powder room?" Rose asked.

Samantha led her to the corridor and opened the right door, remarking they should probably put a sign on it as there were so many other doors to confuse guests. Rose had an immediate and, she admitted to herself, mean-spirited, vision of a small gold-edged painted porcelain sign that said, "The Little Room."

Annie rang the bell just as Rose got back to the family room. She greeted Samantha warmly and said how glad she was to come in out of the cold.

"I have a lovely fire going, Annie. Please do come in and warm yourself."

They all sat and enjoyed their coffee and a remarkably good cake that Samantha had baked herself that morning. Samantha basked in their enjoyment, and Rose envied her the kind of mother who raised her daughters to cook the southern recipes they had been brought up to appreciate. *Now look who's thinking magazine stereotypes*, she thought.

"Would you like me to bring a couple of these to the reception?" Samantha asked.

"Oh, yes!" chorused Annie and Rose. Susan offered a grudging smile.

A pitiful crying, which had been going on for some time, became more strident. Samantha looked uncomfortable.

"You never mentioned you have a dog, Samantha," Rose said.

"Didn't I? He's only a little terrier and he does so hate to be left out of things. He's really sweet, but he does jump a bit. He's always so excited to see visitors and he just assumes everyone else loves him as much as we do! I've got him shut up in the laundry room. Do you mind if I let him out?"

Annie hurried to answer, ignoring Susan's sour look. "Oh, none of us is dressed up. Samantha, please go ahead. We'd love to meet him. I have a dog, too, a young cairn terrier. Terriers are full of character. I just love them. He didn't like my old cat at first, and she certainly didn't like him. They get on all right now, though."

Samantha went to let her dog out. He came speeding toward the guests like a bullet train and then turned tail and dashed back to his bed in the kitchen to get a favorite toy to present for their inspection.

"Oh, a Jack Russell," Rose said. "They are really adorable. He seems so affectionate, even with strangers."

"Yes, he's wonderful—affectionate, responsive, good with people. He doesn't like other animals much, though, so we have to be careful. His name is Jackson."

Susan rolled her eyes as Jackson made his rounds, then simmered down a bit and settled by Samantha, his nose quivering, much like Susan's did sometimes, Rose thought as she tried to suppress a chuckle.

"Samantha, we were all talking yesterday at Annie's house about what we did before we were married and before we came to Salton. It was quite interesting. How about you? What did you do before you married Toby?" Susan asked. Rose could see that Annie was disconcerted by Susan's blunt approach.

"Oh, I was just a secretary for a construction firm, nothing special. I met Toby that way, because his firm was having an office building designed and had invited our company to bid on it. We fell in love almost immediately."

"How sweet," Susan said, earning a frown from Annie.

"Yes, he is the sweetest of men. He got that job and many others because everybody knew he was straightforward and decent."

"How nice for you!" Susan said, her tart voice earning another sharp look from Annie.

All of a sudden, Jackson sprang down and went over to the large armoire near the door. He started to sniff and whine, and pushed his paw under it. The women looked on curiously, forgetting their trend of conversation. He finally managed to hook something with his claws and dragged it halfway out before it got stuck.

Samantha went over to him. "Whatever are you doing, Jackson? What on earth is that?"

She pulled the rest of the package out and brought it over to where the others were sitting. She sat down and set on her lap an oddly shaped parcel wrapped in brown paper and tied with string. She opened it, unfolded several layers of paper with care, and gasped in horror, as they all did. Sitting on Samantha's lap was a ten-inch chef's knife encrusted with dried blood.

Susan looked at them all in triumph. "Time to call 911, I think."

Rose looked across at Samantha with something like pity, remembering Susan's behavior at the party. Again, a gathering Samantha had tried hard to make a success had been marred, this time quite horribly.

"Will this nightmare called Salton ever end?" wondered Samantha aloud, shivering, although it was warm in the house.

Joe Paglietti was a methodical, medium sort of man. He was nearly forty and of medium height and build, moderately good-looking, with hair that was neither fair nor dark, but something in between, like tree bark. He was intelligent, but not brilliant. He had been divorced for five years, had a teenage son he rarely saw, and had little time or enthusiasm for a social life. His instincts had told him for some time he should explore the world of the Salton Symphony.

Detective Paglietti interviewed the Elantros, Rose, Susan, and Annie. The women testified that Samantha was certainly surprised at what she had found and had made no effort to conceal the parcel or its contents.

"Samantha was as shocked and horrified as the rest of us," Annie said.

"Samantha was quite upset, and we were all very shocked, of course," Rose said.

"I suppose Samantha was upset. I mean, she would be, don't you think? She didn't look as if she had seen that knife before, but of course, I don't know her that well. And Annie and Rose had clearly never seen it before," Susan said.

They made statements detailing their movements that morning and the sequence of events up until the gruesome discovery.

Toby came in for a more thorough grilling. A background check turned up nothing noteworthy. A preliminary test showed no fingerprints on the package or the knife. There was no motive that the detective could find, and he had an alibi for both Judy's and Gayle's murders. He had been out of town and in the company of others each time. The blood on the knife was Gayle's. The Elantros were tainted by the investigation, however, as Davey Roberts had been, even though he also had an alibi for the murders and was cleared of suspicion. The three were pariahs in the town and knew they would be until the killer was found. "There's no smoke without fire" was the most overworked cliché of the month. Annie had an alibi for Gayle's murder—she had been in a meeting during that timeframe—but Rose and Susan stated that they were at home alone at that time. Neither Annie nor Susan had alibis for Judy's murder, as Paglietti had discovered surreptitiously—they had no idea he had considered them suspects—and Rose, of course, had been injured in the attack.

He read through the statements again and leaned back in his chair, hands behind his head, staring at the ceiling for inspiration. It was obvious to him that the knife had been planted at the Elantros. But by whom? It was a ploy by the killer to divert attention, but it had not worked—at least as far as he was concerned—and had not been thought out very carefully. It was an impetuous act, a crime of opportunity. That meant that the murderer had not expected to visit the Elantros until shortly before planting the knife.

Almost mesmerized by the regularity of the creak that chiseled into the silence with each revolution of the ceiling fan, Paglietti turned the statements over in his mind. Then it came to him—the dog! Jack Russell terriers were known for their unusually keen sense of smell, even for a dog, and their relentless pursuit of prey. He remembered reading about one that had sat at the entrance of a rabbit burrow for a week before being found and retrieved by his owner, starving and filthy. Jackson would have found that package almost immediately, because he would have picked up the scent without much delay. The package had only been under the armoire for a very short period of time. It had either been put there the night before or, more likely, that very morning. And both the Elantros would have known better, as Samantha had told him they used to breed Jack Russells in Arkansas. He would do some quiet checking and keep this information to himself. He would have to tread carefully and quietly, for these people were not without influence, and he must obtain evidence that was solid to the point where even expensive lawyers would find it unassailable. He knew the society crowd assumed the murders had been committed by an outsider, or outsiders, and he would imply that he was persuaded of that himself. Feed into their complacency, and worm his way into their world—at least to a point—would be his strategy. A smile lingered at one corner of his mouth as he plotted his course. He picked up the phone.

"Mrs. Minhoff?"

"Yes, this is Annie Minhoff. Who is calling?"

"This is Detective Paglietti. How are you this evening?"

"Oh, very well, thank you. What can I do for you?"

"Well, I came to the last concert, as you know, and thoroughly enjoyed it. I've met so many nice people who are involved with the symphony. I would love to become a member and lend a hand. I guess you always need volunteers."

"Yes, how wonderful! What a coincidence! We were discussing the arrangements for the next reception a couple of days ago, and Susan Lazare suggested asking you to volunteer, since you seemed to be taking an interest in the symphony. Actually, we need someone to help Roger, Janet Bakewell's husband, with the wine. I'm afraid you would have to leave the concert about a half hour after the intermission."

"That's fine. I'd be delighted. I have a ticket for the concert."

"And is there a Mrs. Paglietti?"

"I'm afraid not. We divorced some time ago."

"Well, I'll call Susan and let her know. She'll call you to coordinate."

"Thank you, Mrs. Minhoff, you've been most warm and welcoming."

"Annie, please."

"Annie, then, and I'm Joe."

"Well, Joe, I'm so glad you're joining our little group, and I know the others will be, too. I'll look forward to seeing you at the concert. Goodbye for now."

"Bye, Annie."

Well, he thought, *at least one of the group won't be so happy to see me right there in the middle of things. Annie Minhoff couldn't have thought of a better job to give me. The bar will be the best observation post imaginable. But why would Susan Lazare think of asking me? Odd.* He pursed his lips and whistled out his breath. *This is way out of my experience. It's going to take some ingenuity.* He'd have to start thinking outside the box, as they say. *I'm not going to ask for help.* Joe Paglietti walked to his car, with more bounce in his step than usual, to go home to his apartment with its comfortable recliner, the chilled six-pack, and a couple of old *Law and Order* episodes. For the time being, he was a contented man. He'd start worrying tomorrow.

By seven the next morning, Joe was looking down at the dead body of a strange-looking woman. She was lying in front of a large tree in a wooded strip adjacent to a grassy field between two subdivisions. The front of her head had been smashed in with force, probably on the tree trunk. She had a high sloping forehead; the slope made more extreme by its injury, and her large sagging breasts and abdomen were tented by a polyester knit dress in a harsh shade of magenta. The standard poodle sitting next to her had bitten and chased off a curious spaniel whose owner, from a safe distance, had called animal control without noticing the body. The animal control officer found the disconsolate animal whining over his mistress's body and called it in.

The dead woman's name was Anita Pascal, and she lived with her husband nearby. Her husband was a meek, arthritic little man who had become distraught when he heard the news, sniveling and making little whining noises, much like the dog's. He was not a viable suspect. Inquiries revealed a woman who was mostly reasonable, but verbally aggressive when challenged, as she often was in her job as an insurance adjuster. She didn't have many friends and, apart from a visit to the Salton Citizen's Foundation Christmas party with some neighbors, had never had anything to do with the Symphony Seven. Still, Joe was certain that the same murderer had struck again.

16

Pansy

found myself dancing with her at the Christmas party. How in the hell did that happen? Susan was a great dancer, had a smile on her face, and hummed "Let's Do It My Way," although that wasn't the tune we were dancing to. She looked downright joyful. I danced along clumsily although I'm pretty good. At least I've always thought so since I took lessons years ago. I remember gazing into her face, watching her laugh with excitement, and noting the gleam in her eyes she always got when she was the center of attention. It was a revelation to see her happy and carefree, and I will remember her like that for the rest of my life. I often get these flashbacks of my life in Salton, and that picture, likely as not, is in some part of them, sometimes in the center, and sometimes on the edge where I can hardly see it.

I remember dancing to the next tune, and then the next, getting lighter and happier by the minute. She went faster and faster until we were dancing double-time to the music and whirling around in a dizzying display of virtuosity. The Christmas decorations around Samantha's dance floor were the gold and red twirling ones and they bounced before my eyes in what should have been a sickening, disorienting fashion. But it wasn't, it was sheer fantasy, and we were in fairyland. We were young, and we were happy. I stopped focusing on her and thought only of my own unfettered joy. We didn't stop dancing all night, and the other guests gradually fell away. They stood watching with looks of wonder on their faces, as if they had seen a vision of the Virgin Mary. What a strange way for me to think about their expressions, because we were so far, both of us, from the ideals of a Madonna, even in this fantasyland. We weren't our usual troubled selves out there on the dance floor; we were happy, happy forever. The feeling was deeply spiritual and I can still conjure it up sometimes, if it is quiet and I concentrate hard.

It is the only good dream I can remember. They say that everyone dreams every night, but most people forget them when they wake up. I often feel something on the edge of my mind when I awaken that is probably the last tendrils of a dream, but it never holds, except for the worst ones—I remember some of those. So, one happy dream of two lost women dancing the night away is something to hold on to. Especially because I tried to kill her friends later, and she is bound to hate me for it. It's a vision to have and hold on to always.

Latching onto the good memories is an enticing idea I try to keep in mind as I write this journal, although I cannot deny the dark ones their place. You have to face up to things in a journal. If you're going to lie to your own journal, what's the point of it? It becomes mere subterfuge. I intend this journal for posterity and I'm going to leave it behind to help people understand me and know what daunting obstacles I have had to overcome. If I ever leave here, I'll have to become someone else, so why does it matter? Damned if I know.

It's time to stop rambling and get back to my story.

The next year my firm advertised a job opening in Washington, D.C. I'd wanted to leave New York for a long time and this would seem to be the perfect opportunity. I'd pretty much worked my way through New York—Manhattan, Brooklyn, Queens, although I never braved the Bronx—and even my skill with cosmetics didn't provide a guarantee of anonymity. Look at the way Daisy kept showing up. I suppose a sister sees more than others, but still.

I wasn't sure I was qualified for this job as I had only been a human resources officer for just under a year, but I applied anyway. I did well in the interviews as I had studied hard trying to anticipate the questions they might ask me, and it was down to two people.

Unfortunately (for him), my competition, a good-looking, personable young man, somehow got pushed under a train in the Times Square subway station. Several trains had been canceled, leaving the platform overcrowded. It's a horrible way to die, I should think. I hope the power got him before the train did. He was a nice kid, and he always treated me with respect, which I appreciated. But his life was over and he could feel no more. One person dies and others carry on. That's the way of the world.

I wore a sad face as I told the human resources director that I would never have wanted to get the job under such tragic circumstances, but would naturally be proud to accept and do my best to justify his faith in me. I must say it was hard to keep a straight face, but I managed until I was well away from the office. I went straight to a coffee shop, ordered a latte, and sat chuckling into it as quietly as I could while I sipped.

No, I didn't do it.

17

Rose strolled around the lobby of the theater, which teemed with people waiting for another Salton Symphony concert to begin. Annie and Rose had persuaded the Elantros and Davey that it was best to come rather than stay away as if they had any reason not to hold their heads high. Toby and Helen gave out programs and took tickets at the center doors, and Davey helped Annie and Samantha with ticket sales. Rose watched how the patrons reacted when they noticed them there. After an initial sideways glance and a skipped breath, people were civil enough and cool hellos were exchanged.

She knew most of the audience, at least slightly, as they'd been coming to concerts for years. Others rarely came, but were perhaps here tonight, hoping for another spectacular disaster. Rose made her way toward the corner where

Detective Paglietti stood, quite alone but watching everyone. He had come to the previous concert and, Annie had told her, had professed to be enthralled with the symphony and its music and wanted to get involved. She wondered what he thought of these people and their world, a world that must be alien to him, one in which they belonged and he clearly didn't. Maybe he envied their sense of belonging; even though most of them had come from somewhere else, they had been able to put down new roots soon enough. *Well,* she thought with some bitterness, *he could never guess the enormity of effort it could require to belong.* It would bring him no joy. She stopped short of joining him, just smiled a greeting as she continued on her way. It would be too awkward to have him sitting with them under the circumstances. As she continued her amble, Rose amused herself by eavesdropping.

"If only they'd catch him, such things shouldn't happen in a place like Salton," bemoaned some.

"It must be an outsider. People like us don't do things like that. No, these are not people like us," they insisted. "No, not one of us."

"Not all Salton neighborhoods are like ours, you know," one worried matron explained to her companion.

"You never know about people, though, do you? How many people can you say you really know deep down?" interjected Rose, who had come up behind them.

"Well, who do you think it could be? Surely not one of us!" was the indignant answer.

"No, of course not, not one of us. A stranger, a passer-by, a madman."

"You think we have a madman in our midst?" a fearful voice asked.

"Who else would do such things?" replied Rose.

They were still shaken and afraid. Salton had been violated.

Annie and her husband had saved seats for their group. Toby and Samantha, looking more relaxed now, made their way in with Davey, whose hunched shoulders betrayed his unease. It was nearly eight o'clock and time for the concert to begin, so Rose found the others in the auditorium and sat down. The president of the board, Caroline, would open the concert as usual with some announcements and recognition of that evening's sponsor. After the last debacle, she was very apprehensive, afraid of something going wrong. She had told them all over the past couple of days that she was a nervous wreck and didn't know if she could get up on stage and go through with it. They all promised their full support and told her she would be fine. No one blamed her for what had happened. They all said it in one way or another. Caroline's pudgy hands, clammy at the best of times, left wet fingerprints on everything she touched, and she constantly blotted the dew on her upper lip with a mangled tissue.

"Helen, have you seen Caroline this evening?" Annie asked.

"Oh yes. I went backstage to check that she had enough orange juice and to make sure she was all right. She was so nervous. She said her mouth was dry, and she had almost finished the juice, so I got her some more. She was really knocking it back."

"Heavens," Annie said. "I took her a small pitcher to the dressing room only an hour ago. Actually, I took the liberty of pouring a miniature bottle of vodka into it to calm her down."

"Oh God!" Helen said, aghast. "I put quite a bit in the second pitcher I got her. I had the same idea."

"I went back there to say hello when she first arrived, and I saw her pouring something from a flask into the jug," Samantha said tremulously.

Rose said quietly, "I picked Caroline up, and we had a couple of glasses of wine together before we left her house. She said she needed to steady her nerves."

The friends gazed at each other, horrified. As the house lights went down, their eyes pivoted to the podium at the corner of the stage as Caroline emerged from the wings, stepping with great delicacy and caution, as if walking a tightrope. She leaned on the podium with an air of confidentiality.

"Goo' mornin'!" Now she had everyone's attention and rapt silence stilled the auditorium.

"I guess you're here for the music, so let's get on with it without any shilly-shallying. I've got to give this silly thing—where is the damn thing—to the people who gave us some money to put on the show." Caroline retrieved a plaque from the shelf under the podium and dropped it. She picked it up and, grasping the edge of the curtain, managed to hoist herself upright, although at some expense to the curtain and a little pop of flatulence.

"Come on!" she shouted at the figure cringing in the wings. "Get on out here, we're in a hurry."

A portly young man sidled onstage reluctantly, as one who approaches the dentist's chair.

"Well, what's your name? Speak up!"

"Fred Turner, ma'am."

"My friend Fred, here," Caroline said as she draped an affectionate arm over his shoulder, "owns that hamburger joint on Oak Street. The name escapes me for now..."

Fred maneuvered close enough to the microphone to get the name of his restaurant and the nature of his good deed out to the people.

"Good evening, Fred's Home Away from Home is very proud to…"

"Aw, don't waste our time with that crap, just take your plaque and go eat another of your sandwiches. Looks like you really like that shit!" And she grasped his love handles and shook them playfully. A scarlet Fred, waves of outrage and humiliation crashing over him, hurtled offstage.

Caroline, swaying a little by this time, cried, "Come on out, Maestro, start waving your stick and let's get it over with. Bye y'all!" And with an expansive wave, she sashayed out with head held high, carefree now that she was shed of the burden of refinement.

The audience breathed out all at once, producing a curious euphony as several hundred programs riffled gently. Most of them forgot to applaud as the conductor came on and his scowl did not bode well for anyone. The music was unusually militant that evening and sounded more like a marching band than the rich outpourings of a symphonic orchestra.

Rose couldn't concentrate on the music. She was still riveted by the performance put on by Caroline. In sobriety, the woman was all style and manners. Her behavior under the influence had been nothing short of clownish vulgarity. *None of us can hope to hide our true selves forever*, she reflected. When the surface cracks, the naked soul flies loose. She shook herself and pushed away these frightening thoughts.

She was sorry that Fred had suffered such public humiliation. She knew this was the first time he had given significant money to one of the local arts groups, and she suspected it would be the last. She was the one who had persuaded him to become a donor, and he had agreed with surprising ease. His father had always given generously to good causes when he ran the business, he said, and, with refreshing honesty, had gone on to tell Rose that he aspired to come up in the world. *Well,* she thought with some malice, *he has learned his lesson about giving money to uppity middle-class people who expend their energies doing nice things for other people just like them.* No, he'd probably go back to giving his money to people who needed it and appreciated it. Not such a bad thing, on the whole.

After a while, Rose tiptoed out of the auditorium and went backstage to look for Caroline. She found her, chin resting on her copious bosom as she snored and snuffled, happily oblivious. She took Caroline home and delivered her to an irate husband, whom she followed as he carried her upstairs, where he dumped her on her bed and left her fully dressed on top of the duvet. He didn't bother to take off her shoes. Then he stomped back downstairs to catch the rest of the movie he'd been watching. He didn't answer when Rose called goodnight to him.

When Rose got to the reception, it was in full swing now that the audience had awoken from its stupor, everyone recounting snippets of Caroline's speech, which was getting funnier with each reiteration. At least no one was talking or thinking about the murders. Paglietti poured wine, collected empty glasses, and was affable in the extreme. She was surprised that no one commented on his presence, although she supposed earlier events had provided enough diversion. She went to the bar for another glass of wine. While she was in line, she overheard him talking with one of the symphony's major donors and realized that the detective was indeed a lover of classical music and was quite capable of discussing the finer points of a concert. When it was her turn, she held out her glass and was puzzled when he took it and gave her a fresh one.

"We'll soon run out of glasses if you keep giving them out like that," she commented.

"Of course, I didn't think. Put it down to inexperience," he answered with a charming smile.

Rose went over to join the Seven. Annie said she was so ashamed of her role in Caroline's downfall that she wasn't in the mood for a party, so she and Tom were leaving early. The Elantros chatted for a short while and left, followed shortly thereafter by Davey. Janet, her husband Roger, and Rose talked quietly together. Roger mentioned that he felt Janet needed a change of scene. He was so busy at work, though, that he simply could not get away any time soon.

"Why don't you go on a little holiday, dear?" he asked her.

"I would love to, but I really don't think it would be much fun to go alone," Janet protested.

"Well, maybe one of your friends would like to go. I think a week in the Caribbean would do you a world of good."

"Actually," Rose said. "I have never been to the Caribbean. I would love to go with you, Janet, if that would be all right with you."

"Oh, would you! I would love that! I'd love to get away. We could have fun together."

"That's settled then. You girls can look into it next week. You'll be my guest, Rose."

"Oh, no, I couldn't possibly, that's too much!"

"I insist, you'll be doing me a favor, looking after my Janet and helping her feel better."

Roger looked at Janet with sappy adoration, and Rose sighed. He was so good to his wife, a thoroughly decent man. And Janet hadn't always been easy to get along with. Even in public, she was often demanding and petulant, shrill and ungrateful, although she had improved lately. Of course, Roger was boring, just like Victor had been—decent and boring. Although Victor had liked to wear her lingerie to bed, which she considered a little outside the norm. Victor's one secret. She supposed everyone had a secret. She looked at Roger and pondered what his proclivities might be. You could never tell, but she doubted his fantasies ran to wearing his wife's undergarments. Besides, his gut would get in the way, and he'd look like an elephant in a tutu. She had to stifle a giggle at the bizarre image that came out of nowhere.

Rose and Janet spent a delightful week poring over travel catalogs and planning their trip, set for the middle of March. Then they went shopping and Janet started to cheer up. She hadn't changed her priorities to the extent that shopping for new clothes couldn't fill her with pleasure. Even Rose, whose mood was usually somewhat flat, was a little excited. She would have to get a passport. She had a good figure and experienced a fleeting desire for a bikini, then set it aside. It would upset Janet, who was not bikini material.

Caroline resigned from the Board of the Salton Symphony and Rose was voted in as the new president at an emergency board meeting. Rose had held several offices on the board, but never that of president. She was thrilled and felt she deserved the recognition. Caroline, although efficient and hardworking, had not always displayed good judgment. She had alienated many board members in her short tenure and they were relieved to be rid of her. Rose, they opined, could be relied upon to be objective, calm, efficient, and pleasant and, they hoped, could ensure a trouble-free concert in May. At least the audience numbers were up, although that would probably level off when future concerts turned out to be uneventful. It was always a struggle to bring in a good audience year after year.

Rose was gratified and knew she had climbed to a new social level. She would have to entertain a little more. She must inventory her porcelain and crystal and make sure everything was just right. She must practice public speaking, a thought that filled her with some trepidation. And she had better start thinking about the next season. There were several changes she would like to make to the committee structure. Time enough for all that when she returned from the trip, which was all she wanted to think about right now.

The airport was chaotic and none too clean. Janet wrinkled her nose, took Rose's arm, and dragged her off to find their suitcases. Rose looked at the parking lot with dismay. Its only concession to Caribbean loveliness was the uneven distribution of a few tattered palm trees on the periphery. This was not the pristine tropical scene she had envisioned. They found the hotel's courtesy bus and loaded their own bags while the indolent driver leaned on the door, watching. Janet was fuming but, Rose noted, not as assertive as she would have been in her home element. Rose's spirits lifted the farther they drove from the airport. The beaches were cleaner than the trash-strewn dumps they saw at first, the greenery was lush, and the palm trees well-tended.

The pastel hotels and houses radiated a reassuring wholesomeness.

When they arrived at the hotel, an ebullient young woman greeted them with warm courtesy at the check-in counter and sent a porter to retrieve their baggage. Janet and Rose mounted a wide stone staircase to their suite on the second floor. It had two bedrooms with a little sitting room between that had glass doors leading to a balcony.

Rose flung open the doors and leaned on the railing, taking in the luminescence of the turquoise sea in front of them. The contrasts of white, blue, yellow, and pink buildings, sand whose colors undulated between white, gray, and yellow, and the almost shadowless sea, were breathtaking. She'd been transported into a fantasyland and she meant to enjoy every minute.

After they had unpacked, they went down to the plain little dining room for lunch. They had a view of the gardens behind the hotel and admired the flamboyant flowers and birds. "The dining room doesn't need ornamentation," Rose said. "Pretty pictures can't compete with that kind of nature."

To Janet's disgust, Rose decided to try goat stew, which she pronounced "interesting." She disliked its gamy flavor, but put on a good show of enjoyment to annoy Janet. Janet stuck with more reliable choices—hamburger (well done) and fries—which she pronounced "acceptable." After they had finished, Rose wondered aloud if they used beef for their hamburgers. Janet stuck to fish after that. They both ordered the fresh tropical fruit salad, very different from the canned variety available in American supermarkets. Its exotic, sweet, substantive qualities pleased even Janet's limited palate, and Rose decided to have it every day. It was the food of the gods—nectar, the food of paradise. Might as well enjoy it here on earth.

The beach was furnished with several sets of tables, umbrellas, and lounge chairs. They settled themselves and decided to go for a swim. The hot sand burned the soles of their feet, so they had to make a dash for it. From the back, Janet looked rather like an ostrich running across the desert. Later, they bought water shoes from the hotel shop. "There be sharp things on the bottom you don' want to step on," the salesclerk told them.

The water was deliciously warm, divine, they agreed. "Blood warm," Rose said.

Janet caught her breath and said with bravado, "More like a bathtub, I would say."

"Yes, you're right, of course, just like a bathtub."

Over the course of the week, they learned to snorkel and were entranced by the tropical fish they saw scavenging among the coral. Rose felt as if she were in the midst of a movie. The sound of her breathing underwater resounded in her head, and nothing seemed quite real. One morning, she saw two strange creatures approaching that looked rather like jellyfish, except for a little protuberance on their bellies. Startled, she reared up out of the water, only to find that she had been watching the breasts of a young woman who was swimming topless. She related this with great mirth to Janet, but Janet was repelled by the topless sunbathers and certainly not amused. Rose thought it might be nice to go so free and easy in the sunlight.

Rose enjoyed the boost of the flippers that enabled her to swim a long way without much effort, though her adventures scared Janet, who believed in the utmost caution. There was a small island just a few hundred yards off the shore, and Rose was determined to swim all the way around it. As she drew close, the water got rougher. She was snorkeling as she wanted to see whatever was coming her way. She discovered that just underwater there were other outcrops of coral and she would have to swim carefully through the passages to avoid contact with the sea urchins that lay in wait with their cruel black spines. Ahead, she saw a red cloud approach. As it came closer, she realized it was a shoal of jellyfish. She didn't know if they were poisonous, but they looked it with their red markings and orange tentacles. There was a break in the passage ahead, a narrow one, so she dove under the creatures and swam as fast as she could. She was almost free of the red mass when she saw a sea snake pop up from its hole in the seabed, which inspired her to swim on with a strength she didn't know she had before popping up herself, spluttering and coughing up the water that had entered her snorkel. Her pulse raced, and she felt wonderful, embracing life instead of floating along its surface. She cleared out her snorkel and went on her way, the water calmer on this far side of the island, the outcrops fewer. She saw only beauty on the way back, the ugliness far behind her.

When Rose got back to the beach, Janet was standing there with a hotel guard.

"Where did you go? I couldn't see you. What happened? I was so worried. Don't do that again! I thought you had drowned. Madness!"

"Oh, I just went for a swim around the island. I'm so sorry I worried you."

"That island's got bad currents, missy. Best not go there," the guard said. "An' our fish down here got teeth, too."

"See!" Janet trumpeted.

"I won't do it again, so sorry."

Rose reclined in her lounge chair, lassitude overtaking her as the adrenaline rush died away. She promised herself another trip to the Caribbean one day. She would learn to scuba dive, too. She wanted to see what was lurking down deep. A different island, perhaps. A wilder one.

18

Pansy

loved my job and loved Washington, too. I lived in Bethesda first, and then Georgetown. My apartment in Georgetown was much smaller than the one in Bethesda, but it was so much fun in those days. I used to walk along M Street and look in the windows of quaint boutiques, and my favorite restaurant had nothing on the menu but crepes you could order filled with meat, seafood, fruit—just about anything you could think of. Georgetown changed later, no longer quaint and pretty but full of shops and restaurants catering to twenty-something singles, as well as clusters of junkies nodding off in the doorways of boarded-up storefronts.

I met a pleasant young man in Georgetown at a summer party given by one of my neighbors. He was quiet and sweet, good-looking and attentive. We dated for a year and he showed me a new life, the way of life enjoyed by people from good homes and schools. He introduced me to the theater—classical music, ballet, musical theater, drama—it all held me spellbound. We ate in ethnic restaurants and he helped me with ordering. I always liked pasta, but with him discovered more varieties than I'd dreamed possible. I started to read for pleasure, a concept that seemed alien at first. I have been a voracious reader ever since I realized that both self-improvement and entertainment were available in abundance at the local library. Bookstores contained irresistible treasures, and I started to amass books in a way that was remarkable for someone who had, until then, avoided tying herself down with possessions that would be difficult to move in a hurry.

Just after Labor Day, he told me he would like to take me to his company's Christmas party, where there would be dancing as well as dinner. He promised a fine evening. I was excited, but had to hold in my panic. I told him I didn't know how to dance properly and would like to sign up for a few lessons. He said he wasn't very good at dancing either, so we would do it together. I asked him to help me choose my dress, too. I still have it, a poor girl's dream of a dress—black lace over pink silk. I felt like a princess in it and whenever I took it out of its box, as I used to do from time to time, I reached for that memory of my special night, my coming out, and knew the dress to be enchanted still. We had a grand time and danced all night. I'd turned into a swan.

I went to my first party, against my better instincts, when I was sixteen. It was some charitable event put on by the local youth center, and my caseworker more or less forced me into going. She said I needed to learn some social skills. My dress was cheap and looked it, and I didn't know how to dance. My foster mother had given me a home perm that frizzed horribly and I knew I looked a fright. Sometimes I stood, and sometimes I sat, as far away from the dance floor as I could, keeping my eyes fixed on my white patent shoes, and hoping to God no one would ask me to dance.

It wasn't only that I didn't know how to dance; I couldn't stand the thought of a boy's nasty clammy hands on me, their hopeful, wandering hands. I hated the loudness of the music, the boys' crude and noisy showing-off, the stink of their breath—even though alcohol wasn't allowed, most of them had hip flasks—and stale cigarette smoke. I knew, even then, that I didn't belong in that tawdry masquerade. I closed my eyes for a while and dreamed of my next dance—my lovely floating dress, the wine and champagne, the foxtrots and waltzes played by a stylish band—until my eyes startled open at the sudden crashing of drums that was hurled at us by the bunch of yobs from Yonkers that passed for a band.

Years later, when I had a good job and had schooled myself in the fashion and mannerisms of more gently bred girls, I still couldn't bring myself to risk another dance. There were still a lot of missing pieces in the puzzle that made up the new me.

Later, when I felt ready to let another boy touch me—and he touched me a lot—and I didn't find it altogether horrifying, I knew I could get used to it if I had to, but I vowed to wait until I had to. That poor boy's hopes and ego were crushed by my sudden and unexplained rejection before he achieved his goals. If I was going to do it, it had to be for a good reason, and he was not useful in any way. But at least now I knew I could. Not every man was like my father, after all. That was all long before I met Sven, of course.

The nice young man I married when I was ready to take that step was not like Dad in any way I could see. He stayed nice until he got sick years later. Then he started to look at me sometimes like Dad used to look at Mom before he beat her.

I told him very little about myself, except that I was an orphan, and had been raised in foster homes. I probably was an orphan for all I knew and often wondered what had happened to my mother. After all, where could a woman like her go? Did she miss us? Have any regrets? I doubt it. I think love had been beaten out of her, although I'd never known her whole, after all. Maybe she'd always been shallow and cold. She might have gone back to England if she could raise the fare. I understand they have great welfare benefits.

He told me he was also an orphan, raised by an aunt in Milwaukee. He thought both of us being orphans forged some sort of bond between us. I just agreed and looked solemn. He had attended George Washington University, and, after graduation, stayed in Washington. He worked as a financial analyst for a huge corporation that sold large office machines. He would much later become comptroller of that company after they moved us around the country for a few years.

We married in a simple civil ceremony, and I moved into his apartment. I wore a simple knee-length white dress and veil. I felt entitled to wear white—fathers don't count. Thinking about the first night made me jittery. I didn't know how I'd react to being penetrated again, but I'd read enough by that time to know how to fake it if I had to. I took a long time in the bathroom before sliding under the covers. We lay side by side without looking at each other for, maybe, five minutes. He kissed my cheek gently and drew me to him. He was sensitive enough to know I was nervous—I didn't have to say anything—and took things very slowly, kissing, caressing me all over. He was clean and smelled fresh. I liked that.

My mind jogged over to that night I watched Sven, and as I relived the scene, I felt myself melting inside. The heat in me became almost unbearable. I think he was shocked when I grabbed his buttocks and thrust him into me as I moaned and writhed in ecstasy. He liked it, though. If only he'd known the company he was keeping.

I felt very good about the new me—this sophisticated, young, married woman—in spite of the disapproval of his aunt, who loved him like a son. She came to the wedding and, I could tell, disliked me on sight. Some women have a nose for these things and she obviously thought I was not good enough for her family and her wonderful boy. She was right, of course, and her knowing without being told shamed me. The new me wasn't quite finished, I realized. I know now that you can't change all of a person, just some of the bits that show.

I had learned so much about the finer things of life, the beauty of language and color, I felt they were part of me now, that I had grown a new skin. But there are dark imps in dark places, buried deep within my mind that, to this day, sometimes crawl up to the surface, especially when I smell danger. This perceptive woman sensed the imps in me, sensed the dark places. But she kept her counsel; she left me alone. If only the others had left me alone. People can't seem to resist trying to kick another soul down a rung on the ladder, which they think places them up one. They really stay in the same place, though, don't they?

All those Salton socialites are upstarts, *arrivisti*, common folk elbowing their way through their own corner of the jungle, hustling their way through life, the same as everyone else, the same as me. They are nothing. After they have gone, the universe will close up seamlessly after them as if they had never taken breath. There aren't many people who really matter—except to themselves.

Shame is a terrible thing, a cruel thing imposed on you by the ideals of others. It is a cruel master, this thing. Why should I feel shamed by what evil people have done to me? Why should that young girl have been forced to shoulder this burden, this shame hobbling her as she struggled through life, yearning for good things? People will tell you that someone who has had the sort of bad things done to them that I have suffered will likely become damaged goods. But it wasn't my fault, none of it was. It wasn't the bad deeds that birthed the troubles, it was the shame they forced on me in the old streets and the foster homes, and even schools where no one could know my background; but they sensed the destitution, sensed the shame.

My life is exhausting, always taking care not to let the facade slip. All that killing, too. It takes meticulous planning, you know, and nerves schooled and stretched to a steady rhythm while you perform the task at hand. You must be willing to stake your life on a few minutes of action you have thought through many times, always understanding that fate can take a wicked turn. It's a lot of trouble, believe me.

My young man saved me from myself, I thought at the time, and braved his aunt's disapproval, which puzzled him. He was too innocent to sense the imps. He would go to visit her from time to time, but I stayed behind. I didn't begrudge her his visits as she'd taken him in when his parents died and given him a happy home, after all. No one had done that for me. My own sister didn't bother to check up on me in the foster homes. Even the caseworkers didn't check on me, and that was their job. I was entitled to regular medical checkups, but I never got them. It wasn't in the best interests of some of the foster parents to take me to the doctor.

My teeth ached a lot, too. After I was grown and earning money, it took me three years and a couple of thousand dollars to get them right. I'm good with pain, though. Most of what I have suffered since is not as bad as the early torments. It was good pain training; I suppose you could say that for it. You learn to park your mind somewhere else and get on with life in another corner.

When I found out I was pregnant, I had mixed feelings. What sort of a mother could someone like me be? I wasn't even sure I could love a child. I'd only ever loved Sven, and look where that got me. I went on loving Sven for a long time after I knew he was gay, but the love turned in a different direction. I'd like to have had a brother like him. Would you revile me too, Sven? Of course you would, you're too decent.

I knew a lot of the wrong things to do bringing up a child, but had no idea about the right things—no experience, you see, no values to speak of, no path to follow. It's one thing to discard your parents' values, but quite another to fill the void wisely. As it turned out, I didn't do too badly at mothering and certainly a lot better than my parents. And I loved them enough, especially my first. My husband's aunt sent a stiff note of congratulation and a silver spoon when the baby was born. I quit working and we settled down. I've always kept that spoon close by.

We went through some difficult times in our last posting before Washington, as I could never settle down in Rochester—anywhere in New York State was too close to New York City for my peace of mind. I always felt tense and quarrelsome, so I persuaded him to ask for a transfer back to the Washington office. When we got there, we rented for a while and then bought a house in Salton, one very much like my early dream house. It had the white fence, the old trees, lovely flowerbeds, and I made sure to get the polished furniture. It was my finest achievement, I thought then. Now I had left all the rottenness behind, I could build a new life, the life I had always wanted. Yes, I was content to be married to him, and I was grateful, too. He was very good to me. No one but Sven had ever been kind to me before, beyond the casual kindness of work acquaintances.

I had to make sure he never found out about Pansy, so I burned my first journal—the one I had treasured enough to kill Mrs. Layding for. That was my tribute to him, my commitment to him. If he had known my secrets, he would have looked at me in a new light and seen nothing but shadows. He would never have trusted me. And he would have been right. I betrayed him in the end, when he became a burden.

During the good years, his niceness would get on my nerves sometimes, but when he changed, it was unnerving— that look of hate and anger he would shoot at me, his resentment of my fullness of life in the face of his declining health. It was not to be borne, just not possible to endure.

19

Susan stared into the fire. She had been thinking about the disrupted concerts since the day before and was pondering some small points—no more than coincidences—that had been puzzling her. She wondered if they added up to anything. She might call Annie in the morning; she couldn't concentrate on anything other than Molly today, Molly's birthday. She would have been thirty-four and, no doubt, a mother. Susan wondered what it would have been like to have grandchildren to love. She had forgotten what it felt like to love anyone deeply, although apparently, she had loved Aunt Beatrice a little.

Born and brought up in New York City, she'd lived in Indiana for a few years as a young wife and mother. She didn't want to stay in Indiana after Molly died and, as her husband's company had a division in Washington, they were able to move within the year. They later moved into a charming old house in Salton, the same one she lived in now. No one in Salton knew about Molly, as she could never talk about it, especially after her husband died as the result of an accident. A company truck had backed into him in the parking lot as he walked to his car after work in the kind of twilight that merges all quiet colors into the same shroud. The driver's poor record cost the company plenty. Susan had gone after the company like a Fury, but the settlement hadn't made her feel better. The hollow satisfaction of vengeance passed over her in moments and left her mind adrift. She didn't make friends for several years.

One day, she noticed an advertisement in the local paper for a concert to be given by the newly established Salton Symphony and, on impulse, decided to go. Some people in the lobby, whose nametags proclaimed them board members, greeted her with charm and warmth and made her feel welcome. They all chatted for a while and they urged her to become a season ticket holder and a volunteer. During the intermission, the assault was renewed, and they invited her to the donor reception that always followed a concert. She had enjoyed the concert and the reception—as much as she was capable of enjoying anything—and was finally hooked and reeled in by Annie and Rose.

That had been fifteen years ago, and she treasured her bond with the Symphony Seven. She knew most people disliked her, and she didn't blame the recipients of her sharp tongue for keeping their distance. But somehow the Seven all got along and it was a human connection, one that accommodated the emotional distance she required. It was the best she could do. Her rage had taken over from sorrow long ago and had turned her into a bitter woman who enjoyed hurting people. She couldn't seem to stop lashing out and couldn't even bring herself to try—aggression acted on her like a narcotic, deadening the pain that crushed her seconds after she awoke each morning. She certainly did not want to be close to anyone again; the idea of the intimacy of close friendship was distasteful—unthinkable and undoable.

Molly's life had been short and tormented. She'd suffered from cystic fibrosis. There had been illness after illness, endless treatments, daily therapy, and they had watched with feckless hope as their daughter went from bad to worse. They never slept the night through, listening for the slushy coughs that compelled them out of bed to nuzzle and reassure the little girl before they forced the mucus out of her lungs. They couldn't save her. When she was seven years old, pneumonia took hold and leached the life out of her.

She had asked them, "Am I going to live with the angels?"

Susan said, "Yes, my darling. You will be very happy with them and you won't be sick anymore. We'll come along later to stay with you."

"I think I see one, Mommy. Do you see her over in the corner there? She's so pretty, she looks very kind. Do you see her, Mommy?"

It had been heartbreaking to hear her spend her precious breaths with that brave determination to hold on to her angel. Susan remembered the little face peaceful in death, a thin face with its porcelain skin framed by dark curly hair. Susan had kissed the silent blue vein on the side of Molly's neck, the one that used to signal, ever more tentatively, that life still lingered. There was a small grave in Indiana that had no one to tend it. "But she isn't there," Susan said to herself. "Although where she is, I couldn't say."

Molly's father had kept his promise and joined her without much delay. Sometimes Susan felt she should go, too. There seemed to be no point in carrying on. Her life was meaningless when she thought about it. But as she lacked the spark to make her life worthwhile—that had died with Molly—she also lacked the spark to end her foggy existence. Her daily battles took all her energy and, for the most part, enabled her to sleep the night through.

20

Toby arrived home with a happy sloppy bounce, looking forward to recounting the evening—especially his friends' corny jokes—to Samantha. He was too tired to put his car away and so left it in the driveway; he'd be going to the office in the morning, anyway. He fumbled with the key because he'd had a lot to drink, although he would never admit that he was actually drunk. He realized, with some surprise, that the deadbolt was not locked, but the alarm came on when he entered, though, so everything was all right. It was unlike Samantha to be so careless. He toiled up the stairs, knowing that the alarm would have awoken her and that she would be waiting for him, sleepy and soft. She wasn't.

Bewildered, he went downstairs again to look around. He felt uneasy now, accustomed as he was to her presence. He heard Jackson crying in the powder room and let him out, again surprised and confused, because Samantha would never have shut him in there. He went into the kitchen and turned on the light. The keyboard caught his eye—her car keys were missing. He rushed through to the garage and was almost overcome with exhaust fumes. He got the doors open and turned on the light, seeing what he half expected and feared to see. Samantha lying face down on the concrete floor.

He dragged her out into the yard, laid her gently on the grass, and started CPR. He stopped long enough to call 911 and began again, refusing to admit that she was past help. He couldn't lose her, he wouldn't, wouldn't. He tried to look only into her open eyes and avoid the sight of the ugly wound on her head. He felt hands on his arms pulling him away. He saw figures bent over her, somehow ghostly in the bright flashlights, and the slight shaking of heads that pierced his heart.

"She's gone, sir. She's gone. I'm so sorry," the paramedic said with gentle authority.

Toby doubled over and clutched his abdomen, screaming like one tortured to their breaking point. He continued to roar and cry and rage for what seemed like hours until flagging energy reduced him to a pitiable sobbing. Detective Paglietti settled him on his bed and told him he had to look around; he'd be back up later. After he left, Toby stared at the ceiling, his concentration interrupted now and then by a new burst of raw mewling.

A printed note, composed on the computer, was found in the study, in which Samantha confessed to the murders and said she could no longer live with the guilt. "I did it, I'm sorry, but I hated them all. I cannot live with it anymore." Her suicide and admission of guilt shocked all who knew her and devastated Toby, who was only at the beginning of his journey through a nightmare of sorrow accompanied by alternating bewilderment, disbelief, and anger. Most people were relieved that they didn't have to be afraid that a murderer was lurking in their midst any longer, and that it had been an outsider—more or less. But their condolence notes to Toby only expressed sorrow for his loss. No one came to visit except Annie and Helen. He could guess what people were saying.

"We always knew it was an outsider, of course," Salton would be saying, nodding its collective head sagely. "Not one of us."

Toby raged at Detective Paglietti, insisting that he did not believe she did it for a moment and that she had been murdered to divert suspicion from the real killer. Samantha never used the computer and would have written a note by hand. Yes, the alarm was armed, but the front door deadbolt had not been locked. And she would never have shut Jackson up in the powder room. She never confined him unless she had guests who didn't like dogs, in which case she would have put a gate across the kitchen door. She was anything but suicidal and there wasn't a violent bone in her body. She had told him she might go out with a friend that night, although he had been in a hurry to go to a meeting and had not waited to catch a name or where they were planning to go. And why was she face down on the ground instead of in the car?

Samantha might have changed her mind, gotten out of the car, and fallen because she was groggy from the fumes, the detective pointed out. But Paglietti was inclined to agree with Toby that Samantha was not the killer, but a victim. He told him that it was the opinion of the medical examiner that Samantha's head wound was too severe to have been caused by a fall, asking Toby to keep that information to himself for the time being.

Much later, Toby would tell Paglietti that his house-keeper had reported that two Waterford wine glasses were missing, and that she had not broken them. She never broke things, certainly not, no sir!

The funeral was not well attended and Annie and Helen were the only Seven to attend. Janet and Rose had left on their trip the morning after Samantha's murder and had not found out about it until they got back and Roger told them at the airport. Annie was embarrassed by the small turnout, but Susan told her that she had never liked Samantha so wouldn't bother. Sally had confided that Jack had forbidden her to go, although she had written Toby a note on the quiet. Annie watched in distress as Toby sobbed all the way through the service, his erect posture sagging under the weight of his grief. His breath was ragged and desperate at the graveside. After it was over, he refused Annie and Helen's offer to come home with him and even sent his children away.

A couple of months later, he would call Annie and blurt out that he couldn't stay in Salton with everyone thinking his wife had been a murderer. He had put the house and his business up for sale and planned to move to a small town on the east coast of Florida. Even after he moved away Annie kept in touch and, as he slowly recovered, he'd tell her that he had begun to miss his business and that a friend had persuaded him to spend a few weeks from time to time in Toronto to help him revive his flagging company. Annie was pleased he had contemplated getting back into business and hoped he was on the mend.

21

Janet and Rose returned from their vacation, rested and tanned. It had been a marvelous respite, and they had enjoyed their easy familiarity and relaxed friendship. Neither of them would ever reveal much of themselves, but were nevertheless pleased with one another's company. They were shocked and dismayed when they learned of Samantha's death, but were glad to shake off Salton's preoccupation with murder and relieved to have avoided Samantha's funeral.

Rose had felt almost merry on occasion. It had been a great vacation. Why hadn't she thought of traveling before? She had denied herself an important experience. When they were going through customs in the island's little arrival hall, she had listened to the inhabitants speaking in their native French and Dutch dialects, although they all spoke English, too. She wondered what it would be like to be in Europe where everyone spoke another language all the time, ate different kinds of food, and were altogether—well, different. Starting next year, she would go somewhere different every summer. And she would spend a week each winter in the Caribbean. She could afford it. Her scope had been too narrow. It was time to open up her mind and explore the rest of the world. She'd go to Europe on her own, though. Her friends were too provincial to experience a foreign culture as fully as she meant to. She would start with France. And she wouldn't be eating hamburgers. Or goat stew, come to that. She'd have her hair styled in Paris and buy a new outfit. Maybe she should take French lessons at adult education. Yes, absolutely she would.

Janet had eaten well and looked a lot better, to the relief of her husband. Their reunion was sweet and comfortable. Her belief that the murders were behind them further lifted her spirits and she was filled with new energy. She took a nap when she got back from the airport, a refreshing sleep that was free of Gayle's corpse. She and Roger had dinner out and retired early. She had trouble sleeping because of the nap, but finally dropped off. She dreamed of holding a newborn baby girl, but her features kept changing in waves of pale hues, although she knew who it was. She awoke with a start, her nerves taut again.

She had never told anyone about the abortion. She felt so ashamed, and her parents were devastated. Her father had sent her out of town to his aunt in upstate New York. She stayed there for a few months. She bled a lot. Abortion was still illegal in those days, so she couldn't see a proper doctor, only an old crone with tubes and pans who hadn't stayed long, thank God. Aunt Edith, grim and humorless, made her do all the housework. She didn't get much rest, nor did she get much to eat. Janet wrote the required thank you note when she got home and never had anything more to do with the old gorgon. Her father must have known what his aunt was like and how she'd treat her, she realized with growing bitterness. He had never punished her before, but he sure did that time. He'd called her a slut, too. People thought she had gone to visit a sick relative to help her after surgery. Janet had helped her all right; that damned woman had enjoyed having a slave at her beck and call.

Her parents were well off and she could have kept the baby with their help, although college wouldn't have been possible. Her mother never spoke of it again. Her father barely greeted her when she returned home, and things were never the same between them. He felt betrayed, as did Janet. She had expected them to be upset, angry, disgusted—all of those things—but she had expected some acknowledgment of her suffering, too. She'd refused to tell them who the father was, which added fuel to the fire. But if she'd named the strapping young gardener, it would have been even worse. They wouldn't have understood how she could cavort with someone of his class.

After she and Roger got married, she didn't conceive for a few years. She had to tell her doctor about the abortion, and he found she needed minor surgery because it had caused some scarring. Later she had two children, each of them perfect, ten fingers and toes, all the right things in all the right places, so it all worked out without Roger having to find out.

Janet never forgot her first baby, though, and she would dream about her little floating fetus sometimes—she was convinced it was a girl, although the woman never said. She'd wake up with tears on her face as if she were in mourning—not far from the truth. Janet wondered what she would have been like. She could have grown up to have her own children to love, but she would never love anyone because she never got the chance. Janet's face became wet again. When would the mourning stop, when would she stop thinking about her? She was never in her arms, so she felt she must love her always, because she had never had the chance to love her properly like a mother should, like a mother wants to, like a mother needs to, and she never got the good things a child deserves. She believed in women having the right to choose their course, but it took its toll, either way. Janet knew she must carry on, head held high, like a woman with nothing to hide, nothing to regret. She had no choice.

She moved to the spare bedroom where she cried with abandon, a luxury she had never before allowed herself. She hemorrhaged her unacknowledged grief with some of her brittle shell. Roger came looking for her the next morning, perplexed by her absence from their bed and her puffy eyes. She told him everything. He gathered her to him and rocked her like a baby. She cried some more, and he did, too. Janet shared and accepted her grief for the first time since she was seventeen years old. The quintessential woman could begin to emerge from a cocoon spun from indulgence, sorrow, betrayal, and self-doubt.

He was a very dear man and, thanks to him, I had come a long way. He could be boring, I must admit, but even after the initial "in-love" thing had worn off, I still liked him and he was still my friend. And the sex was a good release, allowing me to let off steam. I sometimes wondered why I hadn't thought of it earlier in life, before remembering that it could hardly have seemed anything but revolting before Sven. I wonder what happened to Sven? I hope he was sensible and stayed well. I hate to think of that beautiful body wasting away from that terrible disease.

Of course, if my husband had known all about me, I think he would have felt very different. His aunt sensed that I was not all I seemed, but before she died, she finally had to admit that I had been a good mother and an exemplary wife, and that perhaps she had been mistaken. She left him her estate, which was not enormous, but large enough to make a big difference to us. She died just before he was transferred back to the Washington office and her bequest made it possible for us to move to Salton. Life was quiet and smooth.

He developed a heart problem after he had a bad car accident when he was only fifty-five. He had to be pensioned off and then the trouble began. He moped around and did nothing of any consequence. The doctor told him that he should exercise, but he was too scared of having another heart attack, as the serious one he'd had earlier was traumatic enough. He felt as if his heart was lying in wait, waiting to ambush him at any time. His heart would never have healed to its former state, but with proper care, he could have led a good life. He wouldn't even garden. He became obsessed with money, although we had plenty, and even wanted me to give up my housekeeper to cut down on expenses. She only came once a week for four hours and didn't cost that much. We had great investments in real estate, a good pension plan, and a fat savings account, especially after the accident lawsuit was settled. We were fine, financially, but his dread of death drowned him in oppressive waves of depression. When he demanded I fire the housekeeper, I asked him if he planned to do the housework himself. He looked at me with a hostility so out of character that it rendered me speechless. I don't think he liked me anymore. Perhaps he bitterly resented that he was ill and afraid of dying soon, and there I stood before him in fine fettle and still enjoying life. I was ten years younger than him, too. His bitterness gnawed at him like a cancer.

It wasn't easy to enjoy life around that long face and pouting lips. He was obsessed with his health and became very demanding and bad-tempered. He stank of death. He was insufferable. I became depressed, wondering how many years this unbearable situation would go on for—he'd begun to drag me down with him. I suggested counseling, which sent him into a frenzy, which brought on chest pain, which brought on another round of angry recriminations. He was a damned nuisance, and I had had enough. In truth, he probably had, too. He was a miserable wretch, too afraid of losing his life to live it.

As I handed him his medication one day, it struck me how like one of my vitamin pills it looked. I took a whole regimen of diet supplements each day as doctors recommended on television talk shows. I seldom saw a doctor myself. Since I doled out his medication and water most of the time, I replaced a lot of it with the vitamins. After a couple of weeks, when he was in a particularly foul mood, I suggested counseling again. The tantrum this time was much worse than the last. He clutched his chest and fell to the kitchen floor. This looked like the big one. I had taken the precaution of hiding his prescription bottle. He crawled across the floor and begged me to find it.

I sat and watched him. I thought back to how he was when we first met, so eager to give me the best he could. I felt quite sad, thinking back through the good years, but this was not the same person, this raggedy man sprawled impotently at my feet, a pool of rank urine spreading out under him. It was time for this person to go. He looked up at me just before he died, his eyes wide and puzzled, then petrified as he understood it was all but over. Toward the end, his hand shot out and made a terrifying grab for my ankle that made me cry out. Then he died, and his grasp and jaw fell open. Even so, I scrambled well away from his reach. I wonder where he went, where anyone goes. I wonder if he watches me, if he understands everything now. I wonder if he is grateful to be safe in his heaven. People are never grateful, but maybe souls can be.

I took the phone off the hook, dropped the open container—with the right pills in it—just out of his reach, and went grocery shopping. I "discovered" him when I got back and called 911 right away. I was sorry about it all and wished it hadn't been necessary to put an end to things that way. He wasn't happy, so I didn't feel guilty. I don't know if I have ever felt guilty about anything. Everything I've done has been a logical solution to an immediate problem, after all. But I had my life back now. I missed the old husband, the shared happy moments with good books and little weekend outings, but I was glad to be rid of the petulant whiner.

I liked being alone again. I enjoyed the peace and quiet. It had been a long time. Even though I had liked him well enough until he changed, I realized that marriage had been stifling for a free spirit like me. I got most of the things I wanted in life, so I compromised in many ways. I guess everyone has to do that, don't they? Life itself is a compromise with death.

23

Tipped with the green of fresh limes, the cherry trees prepared for full leaf while their blossoms displayed the last of their blowsy show and birds chirped their attractions to possible mates. *Spring is great,* thought Annie, as she made her way to the usual Thursday gathering in the Salton Family Restaurant. She had always found this time of year uplifting after a dreary winter, and this year it felt better than ever after the dreadful events of the past several months. She'd had a hard time finding parking and had to walk farther than usual, but she enjoyed the exercise and kept up a light, brisk pace.

Only Rose was already seated and Annie moved to the back of their usual table to face the door. A woman sat at a nearby table whom Annie had never seen before. She noticed her because she looked out of place. She had shoulder-length dark brown hair, tinted glasses, heavy makeup, and wore baggy clothes, although, judging by her face, she was thin. She caught Annie's eye and looked down quickly at her menu. Annie rarely came to this restaurant without seeing someone who was at least an acquaintance—most of Salton came regularly, especially for lunch after shopping on Saturdays or church on Sundays. Then the parking lot was full of Mercedes and Jaguars as well as the usual Detroit and Japanese products. As far as dress was concerned, people fell into several categories: on Sundays, there was church gear; at other times, carefully planned casual chic and your standard "preppie" style (Annie's specialty); and then there was the polyester and sensible shoes crowd, usually an older and less affluent group. This woman didn't fit into any of these sets. Perhaps the reasonable prices were beginning to attract new people. Annie turned her attention to the menu to see if, by any chance, there were any new specials. There were not.

"What are you having, Rose?"

"Oh, I don't know. Perhaps we should start going somewhere else from time to time. I'm really tired of this food. They never have anything different."

"Well, we do go to other places when we're not a large group. I know you like out-of-the-ordinary dishes, Rose, but you know very well that Sally, Susan, and Janet won't pay the prices. This place is very reasonable, and the food is always reliable."

"I know. I guess I'll have a grilled cheese sandwich."

"Good idea, I will, too, for a change."

"Wow!" Rose said in mock amazement, and they laughed.

The others filtered in, orders were placed and they started to discuss the next week's house concert. These concerts were given annually at one of the local mansions and were a great favorite with some of their supporters. It was Annie's favorite event of the year, too. The audience usually numbered around fifty—intimate enough for relaxed conversation and easy mingling with the musicians, who tended to enjoy it too. The house had to be big enough to accommodate rented chairs and, preferably, a good piano. It was possible to rent a piano if the owner didn't have one, but that was very expensive, even with the break the local companies would give them—just cartage cost hundreds. The concert had been slated for Samantha's house, but had been switched to Betty Tomlin's for obvious reasons. The symphony would invite major sponsors free of charge and sell tickets to any others who wanted to come. They provided the food and wine, and it was generally regarded as an enjoyable, civilized Sunday afternoon. Most of the corporate sponsors invited did not accept as their objectives for sponsorship lay with public relations rather than the spread of culture. Nevertheless, there was always a smattering of corporate types who attended. The individual sponsors were, of course, interested in the event, and loved the party. Unless board members were sponsors, they had to pay to come, and most did. The musicians played in small ensembles and there were enough solo parts to make it worth their while to give up an afternoon; they sometimes got engagements out of it to play for private parties, too, an added incentive to helping out.

The Seven went over the concert plans before moving on to other topics as they finished their lunch. Annie felt sure that the strange woman was watching them and trying to listen to their conversation. Perhaps she was new in town and wanted to know what was going on. The woman had a book open in front of her, and every time Annie looked at her she turned back to it, but not often quickly enough.

When they left, Annie said "hello" and she muttered a reply, her eyes firmly on her book. Annie, Rose, and Susan wanted to go to a discount mall outside town and asked if any of the others wanted to come. None of them did, and they all parted ways.

They browsed the racks in the discount outlet of Lords and Ladies, a major upscale department store. Annie was looking for a pair of tailored pants, Rose for a jacket, and Susan needed a dress to wear to a wedding. They had good luck finding the right things and disappeared into fitting rooms to try them on. Annie emerged wearing a pair of cream gabardine slacks she liked and went over to a long three-sided mirror to make sure they were a good fit. She turned this way and that and stopped dead. There was that woman from the restaurant ostentatiously looking through a rack of skirts. Annie made a few turns more and surreptitiously watched the woman, who was actually watching the fitting rooms. She approached her with some trepidation.

"Didn't I see you in the Salton Family Restaurant?"

The woman, startled, muttered, "Er, yes, I suppose so."

"You seem to be very interested in us."

The woman looked at her and thought for a moment, as if trying to make up her mind. "Yes, I suppose I am. I can't explain now, but I would like to come and see you sometime, if I may."

"Well, I suppose so, but who are you?"

"You can call me Liz. More, I can't say. Can I call you? It might be important."

"I suppose so."

"Please don't mention it to your friends."

"What about my husband?"

"Yes, that would be fine. It's just those friends. I think I heard your name was Annie?"

"That's right."

And Annie, against her better judgment, gave the woman her cell phone number. Safer than the home number, she felt. The woman turned on her heel and left, leaving Annie bewildered. What could this woman with her grating New York accent want with any of them?

Betty Tomlin's gracious house, designed in the style of a southern plantation, had a small ballroom where receptions could be held. She was generous in allowing it to be used for charitable fundraisers, and it had been the site of many happy times over the years. It boasted the desired grand piano, tuned that morning, and chairs for the audience had been set out the day before. Before the concert, drinks and hors d'oeuvres were served on the flower-lined terrace and would be set out again afterward. The food was delicious and the wine carefully chosen by Betty, who had also been kind enough to pay for it. The wife of one of the new board members was an expert in Japanese flower arrangement and she had placed her arrangements—stunning in their delicacy and simplicity—all over the reception areas. Betty owned valuable antique furniture and many excellent paintings—mostly landscapes—and, together with the flowers, the effect was one of harmonious beauty. A trio played light music during the cocktail hour and the conversation flowed as buoyantly as the music.

The program featured several ensembles, and was to end with a performance by a youth group sponsored by the Salton Symphony. The penultimate piece was a string quartet that announced a change to their program and played for a grueling twenty minutes, a selection quite out of keeping with the occasion, and previously undisclosed to the organizers. The audience had had enough of the dreary selection after five minutes, and the fidgeting should have been obvious to the ambitious players, who, nevertheless, doggedly pursued their course to the finish line. The applause was short, faces had turned sour, and the audience was in no mood to endure the last group with anything more than a steely resolve to behave well.

One of the young musicians, an Asian girl who, polite but shy, had barely spoken to anyone at the reception, introduced the players and the piece they had chosen. Her voice was fresh and clear, her presentation neither shy nor showy, and she showed herself to be in her element in the world of music. The audience was at first touched, and then enchanted by the mastery of these young people, their earnest young faces, and the slender fluid hands that milked the music for a passion and tenderness beyond their years. The applause was long and fraught with elation.

Annie sat back and drew a deep breath, taking a moment to relax after all her hard work. She had enjoyed the concert except for the long, drawn-out tedium of the string quartet. She didn't like string ensembles much to begin with; of course, she could never tell her cello-playing husband that, but there it was. Samantha would have enjoyed having this concert at her house. Such a tragedy.

She couldn't get that strange woman out of her mind, the one who had followed them to the outlet store. She was an odd-looking person, although she reminded her of someone. Was it someone she could have known long ago? Her words didn't suggest a personal connection, though. What on earth was it all about? Could it have anything to do with the murders? If it did, why didn't she just go to the police?

24

Annie called Toby every few days to check on him. He told her that he could hardly bring himself to look at Jackson, the little dog he could see in his mind's eye nestling against Samantha on the sofa while they watched television in the evening. He would have to get rid of him. He couldn't stand having him around anymore. He felt that Jackson's discovery of the knife had set something in motion that had led to Samantha's murder, as he insisted on calling it. He knew it was not the dog's fault, but Jackson had to go. Annie remembered that Helen had said Toni was nagging her mother for a dog, so called her at once as she was concerned for the welfare of this loving little creature. Helen returned her call when she got home from work and Annie pointed out the benefits of adopting a mature dog—no house training, a pet proved to be loving and amusing, and the chance to save him from the pound. Toby hadn't mentioned the pound, but Annie assumed it would be a strong possibility if a new home were not found for Jackson soon. Helen, after consulting Toni, reluctantly agreed, and Toby and Annie brought Jackson over to their house one Saturday morning, complete with bed, food, leash, dishes, toys, and all the rest of his baggage.

Jackson had been excited by the outing and a chance to play with new people, but his elation quickly wore off when he saw Toby leaving without him and he cried and whined for hours. Toni carried him to her bed and tried to cuddle him, but he was inconsolable. After he quieted, he just lay flat, paws spread in front of him, sphynx-like, and only rose to jump on the back of the sofa in the front living room to look out of the window when he heard a car door bang. Then, seeing it wasn't Toby, he would slump again in despair. He didn't eat for three days. Toni called the vet, who explained that a dog could be expected to grieve over a lost owner for months, even a year. Poor Jackson had not only lost Samantha but had now lost Toby and the only home he had ever known.

A week after they got him, Toni came home from school one day and let Jackson out into the backyard. He sniffed around with some interest for a change and ate a few morsels of his chow when he came in. Toni went upstairs and called him to her bed; after a few minutes, he jumped up and curled up beside her. She kissed his little silky head, and he gazed up at her, awarded her a slight tail wag, and rolled over to have his belly rubbed.

"Don't be sad, little one," she said. "We'll love you forever. You'll be happy again, you'll see."

A tentative pink tongue licked her hand once, and she kissed his head again. Toni felt full of love for this sad little dog and was thankful her father no longer lived with them, otherwise having a dog would have been out of the question. She immediately felt guilty. He was her father, so she must love him a little, but she didn't like anything about him, and she didn't want to spend any more time with him than necessary. She grudged the time she spent in his heavy presence, and she expected to grudge it even more now she would have to leave Jackson behind. On the other hand, she was happy to see her mother happy, and she was happy with her dog. She'd seen her mother blossom after her father left, and she vowed to see to it that Jackson would blossom, too. She would make it happen, will it to happen, love him enough for it to happen. She would see that tail stand up, his eyes and ears alert for new happenings, his bouncy spring come back.

Why should she feel guilty? Her father hadn't earned their love.

Helen came home and called out to Toni.

"I'm on my bed with Jackson. I think he's beginning to feel better."

Helen climbed the stairs and reclined on the bed on the other side of the dog. She stroked his head and complied with the clear request for a belly rub. The little tail wagged again, and his tongue thanked her gentle hand. Helen kissed his head, and the three of them stayed there in contentment for an hour or more.

Toni found herself thinking of her father more and more often. Her mother said she had been surprised at the calm way she'd taken her father's leaving so suddenly, once the shock and anger had worn off. Even if they were at loggerheads most of the time, most children were rendered distraught by the breakdown of their parents' marriage, after all. Toni had been surprised, but now the serenity was wearing off, her feelings were confused. She had trouble concentrating on her schoolwork, but felt she must be strong for her mother. She had never told her mother this, because her mother would feel it was her job to be the strong one. Toni had watched the two of them together over the years and couldn't help noticing how her father's treatment of his wife diminished her self-esteem, and Toni sensed how vulnerable her mother was to self-doubt.

Sometimes she felt she loved her father, and sometimes she didn't. Sometimes she even hated him, and that didn't feel good. Sometimes she wanted to see him, and then she didn't like being with him when she did. She understood that he was a deeply flawed person. She hoped she took after her mother. She screwed up her courage and made an appointment with the school counselor. She found the idea of sharing her father's words and actions with a stranger distasteful, but she knew she needed some help to deal with it all. It was probably better than discussing him with someone who actually knew him. She didn't know how to feel, let alone how to act. She was stuck.

"It's hard to be realistic about our parents, to see them as people outside their relationship to us. It sounds as though your father has issues he has never dealt with, and probably never will. Just know that you are not him, and you are not in danger of becoming like him, because you have different values and a different personality."

"But I'm half from him. Why wouldn't I act like him when I'm older? People change. Maybe Mom wouldn't have married him if he'd been like that at the start."

"Sometimes people hide their natures at the start. Then, when they feel they've got the upper hand, they turn ugly. And young women aren't always very clear-sighted when it comes to their boyfriends."

"I suppose."

"Your values are firm and you have a good mother. You know your father for what he is. You can allow yourself to love him, whatever his imperfections, and that is not disloyal to your mother. I don't believe she would want you to hate your father. That would hurt you more than it would hurt him. You can love a person with deep flaws. You just have to keep your eyes open to protect yourself from hurt. And that goes for boyfriends, too—see their faults clearly and decide what you will or will not put up with."

"I've never had a boyfriend."

"You've never met a boy you like?"

"Well, there's one, but he hardly knows I'm alive."

"That'll change. It'll happen for you soon, I'm sure. You're a lovely young woman. And you've got too much on your plate right now to worry about boys."

"Guess so. But what do I do about Dad?"

"While it would be nice, you don't have to find your father fun to be with, or even likeable. You have a good relationship with your mother, so make the most of it. Leave your father to be who he is and keep up the contact. You owe it to yourself not to lose touch because he is your father and, at your age, you are not ready to lose him. You don't need to lose him. You can make other decisions when you are older, but for now, just accept. When he behaves badly, it's not you, it's him. Remember that. Seeing his daughter act with maturity and dignity might even teach him something over time."

Toni thought about the counselor's advice all evening and knew she'd got it right. She could do nothing about her father's personality, she could do nothing to patch up the marriage, and wouldn't want to. Some situations had to be accepted the way they were. None of it was her fault, and she was nothing like him. He would be the ultimate loser because he wasn't capable of healthy human relationships on any level. If anything, she should feel a little sorry for him. She'd considered discussing her counseling session with her mother, but decided against it. She wasn't ready, and neither, she decided, was her mother.

Toni looked down at Jackson and gave him a reassuring hug while he stared up at her with adoration. He had eaten well today. He would eat well for the rest of his happy life, and Toni decided she would go to college locally to keep him with her through his old age and be near her mother.

25

Pansy

J udy called me early the morning after she got back from
one of her trips to New York. She used to go at least three
times a year to take in a show and do some shopping. She
always liked to get her hair done at a fancy salon, as she told
us each time she came back.

"Do I have news for you! I was showing my stylist Danny's
wedding pictures, and guess what! She saw your picture and
said you looked very familiar."

My heart thumped. "I don't think I know anyone in
New York."

"Well, you ought to know this one. Daisy says she's
your sister!"

"That's quite impossible. I don't have a sister," I said.

The pictures from her son's wedding. *Never safe. Even
after all these years.*

"I don't have a sister," I said again.

"Oh, Daisy was sure," she retorted, laughing. "She told me that her sister had moved around a lot when she was young and changed her name and appearance all the time. Daisy said she'd always managed to catch up with you until about twenty-five years ago. She was so happy to see your picture! I'll invite her to stay. What a reunion we'll have. Although I suppose she should stay with you; she's your sister, after all." She laughed again.

It was true that Daisy had often turned up like the proverbial bad penny. I sometimes thought about getting rid of her once and for all, but I balked at doing away with my own sister. She had always been quite nice to me, although she hadn't protected me from him and didn't bother with me in the foster homes. Of course, I should remember that she was only a kid herself at the time and had to look out for herself. I had wanted to cast off my family like a threadbare coat. They would have been an embarrassment, especially after I met my husband. I should have known better and wiped the proverbial slate clean.

"Daisy told me trouble always seemed to follow Pansy, as she said you were known then. She told me about your rotten childhood, you poor little things. Hell's Kitchen, oh my, my! It's all most intriguing. Why don't you come over for coffee now? I'd love to see you and catch up. Bye, Pansy!" she said, tittering, before she hung up the phone. The laugh just about drove me over the edge. Laughing at me like that was unforgivable. Laughing at people like me is dangerous.

I took my gloves even though it was a hot day.

"Good morning! Isn't this fun?" she asked with a conspiratorial little chuckle gurgling out of her smug lips. At first, I was irritated by having to go to all this trouble, but I soon began to feel a little of the old excitement—life had been too dull for too long, except for those delightful interludes with the disrupted symphony concerts. I didn't smell any coffee brewing. Judy sat on the sofa while I stood by the piano. It was a cloudy day, and the light diffused through the sheer curtains in a listless haze. Her eyes seemed to have absorbed any brightness the room might have held.

"I'll call the others later. They'll be so interested to hear about your long-lost sister! It seems you can't keep any secrets in this day and age." And then she laughed again, an ugly, jarring laugh, a wicked witch kind of a laugh.

I put on my gloves and swung the Beethoven bust, which might have been specially made for such an occasion. She was stronger than I had expected. She fought back and hit me with it several times as we struggled. I finally finished her off, but felt horribly dizzy from the blows to my own head. I shoved the gloves in a drawer in her coffee table and ran to the back door. I had walked to her house, so it should be easy to slip home without attracting any attention.

What choice did I have? It only takes a puff of an ill wind to make a whole house of cards come crashing down.

26

One sunny May morning, Sally sat in her family room sobbing miserably. Jack had hit her again that morning. There was a crease in the back of the shirt he wanted to wear and the collar had not been ironed to his satisfaction. He said business was not going well, and it was all because he had to worry about the next stupid thing she'd do, and he couldn't even look smart in front of the clients. What good was she, after all? Even her sons didn't want to come and see her. This last thrust went deep, as she knew it was true. But they didn't want to see their father, either. Was all of this really her fault? Jack was getting more and more angry by the day, and drinking a great deal, too.

Her feelings ebbed and flowed between grief, hurt, and shame to wondering what she could do to be a better wife to Jack. She didn't know if she still loved him, but she tried to act as if she did. She remembered what her son, John, had said to her last weekend on one of his rare visits. He had just about exploded in anger after Jack had complained about the dinner she had cooked and she had apologized profusely to them both.

"Oh, for God's sake, stop apologizing for everything all the time, Mom! The roast is fine and Dad's being a jerk, as usual. You ask for it, you're such a doormat. You let him get away with murder! And you, Dad, you treat her like dirt. I'm ashamed of both of you. I can never, ever invite my friends here." He flung himself from the room. Sally knew his brother, Hunter, felt the same way. They never brought their friends home.

Jack hissed at her, "You stupid bitch, look what you've done, ruining John's visit." And he left the table, went to the den, and poured himself another large drink. Sally looked in despair at the wasted dinner and mourned her meaningless life and her lost children.

She continued to sit, numbed by her predicament. Her friends' husbands didn't talk to them the way Jack did—he even put her down in public. They often made disparaging comments about him, especially Susan and Janet, telling her to make him treat her better, saying she was a good woman and deserved better. Maybe they didn't really know her. Susan had told her only last week that Jack had a serious mean streak and that she should be careful.

"It's not you, Sally, it's him," she'd said. "People like him are good at making women feel inadequate. That's how they control them. Making them feel they are never good enough and always in the wrong. He's the problem, Sally, not you. And lately, you've had more bruises than you used to. You can always come and stay with me if you need to, you know.

You should call the police next time. There is never any excuse for a man beating his wife."

Sally had been surprised and touched. Susan always spoke bluntly, but this was extraordinary. She had offered her sanctuary, too, and Sally knew she never invited people to stay. Susan was a very private person and seemed to have no close friends or family. She wasn't often kind and Sally realized how much it took for her to proffer this gesture of support.

"Thank you so much, Susan. It's very kind of you, but I'm all right, really. Jack is just tense from dealing with business problems. It'll all sort itself out."

Of course, it hadn't sorted itself out and never would. It was getting worse. Sally wondered if Susan and Janet could be right. Was she normal, and Jack an unusually controlling jerk? She had done well in college and had been well on her way to a career as a computer programmer before Jack had swept her off her feet. He had not liked her parents, and they had not liked him. The question of visiting them, even on her own, brought on such rage that she had given up seeing them. They were never welcome in their daughter's home; Jack had made that clear. When her father died, she had not seen either of them in ten years. Jack grudgingly allowed her to go back to Raleigh for the funeral. She had been numb at the time, but now felt searing pain. Everyone has a right to be loved by their parents, don't they? And their children?

She had always been expected to be frugal, but was not allowed to work. Jack frequently claimed to be on the edge of bankruptcy, but always seemed to pull something together at the last minute, making unfathomable deals in his import business. She had often wondered, quickly suppressing her thoughts, if all of those deals were on the up and up.

She thought back over the various comments her friends had made over the years. It was clear they didn't think much of Jack. And Betty Tomlin had treated him with utter contempt at the Christmas party and had ignored him at the house concert. She had been embarrassed. For the first time, Sally started to consider Jack's personality and behavior with some objectivity.   Her anger started to rise. Her sons had had a miserable home life, she had missed her parents' love and support, and she lived a life of cringing subjectivity. The phone jolted Sally out of her reverie.

"Sally? It's Robert Packer. How are you?"

"Robert? From Raleigh?"

"Yeah! Haven't seen you since your father's funeral. I'm in town for a couple of days and wanted to look you up."

"Robert, I would love to see you. I'd ask you over, but Jack is so busy with his business."

"Well then, why don't you come out and have a drink with me?"

Sally hesitated. Jack had told her this morning that he would be out all evening and would not eat dinner at home. He would be very angry if he found out she was seeing an old friend, a man at that. She needed a break, though. She took a deep breath, closed her eyes, and gritted her teeth.

"Where should we meet? I can't be out long."

"I'm staying at the Pear Tree Motel on Oak. There's a little restaurant just across the street. Do you know it? We could have a drink and a quick bite to eat there."

"Okay, I know it. What time?"

"How about six-thirty?"

"Robert, it's so good to hear from you. I'll see you then."

Sally replaced the phone, wondering at herself and her daring. She remembered Robert as a good-natured boy, then a decent man. He'd been born in England, then moved to the US in his teens. His British accent showed a little from time to time, and she'd loved that about him. They had dated for a little while before they both went away to college. She needed to talk to an old friend. She would tell Jack she had been with Helen if he discovered she'd been out. He wouldn't even like that, but it was better than the truth.

She picked up the phone. "Helen, do me a favor, could you?"

"Sure, Sally. What is it?"

"I'm going to meet an old friend from home this evening. I would like to tell Jack I was with you, as he would be really mad. Would you back me up if he asks?"

"Of course, Sally. I'm happy for you. You need a break and old friends are the best!"

"Thanks so much, Helen."

Sally got to the restaurant just before Robert left the motel. She watched him crossing the street. He was quite good-looking and had aged well. Had she? Did it matter at this point in her life?

"Hi, Sally," he said as he bent to kiss her cheek. "You look so good. How do you do it?"

"Thanks, Robert. It's lovely to see you. You look good, too."

They exchanged a few more banalities and then, "That's quite a bruise on your cheek, Sally. What happened? Did you fall?"

"I'm quite clumsy, Robert," she said with an uneasy little laugh, and she bent her head to read the menu.

"I see." The way he said it, Sally knew that he did see. Her parents had told her that he'd stayed in touch with them over the years and he must have known that her parents disliked Jack and always worried about her. And, of course, he would remember that she had never been clumsy and, once, had been smart and lively, cheerful and fun to be around.

They ordered their food and chatted, first about their high school years, moving on to their current lives. Robert had become a corporate lawyer and was a partner in a large firm in the center of Raleigh. Divorced now, he had two children, a boy and girl, both in college.

"My ex-wife is a good mother," Robert said. "But we grew apart. She wanted the country club lifestyle, and I prefer fishing and days reading at the beach. She found someone who could provide her the top country club membership and enjoy it with her. That life seems very empty to me, but some people are more comfortable living their lives on that level."

"I know," replied Sally. "We have this social set that is considered 'Salton society' and I began to wake up to the fact that it is really only a small part of Salton social life when I had a long talk with a friend of mine, the other day. Helen is in the midst of a divorce and can't afford to participate in all of Salton's major social events anymore. She said the more she thought about it and talked to other people, she realized how much we all get sucked into the mindset that tells us this group is the only worthwhile center of social life. There are other groups of people and other activities that can be just as satisfying, if not more so. Lots of people socialize with members of their church, join other not-quite-so-visible charitable organizations, or find people with common interests, such as learning a language or bridge. And then, of course, there is the international set—embassies, World Bank, and so on.

"Yes, I know what you mean," Robert said. "I'm a Big Brother. Best thing I've ever done."

"I can see how good you'd be at it. Helen is joining a group that assists mentally retarded adults with their life skills and residential needs. It's not a very social group, but it does great work. They are decent people, just there to do good rather than promote themselves in some way. She says people like to forget about the mentally retarded or the mentally ill. A lot of families are never touched by these problems, fervently hope they never will be, and are uncomfortable with the whole subject. They would prefer to ignore it. Perhaps some latent superstition holds that one shouldn't tempt fate. I'd love to get involved, but Jack would never allow it. He wants the social set and any business benefits he might get from that association. People don't seem to like him, though, so it doesn't get him anywhere."

That was a long speech for Sally. She was used to keeping her opinions to herself, and she realized that her last remark might be judged disloyal. She looked at Robert anxiously; what must he think of her?

"I know you're unhappy, Sally. You don't have to hide it from me. I heard enough from your parents to realize what kind of man you married." He stretched his hand across the table and rested it on hers.

"Oh, I didn't mean..."

"It's all right, Sally. Don't explain. Just enjoy the evening and we'll try to keep in touch."

Sally's eyes filled with tears. He was so sweet and understanding. She had always liked him the best out of all the high school boys. What would it feel like to be held by Robert? How would his mouth feel? How would it taste? She tamped down these absurd thoughts and turned her head to look out of the window. She froze. A figure had emerged from one of the motel rooms facing the street. He was briefly illuminated under the street lamp, kissing a young woman before she slipped away. Could that be Jack? As he got into his car, she knew that it was. Her confused feelings hardened.

"That's Jack," she said woodenly. "He just came out of a room with another woman. See that white Toyota? That's him." Robert looked at her sadly; he must have seen the lingering kiss her husband had exchanged with the woman.

Sally noticed another woman, this one with long, curly hair and a loose coat come out of the motel office and start to cross the road just as Jack was pulling out. A car screeched around the corner and knocked the woman back onto the sidewalk in a hideous curve. The car raced to overtake Jack's car and cut in front of him too closely, so he had to swerve to avoid it. His car careened over the sidewalk and crashed into the motel. The other car sped away.

Sally ran across the street to Jack's car with Robert close behind. Other people came running to the scene, some tripping over the debris of distorted metal and bricks. Police and paramedics arrived after a few minutes. Jack was alive but conscious and wailed that he had no feeling in his legs. Blood ran down his face, which had little bits of glass embedded in it. Sally felt sick.

The paramedics braced Jack's neck before extracting him from the wreckage with great care and took him off to the hospital. Robert drove Sally's car as she was shaking and crying and not fit to drive, in his view. She had identified herself to the police as Jack's wife, and they said they would talk to her later. The woman with long hair was dead.

Sally told the police the truth. She'd been having dinner with an old friend visiting from out of town when she saw her husband come out of the room. She had seen the woman hit by the other car and it had looked deliberate. This car had caused Jack's accident. The police found the other car a few miles away. It was stolen and there were no fingerprints in it other than those of the owner, who had a solid alibi.

The doctor told her that Jack's spinal cord had been irreparably damaged, and he was now paralyzed from the waist down. Robert remained with her most of the night, but had to get back to his office for an important court date. He clasped her hands between his.

"Anything you need, Sally, anything at all. Just call."

He kissed her cheek, and she liked how that felt. He cared.

Once Jack regained consciousness and understood his situation, he took it badly, as would anyone. He cursed the doctors, then the nurses, but after they ignored him, he concentrated on abusing Sally, and didn't bother to hide it. Pitying his dismal plight, she remained sweet and supportive during the time he was in the hospital. One day, she overheard one of the nurses telling another that she was a saint and that he, even taking into consideration the shock of his awful accident and paralysis, was a nasty piece of work.

It shocked her to hear that from complete strangers, although her friends had been trying to tell her over and over again. It started her thinking with unaccustomed objectivity—she had plenty of time after her unpleasant hospital visits to mull things over. She considered what her parents, her friends, and now Robert had tried to tell her over the years, and what she had just heard the nurses say; she came to the conclusion that while she was no saint, she was too dutiful and compliant. She had done nothing wrong beyond indulging this petty tyrant. And Jack was, indeed, a nasty piece of work.

After three weeks, Jack was able to go home, although he would need to return to the hospital frequently for therapy. Sally had arranged for a male nurse to come in to see to his intimate physical needs (changing his bags and bathing) and put him to bed at night. He had already started to run his business by phone.

They arrived back from the hospital early one evening. Sally had bought a van that could accommodate a wheelchair, which infuriated Jack when he saw it, and as soon as they got through the front door, he let his anger rip.

"What the hell do you think you're doing spending my money like that?" he yelled.

"Well, how do you think you're going to get around, Jack?"

"I'm going to beat this and you know it, you stupid little bitch!"

"Oh, no you're not, Jack. You are going to be in a wheelchair for the rest of your life, so you may as well get used to the idea."

Jack gawked at her, speechless with fury. This was so unlike her usual groveling apology. He noticed a small smile hovering around her lips, and it pierced his brain like an ice bullet.

"Are you happy I got hurt, you fiend?"

"Oh no, of course not. But I saw you, Jack. Didn't you ever stop to wonder how I arrived at the accident so quickly? The wages of sin, Jack, the wages of sin." And with some complacence, she wheeled him into the family room where a hospital bed had been set up.

She stood in the doorway and watched Jack, his mind obviously reeling from this quiet onslaught. His tight face showed his unwillingness to accept his loss of control over her. She wondered if he would risk teaching her a lesson with his hands; he could strike her if he were quick, and she were near enough. But he must realize he needed her to do too many things for him, so that would be foolish. She watched his head slump as he confronted his helplessness.

"We're just going to have an easy supper tonight, Jack. A roast beef sandwich and some chips. I know you always enjoy a nice roast beef sandwich, don't you, dear?"

"For lunch, dear Sally, not for supper."

"Well, what a pity, because that's all I have in the house."

"What have you been doing all day, for God's sake, watching TV and eating candy?"

"Well, yes, dear, when I haven't been at the hospital waiting on you."

Jack took a couple of breaths—shallow panting ones as he'd broken a few ribs and they were still sore. Sally began to wheel him to the kitchen table (she had earlier moved a chair to make a place for him). He waved her off impatiently and wheeled himself, getting stuck on the edge of a table leg. Without commenting, Sally straightened the chair and pushed him up to the table. She put two sandwiches down with a glass of wine for her and a glass of milk for him.

"I'm sorry you can't have wine, Jack. Doctor's orders because of the painkillers."

"I suppose it didn't occur to you to go without."

"Now, why would I do that, dear?"

Jack swept his sandwich and milk onto the floor. Sally looked at him like a reproachful mother and said nothing. She rose from her place and wheeled him out onto the deck. It was a beautiful evening late in May and the air was still balmy. She returned to the kitchen and finished her supper. Then she cleaned up the mess on the floor.

He yelled from the deck, "Get me a proper dinner, bitch."

"Oh, Jack, I'm so sorry, that's all I had. I'll go shopping tomorrow. I guess you'll be going to bed hungry. I'd bring you water for your painkillers, but I'm afraid you might throw that on the floor, too. You really will have to learn to be more civil."

She heard a loud intake of breath that raised a cry of pain. She knew Jack must be horrified and afraid. She held the power now, power over him, his life. She felt gleeful for a moment before she reprimanded herself. Unchristian. Maybe she'd start going to church again. She'd had enough of guilt, though. Next year, perhaps.

The nurse, a stocky, muscular young man called Bill Horton, arrived at eight to bathe Jack, change the bags, and put him to bed. Jack whined and whined.

"She wouldn't feed me, she won't give me painkillers. She's trying to kill me!"

Sally told the nurse she would speak to him when he had finished. She could hear Jack ranting and raving in the bathroom (thank goodness they had one on this level). When the nurse came into the living room where she'd been waiting, she asked him to sit and offered him a glass of wine, which he accepted with pleasure; most of his clients probably treated him like the hired help.

"My husband is a very difficult man," she explained. "I offered him different things for supper and he refused to eat any of it. I gave him a painkiller and I know he's in pain, but I can't give him any more until eleven. Doctor's orders."

"I understand, Mrs. Hartington. I come across all kinds in my walk of life. It must be hard for you, though."

"Well, not nearly as hard as it is for him, I know."

They sat and chatted, mostly about Bill's other cases, while he finished his drink. "Well, I must be going now, ma'am, and I'll be back in the morning to get him ready for the day."

"Thank you so much, Bill. It was nice to meet you. I'm sure we'll all get along very well. We'll see you tomorrow, then."

After Sally had let Bill out, she went into Jack with a glass of water.

"Did you actually sit and drink wine with that bozo? You're going to start fucking the hired help now?"

"Would you like a painkiller now, Jack?"

"You know damn well I would."

"Just 'yes, please' will do nicely."

"You want me to grovel? Yes, please!" he screamed.

She handed him a pill and the glass. "I'll see you in the morning, then. I'll go shopping after Bill has finished getting you ready for the day. I'll think about cooking you a nice dinner tomorrow night. And maybe an omelet for lunch. Would you like that?"

Jack didn't answer, but closed his eyes, looking weary and despairing. Sally smiled as she imagined the torture of a mind used to cruel narcissism having to bend to the etiquette of complete dependency.

27

Annie sat drinking her morning coffee while reading an article in the paper about Jack's accident, when an eye-witness account of the woman's death caused her to catch her breath. A witness said that the driver of the car that hit her appeared to have done it on purpose. The police had identified the deceased as a maid at the motel, newly employed and with no next of kin listed in the office records. The paper had inserted a description of the woman and asked for anyone who knew her to come forward. The description fit that woman who'd been watching the Seven in the restaurant and the discount store. Liz, she'd called herself. Annie had wondered why she'd never called. She called Detective Paglietti to ask if he were free as she wanted to discuss the hit-and-run accident. He asked her to come right over because he wanted to talk to her, too, so she quickly showered and dressed and drove to the station. To her astonishment, she found the woman she thought might have been killed by a hit-and-run driver sitting in his office. The three of them had a long talk.

28

Pansy

That silly young girl was trash—and I know trash when I see it. She had a commonplace mind, but enough low cunning to be dangerous. She'd seen my struggle with Judy through the window. She lived just opposite, had been home from work, and, she admitted freely, liked to spy on her neighbors with binoculars—a peeping Tom. She giggled when she told me I'd be surprised what some of these snobs who wouldn't give her the time of day did when they thought no one was looking. What an irritating sneer she wore as she asked me for money.

"It's just to tide me over," she said.

"I see," I said.

She thought I was just a frightened middle-aged woman who would cry and plead and then pay up. Now she knows— at least she does if there is an afterlife, which I sincerely hope there isn't. I had earned some peace in my life and was angry when she forced my hand. I didn't want to be drawn back into all the unpleasantness I'd managed to avoid for so many years. I don't kill by choice, only by necessity. And Janet's tale about her tenant coming into money told me I'd better act quickly. The little slut couldn't be trusted to keep her mouth shut.

I wore a fetching gown of dark green garbage bags while I killed her, which I had constructed at home ahead of time. I had to staple the sleeves to the bodice and then use rubber bands at the cuff. More plastic bags with rubber bands at the ankles and a string at the waist ensured complete coverage; latex gloves completed my ensemble.

It's much more convenient doing this sort of work outdoors because it helps dissipate that awful smell when death voids the bowels. Everything went off without a hitch and I was able to saunter home afterward looking like a lady out for her daily stroll. After dark, I discarded the bloody plastic in the Salton Family Restaurant dumpster. That place has served me well over the years.

Everyone thought Samantha was quite a sweet woman, and she was, I suppose, but such a sap. I wouldn't have wanted her to suffer much, though, sap or not. I called her one late afternoon, ostensibly about some tickets she wanted for a concert. She told me that Toby was going out with clients that evening straight after work and wouldn't be back until late. I suggested that we go out to dinner, just the two of us, because I wanted to get to know her better. I asked her not to tell anyone because Janet had asked me to go to the movies with her and I pleaded a headache. She was thrilled to have been singled out that way. Poor silly creature.

When I got to her house, she offered me a glass of wine, and we sat and chatted a while. She went to the kitchen to get some snacks, which was the chance I needed. She was twittering on about how she was at last getting to know some nice people and making a life for herself, and she just knew she was at the beginning of something better.

She swayed a little and grasped her temples. She muttered that she wasn't feeling good, had felt fine earlier, maybe she should stay home, flu or something, hated to let me down. Her words began to slur.

I called Jackson, who came at a trot, radiating expectation and trust, and I lured him into the powder room with a cracker from the little dish Samantha set out, and shut the door, ignoring his loud protests.

"Come with me, Samantha," I said, putting on my gloves. "What you need is a breath of fresh air. You'll feel much better after we take a little walk."

I supported her out to the garage—she was heavy, so it was hard going. She was trying to say something, but couldn't get the words out, thank goodness, and I dumped her next to her car. I don't think she understood her predicament at that point. I grasped her hair and smashed her forehead on the ground. If she were aware of anything, it would have been only a passing sense of horror and a momentary explosion of pain, soon over.

It went like clockwork after that. I typed a note on the computer (hard to do with gloved hands), printed it out and left it on the desk, got the car keys from the kitchen keyboard and started the car, leaving the driver's door open to make it look as though Samantha had fallen out. I made sure to close the garage door firmly behind me, shoved the two wine glasses into my bag, and checked that I'd left nothing behind. I'd watched Samantha disable the alarm once—I'm in the habit of collecting exits and entries—and her code wasn't hard to remember—1234—so I set it, turned off the outside lights, and slunk out, keeping close to the shrubbery.

It wasn't difficult to walk the several blocks to my car unnoticed. The houses were few and far between in that neighborhood and there was no street lighting. These people make me laugh with their talk of light pollution and their determination to make believe they are owners of stately homes in the countryside. They need to think more about the things broken people do in the dark, the pollution of darkness that happens everywhere, even in places like Salton.

I thought that date rape stuff might come in useful someday, and had kept it hidden for years. I had traveled to Chicago on an art club trip five or six years before, and one of the participants, a silly young woman, couldn't wait to kick her heels up. A group of us went to the hotel bar the night we arrived, and the girl was soon flirting with a lout sporting puffed-up hair and a gold chain. It wasn't long before I saw him slip a pill into the naïve young woman's drink. Pretending to be drunk, I knocked the drink all over him. He was furious. I made a frantic fuss about cleaning up his pants and jacket and picked the packet out of his pocket. I wonder if he ever realized who took it. He left right after that, puce from the fury of thwarted goals. I told the stupid girl what had happened and warned her to be more careful. I didn't tell her about the remaining pills, though.

The pills were old, so I was relieved that the one I used had proved effective, although I'd put a spare in my pocket, just in case. I knew from what I'd read that no traces of the drug would be detected. I still had some left, too. For another rainy day.

Planting the knife was really stupid and drew attention to a very small group of people, which included me. I hadn't known about the dog's keen nose then, and thought the knife would be discovered by her cleaning lady weeks or even months later—and I would have bet good money that she didn't clean under the furniture very often. Anyway, I made mistakes, got careless. Maybe middle age dulls one's senses—comfortable middle age, at least.

And then there was Daisy. She was so conspicuous in the restaurant. She didn't fit in and she kept popping up wherever I went. And I could tell she was watching me. I have a sixth sense for those things. I think I saw her in a discount store I went to with my friends one day, but that was before I became suspicious. She'd done a good job with her disguise too, so it took me a couple of weeks to recognize her. She's aged quite well, damn her. I left the restaurant quickly one day and hid in a doorway. She looked around, then shrugged her shoulders and got into her car. I followed her at a discreet distance and saw her go into the motel. I hung around in my car at a safe distance for a couple of hours every day until I saw a woman I thought was Daisy, but without the crazy getup.

She wore a maid's uniform. It would seem she was working there. I wondered what had happened to her job in the New York hair salon. Yes, it was her. Since she hadn't come to see me and was hanging around my friends, I knew she was up to no good. Her time was up.

When danger threatens, I become very focused. She had to be dealt with in case she spoke to my friends. I was proud of myself that even after all these years, I could still hot-wire an old car. It proved to be yet another mistake, and I killed a different woman who looked very much like her from a distance. That incident spooked Daisy and Annie and sent them to Paglietti. I suppose I should draw some consolation from knowing that I took care of that bully Jack, though. Sally should be grateful—I relieved her of a life sentence with a brute. People are never grateful, though.

I had to take some concrete precautions. The business with the knife had been sloppy—inexcusably sloppy—and the hit-and-run failure made things worse. I seemed to have lost my edge and was certainly losing my nerve. I had to steel myself to take the kinds of risks that would overawe anyone—anyone normal, that is. Never again. Plan ahead and cover every contingency, always. Make plans B, C, D, and E, too. I took a second mortgage on my house and made the most of my old contacts, although I'm not going to spell it out for whoever might be reading this.

I researched mental illness, paranoid schizophrenia, in particular. I had to think long and hard to come up with some original and convincing voices, but I quite enjoyed it, although the prescribed "stilted formal manner" wasn't hard for me. I should have taken up acting. Well, I suppose I did take up acting a long time ago.

But you all know by now that I'm a lot cleverer than anyone thought. No one could have any idea of how much detailed planning that incident at the concert took. It was a masterpiece of ingenuity, a real test of my abilities. Why did I do it? Boredom, pure and simple. How? I'll never tell; I might want to become an illusionist in my next life. It served as a wonderful diversion as well and took everyone's mind off murder.

I made a nice donation to the animal shelter. I'd taken the little terrier home, saying I wanted to try him out. I reported him missing a few hours later, told them he'd escaped through the front door. He was picked up later and returned to the shelter, so I felt honor-bound to repay them for all their trouble. When they called, I told them I felt I wasn't ready for a dog, that I just didn't have the energy anymore. They were very nice about it. I hope they found him a good home. He was a real trooper. Little ratty didn't fare so well, but there'll always be winners and losers.

29

Sally was carrying the grocery shopping into the kitchen when the phone rang. She put the bags on the kitchen table and went through to Jack. He had his back to the door and didn't notice her.

"Who is it? How do you think I am? What do you want? No, she's not home," and he slammed down the phone.

"Who was that on the phone?" she asked.

He jumped at the sound of her voice and said, "None of your damned business."

Sally returned to the kitchen where the phone had caller ID. She went back to Jack and said, "That was Annie's number. So, you see, it was my damned business."

"Get out! Get out! I hate you. I hate you more than anyone in the world. And I don't want you to keep seeing those bitches you hang around with. They put ideas into your head."

"Ideas of how normal decent men treat their wives, you mean?"

"Get out of my sight, you ugly old hag!"

In spite of her new sense of independence, Jack's rage and the intensity of his hatred shook her. She went up to the bedroom (now only hers, thank heavens) and dialed Annie on her new cell phone.

"I guess Jack's having a bad day," Annie said.

"Every day is a bad day. He never could control his anger and, of course, he can't take it out on me any longer. He feels helpless and out of control."

"I'm so sorry, Sally. Is there anything I can do? Have lunch with me today. Actually, I want to sound you out about something very important. There's a meeting at Rose's house tomorrow at eleven. Can you make it?"

"Yes, but what's it about?"

"The final concert. Apparently, there's a problem with the reception hostess for the opening concert in September."

Sally arrived at the restaurant to find that Annie had booked a table in a quiet corner in the back. It was a quaint little place with crisp, pale yellow linens and fresh flowers on every table. It was a soothing place to relax, although, by the time they had finished lunch, nothing in Sally's life seemed quite real anymore. Her world was warping, twisting a little more each day.

She talked to no one for the rest of the afternoon but lay down in her now feminine bedroom, turning over in her mind the events of the last several months, looking for any indications that might have pointed to the truth. She could find none, and closed her mind to it for the time being. Jack shouted for her, and she ignored him. She had left him enough food and drink, and it wasn't necessary for her to be anywhere near him. It was a good thing he couldn't see the new pale blue duvet with matching pillows, or the pretty glass lamp with its dark blue shade. He'd have gone mad. Madder than usual.

Sally thought about Robert Packer. He was charming, gentle, kind, intelligent, principled, and good-looking, everything she could ask for in a man. She found him very attractive and meant to see him again. Jack could do nothing to stop her now. She wondered if Robert would feel it was too wicked to have an affair with a paralyzed man's wife. She couldn't let Robert go without trying to forge a relationship, but she would have to be quite sure that she was not grabbing the first opportunity to come her way. She had to know it was real, and only time would tell her that, and only if she exercised good judgment for a change. It was time for her to be happy again. Then a sudden and unwelcome realization hit her hard; she could hardly divorce Jack in his present condition. Was it fair to Robert to initiate what could only be a dead-end affair? They would talk, and for once she would talk with honesty rather than saying what she thought he wanted to hear. She would learn to be her own person. Everyone would respect her more if she found some backbone, not only Robert. If they were to have a relationship, it would be based on trust and affection.

Sally decided to call Robert in a few days and propose going down to Raleigh to meet him. She could leave Jack to the nurse, explaining that she had to go and see her ailing mother, which she wanted to do anyway, although Robert had reported that the lady was in good health. She needed to spend some time with her mother—she missed her so much. She had always been warm and comforting, always a reassuring presence.

Sally remembered the time she'd been woken by a nightmare and, frightened out of her wits, had climbed into bed with her mother, who had only stirred in her sleep, but enveloped her in her arms like mothers do. Sally had curved her back into her mother's front and slept like a baby. She hadn't felt such comfort since she left home, although she had once felt good in Jack's arms before they were married. After that, his arms hadn't comforted her, they had imprisoned her. How would it feel to melt in Robert's arms, to feel him enter her, to feel passion again? She stirred, beginning to have feelings she hadn't had in a long time. She lay back, free to let the dreams flow.

The next morning Sally got ready early because Annie was coming to pick her up to take her to see Sergeant Paglietti—he wanted to go over some details with them. They would come back to Sally's house to meet Susan before going over to Rose's, because, Annie said, Susan could not be trusted to be discreet and thus had no idea of the real reason for the meeting.

Sally had wheeled Jack out onto the deck to get some fresh air on this warm June morning. The oppressive heat and humidity of a Virginia summer had yet to take hold and so it was a pleasure to be outdoors. The plants still looked fresh and expansive, the colors not yet bleached out or, worse, marred by rot. She made a sandwich, wrapped it in foil, and put it in the refrigerator. She went out to Jack. He looked at her, wild-eyed.

"Why are you dressed up? Where do you think you're going? You're not going out, I won't have it. You went out yesterday."

"I am indeed going out. I put a sandwich for your lunch in the fridge. There is cold water and juice in the fridge, too. Would you like a cup of coffee before I go?"

"You will not go out today, I forbid it!"

"Who are you to forbid me to do anything? You don't imagine I would want to be here with you, do you, Jack? Why would anyone want to be with you? You're a nasty person, always were. I was just too naïve to see it and didn't have the self-confidence to deal with you, anyway.

"Shut up, shut up!"

"You wrecked the boys' lives, and mine as well. Now your behavior has wrecked yours. And, of course, you don't have the backbone to make the best of it and do something meaningful with your life. You lost the use of your legs, not your brain, you know. Well, now things have changed, and I don't have to put up with your crap anymore. You lost your backbone, and I found mine."

Sally had never gone that far before, and Jack went rigid with shock and rage. Annie chose that moment to come around to the steps that led from the deck to the lawn. "Hi, Sally. Good morning Jack. Are you ready?"

"I'll just get my purse. I'll be right back."

"She's not going anywhere. I won't have it," Jack shrieked.

Sally saw how awkward her friend felt. She knew that confrontation and unpleasantness had never played a part in Annie's life and she clearly didn't know how to deal with it, so she said nothing and stared at the begonias.

"As I said, Annie, I'll be right with you," Sally said as she went inside.

Sally came back through the sliding glass doors and walked toward the steps, her bag slung across her body. Jack propelled himself with surprising speed toward her, his face twisted with fury. She glanced quickly at Annie, who could only look up, appalled.

"Come back here. I will not have you leaving against my wishes. Come here at once!"

Sally, seeing him so close, seeing the violence in his bulging eyes, contorted mouth, and poised fist, jumped aside at the last moment. The wheelchair shot to the top of the steps and Jack, realizing he was in trouble, tried to stop it, but too late. The chair, together with its strapped-in occupant, somersaulted cleanly between the railings and landed upside down on the lawn. Susan rounded the corner to find a white-faced Annie staring at Jack in wide-eyed horror. She looked up at Sally, who met her eyes briefly before running to the kitchen to call 911.

The paramedics wouldn't let Sally ride in the ambulance with the unconscious Jack, so Annie drove her and Susan to the hospital. While the friends waited in the lobby, they discussed what story they should tell the police. Sally decided that they should tell the unvarnished truth. She explained to the officer who came to talk to them that Jack had always been abusive, had become even more difficult since his accident, that he had been angry with her for going out, and had tried to stop her. He had misjudged his direction and speed and had driven himself right off the deck.

"He has been violent all our married life, and his rages are even worse now because he isn't in control anymore. This time he was in a truly murderous rage and I couldn't stop him. I wouldn't have dared get close to him. I just jumped aside."

"I was watching the whole thing from the lawn," Annie said. "He was screaming obscenities at Sally and it looked as if he were trying to hit her with his fist. She jumped out of his way, and he couldn't stop the wheelchair in time."

"I arrived just after the accident, officer, so I can't add much, except to say that yes, indeed, Jack has always been at the very least verbally abusive toward Sally, and, to my mind, has never displayed good judgment in any respect," added Susan in her usual acidic tone.

30

Rose heard the half-hour chime and looked at the clock again: twelve-thirty. She tried Annie's number again, and then Sally's and Susan's. This was very odd. Why would Annie make such a point of having a meeting and then not show up? Perhaps they had had an accident. She called the police station and asked to be put through to Detective Paglietti.

"Joe, I'm very worried. Annie, Sally, and Susan were supposed to come to my house this morning at eleven and they haven't shown up. They're not answering the phone at their homes, either, and this is so unlike them. I was worried that perhaps they have had an accident."

"Hold on a minute, Rose, I'll inquire."

Rose wound and unwound a strand of hair around her fingers as she waited.

"No, Rose, nothing has been reported. Are you sure there was no misunderstanding about the day?"

"No, not at all. In fact, I am a little confused as to why Annie needed this meeting, as I had understood everything was set for the next reception."

"I just know I was roped in to handle the wine again, but when Annie called to ask me, she did tell me there might be a change in venue because of a scheduling conflict with the hostess. I haven't heard anything since. Well, sorry I can't be more help, Rose. I'll be sure and let you know if I hear anything."

One o'clock, two hours after their appointment. Annie sometimes ran late as she hated to cut anyone short on the phone, but, even so, you could always rely on her to be nearly on time. Rose sat thinking for a while longer and then sprang up, went upstairs, and packed a small bag. She left a message on Annie's voicemail to the effect that she was surprised and disappointed that she and Sally hadn't kept their appointment for coffee at her house and that she had decided to go away for a few days. She got into her car and drove north.

Sally and Annie had not called Rose, or anyone else, for that matter. Jack's shocking violence and its outcome had numbed both of them and it was well into the evening before Annie thought about it, prompted by the arrival of Paglietti. He told her he'd driven by their houses after Rose called and found no one home, and he'd gotten to Rose's house just as she drove off. When he got back to the station, he found out what had happened and rushed to the hospital. He surreptitiously reminded Annie to take off her wire. She left a message on Rose's answering machine and spoke to Tom, who was frantic with worry by then.

After an interminable wait, one of the doctors who had treated Jack after the car accident came to speak to Sally.

"Mrs. Hartington. Your husband is alive, although he is not yet fully conscious. He faces surgery and a long hospital stay. He has suffered too much trauma in a very short period of time for the outcome to be a happy one. You may wish to look into a nursing home for him. He will not be able to take care of himself; in fact, he may never be able to breathe on his own. He will be very susceptible to infection and other life-threatening problems. His prognosis is very poor. I'm so sorry I can't bring you better news."

He went on to explain the intricacies of Jack's injuries.

"I'm very much afraid, Mrs. Hartington, that your husband is now paralyzed from the neck down."

Sally felt a stab of pity when she understood the totality of her husband's confinement. He was finished.

Joe Paglietti was unnerved, and this was only the beginning of a week of total frustration from his point of view. His competence was beginning to be questioned both by his superiors and the press. He stared at the recording device in the palm of his hand and cursed his bad luck. He, too, was beginning to question his competence.

31

Pansy

A nnie called me about the reception for the opening concert of next season. I thought it was all set, but she told me that the hostess had called her and said she might have to be away and would let us know soon. Annie, who chaired the reception committee, said she thought we should make other arrangements as a backup plan and asked if I would have a meeting at my house to discuss it. She said it would only be necessary to invite her committee, Sally, and Susan. She seemed to be in a hurry to make these arrangements, although it was only July, so I agreed to have them over the next day at eleven.

I was very perturbed when they didn't show up. I sat in my living room and got more and more tense as the hours passed. The ticking of the clock in the hallway got louder, and it chimed the quarter hours with what seemed like a piercing warning tone. The newly polished furniture that had smelled lemony fresh and clean when Mrs. Jones had left the day before began to reek of rotten orange peels. My instinct has always been sharp, and it was telling me now that things were turning sour. I had too much to lose—even my life, if my luck ran out. The Commonwealth of Virginia kills far more people than I ever have.

Of course, when I returned from my trip, I found out the real reason for their absence. A double-whammy for Jack. But I shouldn't press my luck by talking about the wages of sin, should I? I also ran into the woman who was giving the supposedly problematic reception in the drugstore. She was quite surprised that I was under the impression there was any sort of question about it. She had just come back from visiting her daughter in Philadelphia and would not be traveling anywhere else for the rest of the summer. Everything was all arranged as far as she was concerned.

So, I was right; there was something fishy going on. My nerves were on full alert and I had to take action. Annie called to reschedule the mysterious meeting. Sally would be able to make it, she told me, as Jack was at last in a nursing home. I decided to make some special preparations. I told Helen, Susan, and Janet to come later and keep it a secret because we were going to celebrate Annie's birthday with a surprise party. Conveniently, her birthday was only a few days away and would fall on a weekend when most people might be otherwise occupied, so it would make sense for us to celebrate a few days early.

I had to search for Victor's digitalis for a couple of hours because I'd hidden it too well. I found it, long expired of course, but I'd had such good luck with the old date rape pills, I was quite confident. I think the drug companies are just afraid of getting sued. Or they want to sell more drugs.

I remembered I'd held them back from Victor for almost a month. There were a lot left. Enough to set some hearts fluttering.

32

The doorbell rang just as Rose dropped the mint into the iced tea. Two pitchers, just in case. She closed her eyes and counted to ten. Had to keep smooth, had to seem relaxed, had to wear the right face.

Annie caught her breath when she noticed that Rose had set out six glasses and napkins.

"Isn't it just us, Rose?" she said.

"Oh, I asked the others to stop by in an hour or so. We've got plenty of time to finish our discussion," Rose said.

"Oh!" Annie said. She seemed agitated.

"Is anything wrong, Annie?" Rose asked.

"Oh, no, of course not. It's always lovely to see everyone."

Rose was amused by the clumsy recovery. Good old Annie. "I'm glad you see it that way."

Annie seemed startled. That came out too strong, vicious even. Tone it down. But look at her, all sick-looking and clammy. Annie knows I know.

It was unlike Annie to be involved in unpleasantness. She'd avoided any sort of confrontation as long as Rose had known her. Maybe she was coming out of her suburban bubble.

Annie sat down on the Queen Anne. Rose had a sudden memory of Susan sitting there when she'd visited after Rose got out of the hospital. Old friends, but intrusive sometimes. Often. *Are they for me or against me?*

Annie hadn't glanced Sally's way since they arrived, just stared at a vase of flowers on the end table. Didn't want to show anything.

Rose was getting a stomachache. *Get a hold of yourself!*

Sally sat on the chair next to the philodendron. She accepted a glass of iced tea from Rose with mumbled thanks, as did Annie. Rose went and stood at the side window, gazing out onto her beautiful rose garden. Velvet petals and thorns.

"Well, Annie," Rose said, still with her back to them. "So there's a problem with the reception?"

"Yes, Sarah Biggs isn't sure she wants to host it after all. Do you have any ideas for other arrangements we could make, just in case? She can't let me know for sure until next Saturday. We can't wait until the last minute to scramble around finding another house."

"Well, that's funny, Annie. I spoke to Sarah yesterday—I happened to run into her in the drugstore. She was unaware of any problem and is expecting us as planned. Quite strange, isn't it? How could such a misunderstanding have occurred, do you think?" She turned to face them.

Sally stared at her hands, which held still for once. Rose smiled at them. Annie colored, probably wishing she hadn't made such a poor excuse. She made a visible effort to pull herself together.

"Yes, that is odd. I thought she was still away visiting her daughter in Texas. She gave me to understand before she left that she'd had second thoughts."

"I see." Rose turned to look her straight in the eyes. "I believe she mentioned Philadelphia, from where she has just returned. Shall we call her now, Annie? I can put her on speakerphone."

"No need to bother her if you're sure…"

The doorbell rang again. "I'll get it," Annie said as she rushed to the door. Rose hoped the others hadn't come early.

A husky middle-aged woman strode in and planted herself with folded arms in front of Rose, who felt her face lose color when she realized who it was. She wore well-fitting clothing this time, had short, dark, curly hair framing a thin foxy face, and no longer wore glasses. Lucy had her features. *That's neither here nor there. Concentrate. This is where it starts. Daisy's not supposed to be here. Here on Earth.*

"Hello, Pansy. Recognize your sister Daisy after all these years? Don't bother with any play-acting. Some of your friends know everything."

"I thought you were…"

"Dead? Yes, I know. You made a mistake. Another one."

"I don't know what you're talking about."

"Come on, Pansy."

"My name is Rose. Rose Hale." *Pansy! Hateful low-class name.*

"Give it up, Pansy," Daisy said.

"I've got some more iced tea in the kitchen. The least I can do is offer even a stranger hospitality." Rose took the pitcher out to the kitchen and brought back the second one. She poured a glass for Daisy and refilled the others.

"Trouble has always followed Pansy," Daisy said. "People who annoy her don't seem to live to tell the tale. Some would call her idea of problem-solving extreme."

"This woman is quite mad!" Rose said. *Bitch. Common bitch!*

"No, Rose. You're the one who's mad, I'm afraid," Annie said. "You killed Judy, then that young girl, Gayle, and then poor Samantha to try to throw suspicion on her for both murders. Judy met Daisy in her New York hair salon and showed her the photos from her son's wedding. Daisy recognized you, even after all these years."

"If everyone knows so much, how come I've not been arrested? No proof of anything, that's why!" Rose said. She could feel her face contorting. The Seven had never seen her anything but composed. Flat, that's what she'd always tried to be. *Get a grip.*

"I suppose Judy couldn't resist taunting you. Was she going to tell everyone? Daisy told us she told Judy all about your childhood, your father, and what he did to you," Annie said.

"Judy was a conniving bitch. And you, Daisy, you're no better," Rose said.

"Oh, so you know me now, do you?" *She is so coarse.*

"I suppose I have to admit to that. I'm not proud of my family. But there's nothing else to tell, nothing!"

Annie asked, "How did Gayle fit in to all of this? Did she see something from across the road? Was she blackmailing you?"

"I told you, I have nothing to say. You've got some nerve coming here with all these accusations, and after all we've been to each other through the years."

"And you spotted Daisy watching us in the restaurant. You tried to kill her, too, but instead, you killed another poor woman, a maid in the motel. She worked hard to save enough to bring her son to this country. Now he's an orphan," Annie said, her voice low and sad.

Rose realized she'd been staring at Annie. She turned her face aside with a monumental effort and went back to the window. She wished that damned clock would stop ticking. Rose turned back again and looked at each of them in turn as her own face twisted again, and she didn't try to control it this time.

"My, you all seem to like my iced tea. Your glasses are nearly empty, and Daisy, you've already finished half of yours. Let me top them up." *Curtains for you lot, and serve you right!*

I'll never have friends like that again. Having friends was good.

God, they were drinking the tea fast. Nervous, she supposed.

Rose refilled each glass, moving with the precision of a robot. They stared at her, speechless. There was an agonizing silence as they held their glasses and stared into them.

"There's no proof," Rose flung out defiantly.

"Yes, there is proof," Annie said, her voice shaking now. "They found your gloves in Judy's house last month. They were in the coffee table drawer where you left them. It took Davey a long time to realize they weren't Judy's. And some of the fibers were caught in the bust you used to kill her. The crime scene people assumed they were Judy's gloves until Davey found them and called Detective Paglietti. Your fingerprints were on the leather palm of the left one."

"Judy lent me her gloves months ago. I returned them. She must have stuck them in the drawer," Rose said. "And anyway, that was last month, so how come Paglietti hasn't questioned me about it?"

"He will. They know Samantha's head wound was too severe for having merely fallen on the ground. And they found your prints on Jackson's collar and a little plate of crackers on the end table. And Toby said Samantha didn't know how to use a word processor, but we know you do."

"Why did he tell you all this? Cops don't do that. Why didn't he arrest me if he has all this proof? Of course, because it's not real proof, all circumstantial stuff that a good lawyer can shoot down in flames in five minutes, and he knows it. Did he tell you to come?"

"No, Rose. He doesn't know we're here. We just wanted to talk to you, to ask you why. Why would someone like you do these wicked things? We didn't want to believe it. We told him you're not like that, you're one of us. But now we have to believe it, there's too much evidence," Annie said sadly as she leaned back in her chair.

"Well, thanks for the vote of confidence. Sally, don't you have anything to say?" Rose said. Her armpits were sticky, and she thought she could smell her own sweat. She felt shaky.

"I don't know what to say, Rose. Did you really do those awful things?" Sally asked, her voice back to the plaintive little girl tone she'd cast off bit by bit since Jack's accident.

"Of course I killed those women! I had to. It's your fault, Daisy. You started it, shooting off your mouth to Judy. She was a gossiping harpy and would have destroyed everything I've built up all these years."

"Oh, Rose, how could you? Judy was one of us. We were special," Sally said, her voice stronger now. *Silly little cow.*

"Gayle saw me through her binoculars and blackmailed me. Samantha—just a convenience, a red herring. I've got a special voice inside me, you know. Angelica told me to do it all. She talks to me often." Rose laughed, harsh and high-pitched. She stopped with a sudden deep breath. *Mustn't laugh. I might not be able to stop.*

"Oh, Rose, was it Dad that turned you?" Daisy said.

"Don't be a fool, Daisy, any more than you can help. I made something of myself. What are you? You used to be a hooker. I know all about that. I saw you picking up cruising johns. And now you're a hairdresser, tarting up rich cows for a living. Big deal!"

"You're right, I'm no one special. But my sister is, she's a murderer. Do you really think that makes you better than me?"

"Yes, I'm a killer, but I'm damned clever. You've got to give me that."

Daisy said, "Your friends would have understood about your family. Lots of famous people come from bad places."

"Famous people aren't like Salton people. Different code. But you wouldn't know anything about places like this."

"The people who matter would have supported you, your friends. Your former friends."

That last remark cut deep. "Aren't you starting to feel a little sick, ladies? Hearts beating a bit fast, blurry vision, nausea? After all that nice iced tea, you can't be feeling that great. I made it specially," Rose said, her tone low and venomous.

"I do feel weird," Annie said. "What have you done?" Sally and Daisy remained silent.

"Digitalis. A lot of it. Glad it still works. It was Victor's, you know, so it's pretty old. Oh, well, I'll be out of your way in no time. I've got a car ready and waiting—not my own, of course. I wouldn't have wanted it to come to this, but you would meddle, wouldn't you, Daisy? And Annie and Sally, you had to stick your noses in, too. So long, everyone. It's been nice. Until now. And, by the way, I didn't know that

Anita woman. I had nothing to do with her murder. So you have another killer in your midst!"

The other women still said nothing.

"I feel sorry for our friends when they find you. Not the surprise they were expecting!"

Rose glared at them all, feeling something like regret. She laughed again. *That sounded hysterical. Stifle it!*

"I pride myself on being a positive thinker. Just another road to travel," Rose said with a sigh. *I'm so tired.*

She went to the front hallway and got her coat and bag out of the closet.

She opened the door to be met by Detective Paglietti. "Hello, Rose," he said. "That was quite a story you told us."

"You're too late."

"No, I don't think so. They had strict instructions not to eat or drink anything. And I was listening." He stepped aside. "Officers, take her away."

"Thank God it's over. She was going to kill us all," Annie said. "I thought she'd be suspicious when our glasses emptied so fast."

"I was afraid she'd notice. What did you do with it?" Paglietti asked.

"Mine went into the philodendron, and I saw Sally pour hers in there, too," Daisy said.

"I poured the first glass into the vase, but then I'm afraid the rest went down the back of the seat cushion," Annie said. "She really is insane, isn't she? Did you hear what she said about Angelica? What was that all about?"

"I think she's just a cold-blooded killer trying to act crazy. Anyone gets in her way, she wipes them out," Paglietti said.

"But normal people don't behave that way. She must be ill. Anyway, she thought we'd all be dead. She didn't know I was wired. It doesn't make sense," Annie said.

"Trying out her story, I guess," Daisy said. "Our father used to make us do some of Shakespeare's plays. I hated it, but Rose loved it. I remember her practicing the parts, and her voice would change as she got into it. It used to surprise all of us. She could have gone on the stage."

"I think she's probably been on the stage all her life," Paglietti said, grunting as he left to go back to the station. "The crime scene people will be here shortly. Don't touch anything. Annie, would you mind staying until they come? Show them where you all poured the tea."

"No problem, Joe."

"I'll keep her company," said Sally.

His hands trembled as he gripped the steering wheel. That had been risky, even though he'd coached them all. She'd been ready for them. The first meeting must have aroused her suspicions, the pretext more flimsy than he'd realized. And then the accident at the Hartington's had made the women miss it. Suspecting something was out of kilter must have sent her into alert mode. He had no doubt that Rose had a well-honed sense of self-preservation. And then Annie's feeble excuse falling apart had clinched it. He wondered if his boss would go down that road. He hoped not. He hoped that closing the cases would deflect any questions about risk-taking.

Daisy sank into an armchair and looked around the living room. She gazed at the tall green plant in the corner and wondered what digitalis might do to a philodendron.

A lingering smell of sweat was juxtaposed with the fragrance of the potpourri in a bowl on the table next to her. The room, so genteel, held brutal truths. She supposed Pansy had lived mostly on the surface and only delved deeper for the dark resources she needed when she felt threatened. She was thankful she didn't have all those demons lurking. There were other things that had happened earlier in Pansy's life that had made her wonder. But she had been efficient and there was never any proof, just a feeling in her gut. And she could hardly just come out and accuse her, after all. Where had it all started? She supposed she knew, but it had happened to her, too. Daisy hadn't turned bad. She just didn't let men touch her—only women.

She remembered her father's face hovering above hers, the glaze in his eyes that masked his lust. She hadn't thought of him for years. The smell of sweat in this room had brought to mind his foul body, his breath that filtered up through cheap brandy fumes, cigarette smoke, and a perpetually rancid stomach. His soccer ball paunch protruded over a long skinny cock, which always drew her eyes like a magnet as it rose from its hairy nest.

He'd hurt her so much at the beginning until she learned to force herself to focus on her multiplication tables. She hadn't been very smart in school, but she always got kudos from her elementary school teachers for knowing her multiplication tables so well she could say them forward and backward.

After Mom left, she'd had no choice but to work the streets. She had to eat and no one would help; people treated them all like lepers after the truth about Dad came out. Most of the johns had been better than Dad, although she had been roughed up a few times. They were all different, even their cocks were amazingly different in size and shape, and she'd seen all sorts, even one with a kink in it. Then she got her chance. James, the owner of a beauty parlor, fell in love with her. He gave her a job, trained her, and treated her better than anyone else ever had. He'd gotten her cleaned up, bought her a few nice clothes, and styled her hair. As long as she reserved her favors for him, everything went along fine.

But there had been another woman in the salon, Karen, a bit older than her. She'd fondled her one day in the back room. Daisy recoiled. "What the hell do you think you're doing?" she whispered.

"Don't you know about women making love together? Haven't you ever tried it? We're softer than the guys, gentler. You'll like it, I promise."

Daisy recalled a few things she'd heard at school about lesbians. Lezzies, they'd called them. The girls said mean things about them, laughed at them. Anyway, she left Karen without replying and went back to work. But the idea took hold and wouldn't let go. She found herself eyeing Karen as she worked, and Karen's smirk showed she'd noticed. Karen invited her over for pizza one evening. They drank too much wine and ended up on the floor, Karen in a frenzy, and Daisy not far behind after a few minutes getting used to the idea. Gentle, even in passion; and better. Of course, her boss eventually realized what was going on and fired both of them. Daisy threatened to tell his wife about their affair if he didn't give them good references. They found jobs in a better salon and were still together. She hoped Karen would stay with her if she needed to move away. She couldn't imagine life without her.

When she was thirteen, Daisy got her period. The first time Dad came to her while she had it, she tried to tell him, but he hadn't believed her at first and made her show him the stains, another humiliation. When he saw it for himself, he had hit her so hard she banged her head on the wall and lost consciousness for a few minutes. He didn't even notice. He never looked her in the face again and barely spoke to her, except to demand another beer from the cooler. She kept out of his way if he was drunk, which was most of the time. That was when he'd started on Pansy. Daisy was ashamed now, thinking of her relief when she'd heard it the first time through the thin wall that separated her room from Rose's. Those loathsome grunts, the high-pitched cries, and later, the heavy footsteps out to the kitchen, the fridge door opening, and the pop of the beer can tab—all so familiar, but now nothing to do with her.

Her mother knew what was going on, but felt powerless to do anything about it. She'd been a stupid, ignorant woman with a husband who kept her in line with the flat of his hand, and he did turn over some of his pay when there was any left over from the liquor store. They'd needed every penny. Her mother had been so mired in poverty and degradation, she hadn't even grieved much when the baby died, just a few tears for a couple of days. What was the baby's name? Daisy couldn't remember. She hadn't taken much notice of her baby sister and hadn't been sorry when she died—who would want to bring up a child in that hellhole? She would only have suffered the same fate as her sisters, and if Dad hadn't been put away, they would all likely have ended up like their mother. It must have been rough on Pansy to have seen Dad kill the baby, though. Perhaps that's what had turned her, not the abuse.

Daisy had always found it hard to believe that her father had done that. He was a drunken lout who might have hit the baby in a rage if she cried too much, but smother her? And then to have tidied up after himself? That had always puzzled her. Didn't track right. Daisy straightened up with a start. Pansy? No, she was only fourteen at the time. It wasn't possible. No one did things like that at fourteen. Did they?

33

Pansy

Well, here I am. It's all over. I had a pretty good run, really, so I shouldn't complain. I started to write this journal a month ago when I realized that almost a whole year had gone by since I was caught and stuck in here. I promised myself I wouldn't suffer this humiliation much longer than a year and I do want people to understand everything before I go, especially the children. They've got no parents now and no inheritance, either. I cleaned everything out after the Samantha debacle, as I knew I might need it someday soon. I've always been able to smell danger. I made other arrangements after Daisy's death (Well, I thought she was dead at the time). And wait until the children read about me killing their father—although I didn't really kill him, I just let him die. I suppose I could have left that bit out as no one ever suspected—just like my baby sister. It feels good to get it all off my chest, though, and it will help people understand "where I'm coming from," as they say these days.

You have to feel sorry for my children, even though I've never been one for feeling sorry for people. Some have had it worse. God knows I did. I've lost them for good and I'm resigned to that now. I loved them in my own way. Nothing showy, but I took care of them, listened to their woes, and tried to help with their little problems. Lucy never knew I had anything to do with that rotten cad Danny's arrest for drug possession. She saw the light, and he saw the inside of a jail cell for a few months. He would have dragged her down and I couldn't have allowed that. I don't know where Justin and Lucy got their idealism—certainly not from me. Don't get me wrong, I respect them for it. I'm proud of all of them. They loved me, although I don't suppose they do now. I just want them to stop and think objectively about all the hurdles I had to jump. I got respect, social position, three lovely children, and, my finest achievement, the house of peace with its white fence, polished furniture, spreading trees, and masses of flowers, in and out. They all loved that house, gone to strangers now.

Andrew must be devastated and I'm most sorry about him. He thought well of me and treated me like a queen. I loved that boy a little more than the others. Actually, a lot more. Andrew deserves the perfect wife, the kind of woman I pretended to be. I knew that would be out of the question if details of my background ever came out. That's part of the reason I had to kill Judy—it would have ruined all of us, not just me. Of course, it backfired and my poor Andrew will never find a good partnership now, either in law or in marriage. People tend to think that sort of thing runs in the family. Andrew needs harmony and a mother's touch. I hope he finds the right woman now his mother is lost to him.

I wish him happiness, always. But it will be hard for him to find happiness, and he may not be able to grasp it should it come his way. Poor, dear Andrew, staid on the outside, but sensitive to a fault when you get past his layers of postures.

Justin, I think, will be happy. He will melt into his music and causes and float through reality. Lucy will intensify her assault on life through the ambitious pursuit of her career and, perhaps, even a political vocation—if she can get past the handicap of having a murderer for a mother. Her ruthlessness and ability to rationalize suits her to politics, I think. Perhaps we are more alike than she would care to believe.

I wonder if any of them can keep even a tiny nugget of love in their hearts for me. All their lives they loved me, but did the truth shatter every last shred of it in a moment? Did I kill that, too? Will reading this help, or will it condemn me forever in their eyes? I hope they are not afraid they might turn out like me. It was the degradation of poverty and violence that shaped me, not my blood. And they must remember that they have their father's blood in them, too. He never even spanked them when they were growing up, not once. All in all, he was a good man.

Daisy came to see me a couple of weeks ago. She told me my children will all move away where no one will know who they are, and where I can't track them down, because they don't want to hear from me ever again. She remarked how fortunate it was that Hale is not that unusual a name, although the kids were talking of changing it slightly.

She said she exposed me for my own good and to save anyone else who might cross me. For her own glorification, more likely. I think she just wanted the limelight, although that had its drawbacks. The owner of her salon said this sort of thing runs in families; he had to think of the welfare of his customers, he couldn't afford the notoriety, and she must see that he would have to let her go, and so on. She sued him and got a nice sum out of it, so that worked out for the best. She said she would move away from New York and change her appearance.

She never married—didn't fancy it, she said. Women were safer, softer (except for me). Maybe I'll find her one day. I guess she was mad at me for trying to kill her—twice—and perhaps this was her way of killing me back. She talked about what happens to people who cross me. Well, she crossed me, God, did she cross me. I'll find her one day and she'll know how right she was.

What am I thinking? If I ever get away from here, all that has to stop. It draws attention, and the last thing I would need on the outside is attention of that kind.

I feel as if the stench of this place is permanently in my skin. I haven't tried to dissect it. I don't want to know all its ghastly components. Of course, I don't belong here, in a facility for the criminally insane. At least it's not too far from a town, which might matter later. I'm not insane at all, just practical and of a logical turn of mind—I did those things for good reasons, reasons I've explained here. You're allowed to shoot someone who is trying to steal your property. Well, all those people were trying to steal my way of life. I just couldn't let it happen. All those people were out to destroy me.

The voice saved me—so glad I'd thought it all through. Angelica was my guardian angel, I said. And she told me to do all those things to protect myself, I said. I said it over and over again to so many "experts." I dreamed about Angelica one night. She was lovely and hovered just out of reach, watching over me, just me. And the "stiff, formal posture" came naturally, especially in this place. I slipped in extra little tidbits of instructions from the voice from time to time. They lapped it up.

I talk to Angelica sometimes; she never talks back (then I'd know I have a problem), and that's one of the things I like best about her. I'm just Pansy to her, and she likes Pansy just fine. She seems quite real sometimes.

There's a psychiatrist here who "treats" me, Dr. Bolton. I liked him at first. He listened to everything without being judgmental and seemed to understand my point of view. It was so nice to let down my guard. I felt more relaxed than I had in years. Keeping up appearances and guarding secrets is more exhausting than I realized. Once I felt I could stop talking about Angelica, I could just be matter-of-fact. I felt at peace. The only tough bit was pretending to take my medications and then finding a good hiding place for them. They check your mouth pretty thoroughly, so I had to swallow them a couple of times before I got it right, found that special place behind my right back molar. They made me feel terrible, almost crazy. They came in useful later, though. I traded them for better stuff. Useful stuff. Sedatives, mostly, at least that's what they claimed. I said mine were happy pills. I discarded anything the other patients gave me that looked like the pills I was supposed to take.

After a few months, the sessions started to take a different turn. Dr. Bolton tried to break down my reasoning.

"Rose, I want you to close your eyes and imagine someone is trying to strangle you. What do you feel?"

"I feel like jabbing him in the belly and killing him."

"Supposing he is too strong for you. What then?"

I knew what he wanted. "I'm scared, sweating, terrified, actually."

"Isn't that what your victims might have felt?"

"Yes, you're right. I know they must have, and I'm sorry." Idiot. I don't think most of them had time to feel much of anything.

I started to get tired again. But I realized that it was in my best interests to let him think he was getting somewhere. He has a reputation as a ladies' man. I've been flirting with him for a few weeks now, nothing too overt, and I think he'll be useful later on. I may be coming up on 57, but I look years younger. I'm still quite good-looking and I've kept my figure, especially as I lost some weight after my arrest. I suppose I can be alluring if I must.

I think about the Seven a lot. Why did I try to kill Annie and Sally? They were valued friends, and there was nothing to hide anymore because I found out that day that they knew everything. Daisy may have been right. Maybe people would have forgotten and forgiven my background. I could have just drugged them and escaped. I do regret that whole episode. I would have liked them to remember me kindly. How can you feel kindly toward someone who tried to poison you? But I was like a cornered wild animal slashing its way out of danger—no logic to it. I guess I might have been a little mad at the time, although I hesitate to put that in writing in this place—off-balance, let's say. I'll have to think this through some more, but some other time, far away from here.

I truly miss Salton. I wonder who killed that woman in the woods? Detective Paglietti will have to look to some other rage-filled person to pin that one on. I told him it wasn't me. And I'm saying it again. I did not kill that woman.

I put in a lot of years casting Rose as a solid citizen. When you've paid your dues in that kind of place, you can just coast. It's comfortable, although the dullness can be crushing sometimes, and you wonder what your life's all about. I'll tell you what it's all about: it's about crawling up out of the dirt so you can spread your wings in the sunshine.

I started this last entry two days ago and have been sunk in thought ever since. Now I have had more time to reflect, which I often manage to do in spite of the constant mayhem in this madhouse. I realize that the children were my finest achievement. Not the house. I hope I haven't destroyed them. I hope I made them strong enough. If there is any hope of happiness for me, it lies in knowing that my children are at least content. But I'll never have any way of knowing, will I?

I don't belong in a mental hospital, but on the other hand, prison isn't the place for someone like me, either. The women in prison are so crude and vulgar. Brutish. Some of them are far crueler than I could ever be. I cannot and will not be compared with people like that, and I have no place among them. They knew I looked down on them and took it out on me at every opportunity. The weeks I spent in jail were pure hell, and at least this place is merely purgatory.

I'm very bored and feel angry most of the time now. I need a completely new start. Well, I have plenty of time to think and plan. I'm a very good planner, but I won't be careless like last time. Plans B, C, D, and E. I've hidden this journal well, but I'll leave it under my bed where they'll find it after I leave.

To whoever reads this after I've gone: I promise not to kill again, not unless I absolutely have to, not unless I'm forced into it—you know how people are.

I've been thinking a lot since I've been here and I realize now that, for the most part, there are better ways to handle things. Most things.

34

She walked quickly toward the town, keeping to the shadows cast by tall trees on the edge of the road. She'd collected a few clothing items and even a little money during her year in that place and had cut her hair before setting out, discarding it amongst the trees as she went. She had to get to the bus station early, but didn't know where to find it. She'd left the place in a secretary's car whom, with her new haircut and clothes, she now resembled. The secretary had a boyfriend, a nurse's assistant who lived on the grounds, so she often stayed over. Rose knew about it, but the guard didn't, and he'd smirked seeing her leave at that hour, assuming Dr. Bolton was having it on with the woman. He was more right than he knew, as the secretary hadn't confined herself to her boyfriend.

She'd dumped the car on the outskirts of town and left it in the woods. With any luck, they'd waste time looking for it before checking anywhere else. And they'd also find out about the call to directory inquiries for the number of a small hotel in St. Petersburg, Florida. She'd posed as Dr. Bolton's secretary and made a reservation in his name guaranteed by his credit card, upon which the police would find her fingerprints. Those extra few minutes spent sending the police in the wrong direction should be well worth the delay.

She arrived in town as it was waking up and its first early risers leaving for work. She asked the way to the bus station in what she thought might be a French accent—no one around there would know the difference—and was relieved to find she was quite close. She bought her ticket to Richmond, targeted a plump, untidy young mother with two tired children, and sat down next to them.

"I want some juice. I'm thirsty, Mom," whined the small boy, sleepy and irritable.

"You'll have to wait, Jason. Your sister's asleep and I'm too tired to carry everything over there," said his mother, also sleepy and irritable.

"I'll look after the baby and your things while you buy some breakfast. I remember what it's like traveling with children, so exhausting," Rose said.

"Oh, would you? That's so sweet. It's just over there. I won't be a sec."

"You go ahead, my dear. I'll be right here in case she wakes up."

Five minutes later, the grateful mother was back with a happier Jason and a bag of snacks and juice. She offered Carol (as Rose had called herself) a doughnut, and Rose thought she had never tasted anything more delicious—a freedom doughnut. She got the conversation moving, inventing a home in Indiana and an old friend she'd been visiting. She wanted to get back in time for her husband's birthday and would catch another bus in Richmond. She talked a lot about her husband, painting a vivid picture for her new friend, Darleen. She almost began to believe in him, this diner-owning husband of hers. Soon enough, it was time to board the eight o'clock bus and off they went, looking like a family traveling together. Rose had Jason sit next to her, and she read to him and helped him read to her. She enjoyed his company with a mixture of sadness and pleasure as she remembered how Andrew had loved to be read to at that age. They all had.

Her eyes filled as she remembered Andrew's special book, the one they'd read to him over and over. It was about a little tailor who killed seven flies with one swat, but when people overheard him telling the story, they thought he meant he'd killed seven giants. He was forced to confront the local giant, whom he somehow vanquished. She couldn't remember the details. A little hand pawed her arm.

"Why are you sad? You stopped reading."

"Oh, sorry, dear, I was remembering when I had a little boy your age."

"What was his name?"

"Jake. Let's get on with your story."

The hour went quickly and they said a regretful goodbye.

"You're a lovely woman," Darleen said. "You made it all easy for me."

"You enjoy those precious children while you can, my dear. It all ends so quickly."

Plenty of cabs waited at the bus station, and Rose took one downtown to the Grey Eagle Health Club. The early exercisers had started to hurry out by the time she signed in. The receptionist looked up at her for only a second and she found the women's locker room almost empty. She had repeated the combination to her locker over and over again in her bed every night and she opened it without difficulty, although her heart pounded and her hands were slippery with sweat. The bag sat where she'd left it and she slipped into the bathroom without being seen. In no time, she'd transformed herself. Wig, glasses, makeup, and cheek pads, sweat suit, and sneakers brought to life Monica, whose picture was on the membership card she'd flashed at the receptionist when she signed in. She had enough money now to complete her journey, together with the key to an apartment in a nondescript complex in Syracuse.

Another cab took her to the train station. Next stop, Chicago. The movement of the train lulled her to sleep. She dreamed of falling down a big hole. There was Annie, leaning over the top. She was shouting, "You're not one of us, never one of us, go away!" She woke panting in panic just before she hit the bottom.

A young man sitting opposite her looked concerned. "You all right, ma'am?" he said.

"Fine, thanks. Just a bad dream." She hoped she'd done a good job with the makeup. The wig was pretty good, too. She tried to bury herself in a corner for the rest of the journey.

Two days later, she woke up on a Greyhound bus reciting account numbers aloud. At least, she thought she had. Luckily no one was sitting near her. She was lying stretched out on the back seat, so the driver couldn't have heard her. She closed her eyes and remembered how Dr. Bolton had looked when she left him.

The good doctor had submitted happily. Well, he'd been happy until the last few minutes when he realized that the amazing gin fizz cocktail she'd served him was causing a certain wooziness. He could only call out in a whisper by that time. She'd not been confident it would work because she couldn't be sure that the mix of drugs she had traded her antipsychotics with other patients for really were sedatives; those people could hardly be considered reliable, and in any case, she'd lied to them too, telling them hers were happy pills. She had to take the risk that the amount she dispensed would be effective, especially as he had told her that he had suffered a heart attack a few years back and took medication for high blood pressure. She didn't want to kill him, only to humiliate him and ruin his career. He had only himself to blame—he had been unforgivably careless for a psychiatrist. He had no business sharing personal information with her, and certainly no business screwing a patient. Especially as he thought her a mass murderer. *What did he expect?* she wondered. A convenient and submissive lay for the next few years? Definitely his fault.

His liver-spotted hands on her the first few times were a loathsome memory. The long, sharp index finger that wagged in admonishment at his students and patients poked at her and probed until she thought she would kill him then and there. Sometimes she threw up afterward. The memories made her hot behind the eyes and it took a herculean effort to suppress them. That all had to stop—the rage and the killing. Her eyes snapped open. She would be a forward thinker from now on, no clinging to the past and no lingering in the present.

Rose closed her eyes again and gleefully recalled the final scene, a calming memory. Dr. Bolton would have been found lying on his back, naked from the waist down (except for his socks), hands and feet bound, and displaying damp evidence of his misdoing. The little American flag he kept on his desk, tied with string to his penis by its wooden staff, held him stubbornly erect and provided a wonderful counterpoint to the narrow white beard he affected, which also pointed heavenward. Very creative. She fell asleep again for a few precious, peaceful hours.

She continued to hopscotch from town to town on her way to upstate New York, resting overnight in dingy motels. Relieved and exhausted, she let herself into a dusty little efficiency apartment five days later.

Rose had rented the furnished apartment eighteen months before. She'd paid rent for two years in advance, explaining that she was working abroad most of the year, but wanted a small place to come back to from time to time to be near her cousins. All utility costs (except telephone, which she didn't need) were included, so it didn't matter if she wasn't around to pay bills. She'd deposited plenty of cash in a safe deposit box in a Syracuse bank, stashed some in the apartment, and placed a smaller amount in the health club locker. She had a couple of bank accounts in Syracuse and told them that since she'd be abroad, they should hold her statements. She'd covered her bases, still had her smarts.

She needed groceries. Another wig and change of clothes to produce the woman who had formerly shown her ID at the rental office, and she could show herself at the corner store. She bought a newspaper along with enough food to last a few days and walked back to the apartment. She must lie low for a couple of months before making her final move.

Rose had planned a very intricate support system. She'd taken most of the equity out of the house and sold her stock portfolio. Her savings account was cashed out, too. The money was distributed in several accounts in various cities. She had to remember which name she had used where, of course. She thought through it all in the hospital before she went to sleep each night so that she wouldn't forget. She couldn't rely on being able to make it to the apartment or the health club, after all.

A large amount of the money had ended up being wired, in smallish amounts, to a numbered account in the Caymans on a regular basis. She'd kept up with her old contacts in New York and got some passports (including one with a resident's visa for Canada), Social Security numbers, driver's licenses—the full kit. She'd never been to Richmond before that first visit to get the health club membership downtown and hoped that was the last place anyone would think of looking. Documents were also scattered, including the visas and passports. Photographs in the documents must match her appearance. There were cryptic notes left in the apartment to remind her which persona she'd used to open which bank account and to rent the apartment. Her friends thought she'd been on a trip to New York to do some shopping, or had visited a discount mall in Pennsylvania, or had gone to visit this friend or that. They were used to her doing things on her own, so it hadn't raised any questions. Of course, she'd made sure to come back with something to show for it. Superb planning.

Rose made herself some coffee and lay on the sofa. She needed a rest. She must clean tomorrow. The place smelled stale and dusty and dust motes bobbed in the beams of sunlight that poked through the venetian blinds. Damn! She'd forgotten to buy cleaning supplies.

Rose jumped when the doorbell rang. She went to the door, pulse racing, panting with fear. She took a deep breath.

"Who is it?"

"Super, ma'am. I saw the light under the door and there's been no one here for months. Everythin' okay?"

"Everything's fine, thanks. I'm Mrs. Munroe. I'm abroad a lot, I just got in."

"Very good, ma'am, just wanted to check."

"That's very good of you, thank you. I'm about to take a shower, otherwise I'd open the door."

"That's fine, ma'am. Have a good evening."

Rose lay back down on the sofa and took a sip of coffee. She'd be like this every time she heard the doorbell? Probably.

A pretty vase and some roses would be nice. But she was too tired right now. She dozed off for an hour and woke to cold coffee. She made some more and opened the paper. She found her story on page three. She was portrayed as "Female Mass Murderer," which she considered a gross misrepresentation. How these papers liked to sensationalize things. Poor children, reading things like that. They'd found the car, but had drawn a blank on her whereabouts. "Thought to be in an unknown location in Florida." So far, so good. The article went on to say that Dr. Bolton had been found by another doctor, drugged and bound, the morning after her escape. The police had stated that Rose had been responsible, but gave no further explanation. She chuckled. The hospital would want to avoid a public outcry at all costs.

Yes, a few months in Syracuse would be restful, and then she could slip into Canada, perhaps with one of those bus trips seniors take to buy cheap medicines. She'd take a few practice runs first. A new beginning. Frightening and exciting, tiring and exhilarating. Alone and lonely—the best way for her. She was the type of person who should always keep to herself. Salton had just been a pleasant interlude, a nice long respite. Tabula rasa. Perhaps she would try her hand at writing, starting with a very long and detailed biography for Lily. Lily was a nice name. She liked flowers. Except pansies and daisies.

You needed to be alone to write, so this was the time to do it. And she might start writing a romance novel while she was waiting, too. She'd buy a few in the market to see what they were made of. Marvelous male heroes and happy coupled endings, she suspected. She'd felt romantic with Victor a few times in the beginning, so should be able to rekindle the feelings.

After she got to Toronto, she'd have to take a few short trips to fill in the missing biographical details—the gap after Lily moved to Canada to get married twenty years before. A farmer, name of John, bowled over by a heart attack before his time, poor darling. Or something like that. She might even take a course in creative writing once she settled in. Well, she had time and solitude to take a stab at it now. She should wait a good six months before making another move. All she needed was some notebooks and pencils, a vase of flowers, and some good wine. She had plenty of ideas. She'd never lacked for ideas.

She reached into the bag she'd brought from the health club and drew out the American passport with its attached Canadian visa. Rose looked into the passport photo and Lily Porter stared back. She wore a rather confrontational look, poised and ready for whatever lay ahead.

Rose was fading out now and Pansy was long gone. Soon, Lily would take the field. And she would keep things quiet. Dormant, so to speak.

Epilogue

"Hello, Mrs. Minhoff?"

"Yes, who is this?"

"This is Andrew, Andrew Hale."

"Oh, how are you? I'm so glad you called. I've been thinking about you since I got that package."

"I'm doing all right. Thank you, Mrs. Minhoff."

"Please, call me Annie."

"Oh, well, thanks. Did you read the journal?"

"Yes, twice. It's hard to believe all the dreadful things it described, especially your mother's awful childhood and what it led her to do. But, you, it must have been terrible for you, Andrew. And your brother and sister, what did they make of it?"

"I haven't told them about it. I talk to them on the phone occasionally, but we don't seem to be able to talk about things.

250

It always feels awkward. I keep in touch with Detective Paglietti, and he decided to send it to me. He swore me to secrecy, because the FBI is not going to publicize it, thank heavens. All that sex stuff, for God's sake. It made me cringe, so embarrassing when it's your own mother."

"I know, I was shocked. She'd always seemed so, well, proper."

"I know. Paglietti made a clandestine copy before the FBI took it away, and I made a spare for you. He felt I deserved to know, and I thought you did, too. You haven't told anyone, have you?"

"No, Andrew. I respected your wishes. No one knows about the journal or where you are. Are you working?"

"Yes. The senior partner in our firm was very decent. He had a quiet word with a friend of his who is the senior partner in a Seattle law firm. They hired me. I told the new firm I wanted a change of scene, and I guess I got a very strong recommendation. The senior partner told no one about the real reason for my move. I use my middle name now. Answering to Simon takes some getting used to. What's happening with the other Sevens? I would love Sally to know that Mom regrets trying to poison her, but I suppose there's no way of letting her know without spilling the beans."

"No, there isn't, Andrew. And besides, even if she regrets it, she still tried to kill us in the most horrible way."

"Yes, I suppose so. Anyway, how are they all?"

"Well, Sally's husband, Jack, died of a massive stroke several months ago. Just as well, because he had no quality of life. Sally has been seeing a lot of her sons, and one of them moved to Raleigh, where her mother lives. Her mother isn't in very good health—had a stroke a few months ago—so she's probably going to sell the house here and move down there to take care of her. She's been seeing an old boyfriend from there, too. He's a really nice man. I hope it works out."

"I hope it works out for her. Not to speak ill of the dead, but Jack was a real jerk."

"Yes, he certainly was that. And Janet doesn't involve herself in symphony affairs too much anymore. She's very tied up with volunteer work in a shelter for battered women and, through Helen, a residential support group for the intellectually challenged. She started to change after she found Gayle's body, you know, and after that unfortunate experience we had with your mother, she became very altruistic. She was supposed to find our bodies, remember? I guess a brush with violent death really rearranges your priorities."

"Yes, I guess so. I know mine have changed, you know, what with my foundations getting knocked out from under me."

"Yes, poor Andrew."

"Oh well, got to make the best of it."

"Susan is president of the symphony board now and enjoying herself immensely. She even entertains. Tom and I were over there for dinner last week. She's mellowed, too. Everyone's different now, Andrew, even me. We're very excited because Beth's moving back here and she's expecting. Her husband got a great job in Washington. I'll probably be much less involved with the symphony after that. I hope they can cultivate more volunteers, but enough is enough as far as I'm concerned. I'm looking around for a more needy charity to get involved with."

"That's great. You'll be a terrific grandma. I always liked Beth. There are lots of organizations that need our help. And, let's face it, the symphony was fun for you all, but it's basically a bunch of middle-class white people catering to themselves. I'm doing Reading for the Blind. It's a lot harder than you'd think. You just try describing a map or a photograph for someone who can't see it."

"It must be really difficult to do that in a coherent sort of a way. Who have I forgotten? Oh, Helen. She got accepted to law school at Georgetown and is doing very well. She's almost finished her first year. She's trying to find a way to go full-time. That way, she'll be through in three years. Her daughter, Toni, is doing well, too. Doesn't see much of her father, I don't think."

"Another jerk, I remember. Well, I'm glad everyone's doing okay. I miss Salton. It's one thing to leave by choice, another to feel you're in exile."

"Oh, Andrew, I'm so sorry."

"Thank you, Annie. Can I call you sometimes?"

"Of course, my dear, I've known you since you were a little boy. You can count on me. How are Lucy and Justin?"

"They're fine. Justin didn't leave yet, but he just got a job with an orchestra in Dallas, so he'll be moving next month. God knows what they'll make of him in Texas with his ponytail and vegetarian diet. Lucy moved to California and is working for an environmental group. She's thinking of going to law school, too. She'd be quite good in litigation, I think. She can certainly argue and never gives up once she's got her teeth sunk into something."

"Yes, I do remember."

"But, promise me, Annie, that you'll never tell anyone where I am. Only Paglietti knows, and I can trust him. He's a very decent sort."

"No, I won't—except Tom. I'll not keep any more secrets from Tom, and you can trust him to be discreet. And yes, Joe is decent. I forgot to tell you—he and Helen date from time to time, and volunteer at concerts together, too."

"Well, I'll be damned. I'd never have thought it."

"I was really surprised at first, but now, the more I see them together, the more I understand how well-suited they are. But Andrew, dear, we've talked about everyone except you. There must have been so many emotions boiling up in you when you read the journal."

"Yes, it was terrible. But, I feel much better about things now, believe it or not. When my mother was arrested, I was horrified, refused to believe it. When I heard the evidence, I was angry, so angry. How could she have done all those terrible things? It seemed to have nothing to do with my mother. Then the insanity defense, and it worked, thank God. I did believe she was insane, until I read the journal, and although I worried about it running in the family, at least I could believe that it was the sickness doing the killing. But now she claims she just pretended to be mentally ill. But I think she must be sick. Maybe not the paranoid schizophrenia, but something else. Don't you think she's sick, Annie?"

"Yes, Andrew, I do. After I read about the horrors of her childhood, I wouldn't expect her not to be sick. Although I suppose Daisy has come through it. But she never had the drive your mother had. Didn't have as much to lose, either."

"No, poor Mom. I won't tell Lucy about Dad. She wouldn't be able to get past it. He was unbearable when he was sick, you know. I can see how he might have sent Mom over the edge."

"Your Dad was a good man, Andrew."

"Yes, I know, you're right. But after I read the journal a second time, my horror turned to pity. And understanding. I wish I could let her know I understand. I know the awful things her father did to her made her sick. It's really not her fault. I hope she can hold it together on the outside, that nothing bad happens again. I wish I could tell her that I love her, in spite of everything. But I guess I never can, can I?"

"No, Andrew, I don't think we'll ever see her again. And if you did hear from her, you'd have to report it. You are an officer of the court."

"I couldn't bear it. Now she's escaped, I can't imagine she'll risk being seen anywhere near Salton again. Do you think she can ever be happy and find some measure of peace?"

"No, I very much doubt it. Although she does have a tremendous ability to bury her old selves, as we all discovered."

"You know, I went to New York for a few days after I read the journal. I researched Mom's and her sisters' birth certificates. I found their street. I went by the building, but it's all prettied up now. There's a shoe salon and a café on the ground floor, and offices on the other floors. No one actually lives there anymore. I don't know why that surprised me so much, but it did. The baby was buried by the city. I couldn't find out where. I'll try again, though. If I ever find her, I'll give her a proper burial with a nice headstone. She deserves that. Probably Mom did the best thing for her she knew how. She was only a kid."

"I can't help crying a little, Andrew."

"Me, too, Annie."

"Such a heavy weight on your young shoulders. You've got to move on, now. In your mind, I mean."

"After I've taken care of the baby. Her name was Rosemary, by the way. Rosemary for remembrance."

1. Do you think Pansy's abuse led her to become a killer?

2. Was making her first kill the trigger to killing again?

3. Why do you think Pansy's sister, Daisy, turned out differently?

4. Did Pansy's intelligence and drive work for her or against her?

5. Rose stayed on the straight and narrow for years after she attained the social status she craved. Why didn't it

last? Would Salton society really have looked down on her for her terrible upbringing?

6. Do you think Rose was fully self-aware? Did she know right from wrong? She seems to have brought her children up to know the difference. Did she feel fully justified in her actions?

7. Was Rose victimized to the point that she had to think of protecting herself above all else? Do you think this might be common in abused children?

8. What did the Salton Symphony reveal about the culture of Salton social life?

9. Were you glad that Rose escaped? Did you pity her?

10. Did the story make you want to know what happens to Rose?

Author Bio

D. A. Spruzen grew up near London, U.K., graduated from the London College of Dance and Drama Education, and earned an MFA in Creative Writing from the Queens University of Charlotte. She teaches creative writing in Northern Virginia when not seeking her own muse. She is the author of *The Flower Ladies Trilogy* and the *Sleuthing with Mortals* series. Other publications include a historical novel, The Blitz Business, and a poetry collection, *Long in the Tooth*. Her poems and short stories have appeared in many online and print publications. She resides in Northern Virginia and Southern Maryland. Her faithful companion, a Cavalier King Charles Spaniel named Sam, is always by her side, whether she's writing, painting, gardening, or reading yet another British mystery.

Discover more at
4HorsemenPublications.com

10% off using HORSEMEN10

www.ingramcontent.com/pod-product-compliance
Lightning Source LLC
Chambersburg PA
CBHW020907160726
47993CB00005B/1849